SOUL MURDER

Thomas Domenici

RATTLING GOOD YARNS
PRESS

Rattling Good Yarns Press
33490 Date Palm Drive 3065
Cathedral City CA 92235
USA
www.rattlinggoodyarns.com

Cover Design: Rattling Good Yarns Press

Library of Congress Control Number: 2023940917
ISBN: 978-1-955826-45-7

First Edition

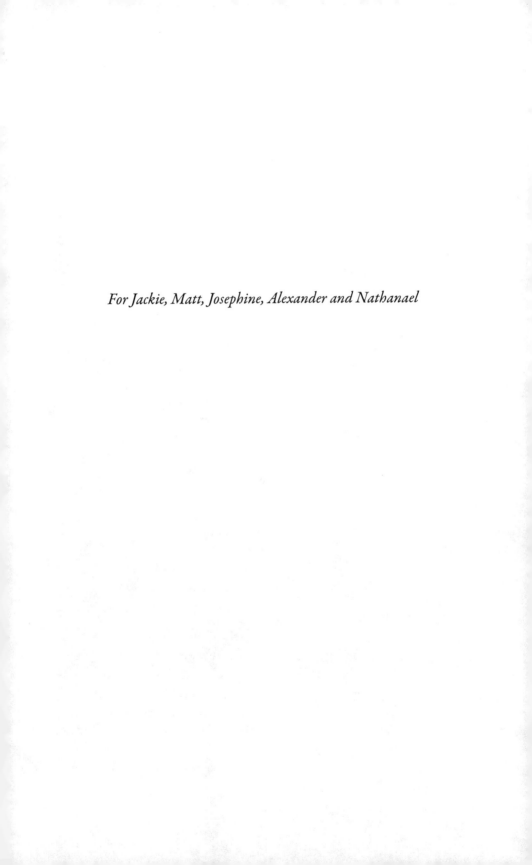

For Jackie, Matt, Josephine, Alexander and Nathanael

"When truth is buried underground it grows, it chokes, it gathers such an explosive force that on the day it bursts out, it blows up everything with it."

—Émile Zola

"Nothing fixes a thing so intensely in the memory as the wish to forget it."

—Michel de Montaigne

One

Standing in the gloom of a warm moon-washed night, John stared back at the house. Something was nagging at him. He adhered to the routine so as not to leave anything behind. However, this time a sliver of doubt sliced through the orderliness of his process. His eidetic memory could be both a gift and a burden. Again he counted each item.

What am I ... The boys! Shit! How did I forget to check on them? He exhaled loudly.

Standing on the backyard lawn, he considered packing up his gear and leaving, but the boys' welfare drew him back. He thought about redressing in the blood-spattered surgical scrubs, but instead, he covered his shoes and head. He checked himself over. After pulling on a pair of clean latex gloves, he entered the house through the French doors that opened to the family room.

He quietly walked to their bedroom. Connor was as he had left him, sleeping on his back, propped up on his pillow. Dylan had moved and lay beside Connor on his stomach, his arm over his brother. He moved Dylan gently, turning him over so that he lay as Connor did. Finding another pillow, he placed it between the boys and against Dylan. As he tightly tucked in the sheets of the bed, Dylan opened his eyes. They made eye contact, and then Dylan's eyelids fluttered and closed.

They'll be okay, he assured himself as he looked down at them. *Certainly much better than they were before tonight.*

He exited the house and then removed his cap, gloves, and booties. He again took inventory, making sure nothing was left behind. He knew that no matter how careful he was, mistakes would be made. Even a genius would eventually leave something behind—finger or shoe prints, fibers, hair, and so on—and he was not a seasoned criminal. He laid out and recounted each item before he put everything in his duffle bag.

He stood in the shadow of a large maple tree at the edge of the property and glanced up and down the street. Except for the din of the traffic rising from Sunset Boulevard, everything seemed quiet. He glanced back at the house, thinking about what he had just done. It gave him no satisfaction. In truth, it only added to the tortured memories that, like acid, ate away at his remaining humanity. Then, satisfied that he would not be seen, he removed Romeo's shoes, put them into the duffle, and put on his own. *Romeo was always such a prick.*

Another deep breath. His chest quivered. The only way to cope with his pain was this, regardless of the inexorable consequences. He needed to stay focused on what this was all about and quash any qualms, sentimentality, or guilt. His only concern now was finding and killing the one remaining man who was primary on his list before he himself was caught or killed.

He slipped his arm through the strap of the duffle bag and slung it over his shoulder. A welcomed cooling breeze blew in from the west, making the trees rustle like living things, their branches scratching at one another with wooden fingers. Heading down the hill toward the boulevard, he thought about Connor and Dylan tucked in their bed sheets. The violence of childhood memories and a fog of despair enveloped him as he relived being washed with bleach and wrapped in a sheet. Struck with a large stone. Buried in a shallow grave.

Clear your mind. Stay present!

He had learned that memories fueled his rage, and rage could lead to mistakes.

Music. I need my music.

John reached into his pocket and retrieved his iPhone and earbuds. He needed to stay focused on what this was all about—finding his kidnapper. This was not the beginning of it. This was not to be the end. There was a voicemail. He ignored it. He turned on his music and put in his earbuds. With a stiff spine, he made his way into the night.

Two

Detective Edward Coyne lay stretched out on his queen-sized bed, clutching a pillow under his left arm. He was in REM sleep. His cell phone chimed into the narrative of his dream. As he moved into reality, his phone went silent. He opened his eyes. Staring into the darkness, he rolled onto his side and pressed the pillow to his chest. He missed the sound of Kristen's breath while she slept, the feel of her naked body lying close to his and her cold feet. A tear came to the corner of his eye as he thought that he, like so many people. slept alone. He closed his eyes, trying to fall back to sleep, when his phone chimed again.

He sat up and felt for his cell phone, which sat face down on his nightstand.

"Coyne," he said, staring at his digital clock. 4:42 a.m.

"Detective Coyne, hold for Assistant Chief Henson."

"Coyne," Henson said. "We had a unit report to a 911 off Sunset. Adult male and female killed, bodies mutilated. Same M.O., last week—male killed and mutilated, and another in Santa Monica. I want Major Crimes on this."

"I'm currently working on..."

"Pass it off to someone else there, whatever it is."

"Isn't homicide already there? I don't want to step..."

"I don't care about the politics..." Henson growled.

Clearly, someone had just woken Henson up, Ed thought.

"...I want you before it turns into a fucking shit show."

"Yes, Sir."

"This is looking multijurisdictional, so we'll need the FBI on this. What's today anyway?"

"Thursday, sir."

"I want you and whoever you're working with in my office on Monday afternoon for a meeting. A full report."

"Monday?"

"Am I garbling, Detective?"

"No, sir. Monday afternoon."

"I'm going to have you transferred to the officer on the scene. Hold on."

Edward Coyne had served four years in the Marines, after which he graduated from UCLA with a degree in Criminal Justice. He then worked his way up the ranks of the Los Angeles Police Department.

He swung his feet over the side of the bed, sat up and twisted his torso to the right, then the left, trying to get the stiffness out of his back.

"O'Neal here."

"Detective Coyne, Major Crimes."

"I have the house cordoned off."

"Text me the address." Ed heard his phone chime. He glanced at the screen. "Got it. I'll be there in 45 minutes. I don't want anyone in the house—no one until I get there."

"We have two tender age boys here. The older one called it in. But he went back to sleep after he let us in. He seemed drugged. The younger boy never woke up. I've got three guys outside but I'm standing in their room now. Thought I should..."

"If they wake, keep them in their room." He hung up and turned on the nightstand light.

Coyne had one of the highest solve rates in the LAPD. For that reason, he was given as much latitude as was allowed and access to whomever and whatever resources he needed. One of his demands was that once he assembled a team, that team worked with him until the case was closed.

He scrolled through his contacts list, deciding to call Mark, a CSI with whom he'd worked successfully and found him to be meticulous. He was a Penn State University graduate with a B.S. in forensic science and a specialization in evidence collection. It was there that he met the man with whom he currently lived.

"Damn, Ed. God isn't even awake yet."

"Got a possible serial. Body mutilations. I'm texting you the address."

"Hey that's not far from me."

"I'll be there in 45. Get a couple of people you're comfortable with, then they're yours."

He stared at himself in the bathroom mirror as he pulled a Gillette razor over his face. *You look worse than you feel and you feel like shit.* He stepped into the shower after he shaved. His mind raced. His partner was on her honeymoon in Hawaii. He would need to call in for someone to work with him. If they used the FBI, he could work with Bill Russo, FBI special agent, and godfather to his son Justin, as he was godfather to Russo's son Andrew.

After he dressed, he stepped toward his son's room. He was supposed to drop Justin at the pool. He would have to wake him. He opened the door a crack. Justin was a junior at North Hollywood High School and swam on the varsity swim team. His alarm was set for 6 a.m. so that he could make an early morning workout.

Ed sat on his bed and stared at his sleeping son. *You look so much like your mother.* He had dark brown hair, which he cut short, big brown eyes, and high cheekbones that gave his face a sculptured look. His lips were full and ran at a right angle to his straight nose. *She'd be so proud of you.*

Ed's wife, Kristen, had died after an undetected aortic aneurism burst two years earlier. Justin had found his mother on the kitchen floor. Ed put his hand on his son's shoulder and lightly shook him.

"Justin."

Justin opened his eyes, glanced at his father, and then at the digital clock. He rolled onto his back and sat up, pulling his knees to his chest. "You're getting called in...will you be home for dinner?"

"I'll let you know."

"Oh wait, I'm supposed to have dinner with Uncle Bill and Andrew." Out of respect, the boys referred to their godfathers as "uncle."

"He may be working on this case with me."

"Maybe you can have dinner with us."

"If you get up now, I can drop you at the pool."

"I can get a ride."

He drove on Coldwater Canyon Boulevard, where houses seemed to grow out of the hillside like pinecones on an evergreen. As the sunrise turned the night-sky blue, he thought of his wife, of the early mornings when he and Kristen went for a run. Coyne again felt the pull of grief.

Following his GPS, he arrived at the given address and parked. The neighborhood was quiet. A police officer approached him as he stepped out of his car. He flashed his badge and was informed that a team of CSI was waiting. "I want the property cordoned off, including the sidewalk." Mark and two other CSI waited by the front door. He motioned them to follow.

Ed pointed to the CSI with a video camera. "I want everything in that house documented before anything is touched."

The officer in the house met Ed at the door. "The kids are still asleep."

"Take me through." He waited for the CSI with the video camera to turn it on. They went into the boy's room and saw them asleep in a queen-sized bed. Then they walked the hall to the master bedroom. On the French doors to the room, written with a marker in big bold letters was, DO NOT ENTER. DOORS LOCKED. CALL 911 <u>NOW!</u> The doors were ajar.

"He kills their parents and then warns them off," Ed said, shaking his head. "They were locked?"

"Yes. I went out to check through the bedroom window. But then I thought if the guy locked these doors he had to exit through the window and there might be footprints there, so I decided to break open the doors."

Ed pushed the doors open and stood in the doorway. Before him were a male and female corpse tied to chairs. The rug under the male's chair was soaked with blood. The female was slumped over with blood on the tee shirt she wore.

"Before we do anything here, I want to get the kids out of the house. I don't want them waking up and seeing this."

Ed woke the boys. When he noticed that they were both naked, he asked that the video camera be turned off until they were dressed. After talking to them briefly, he called for a police car to take them to Children's Hospital.

To the officer, he said, "You're right. These kids do look drugged. Tell them I want a complete physical and blood workup done for drugs. And you stay with them. I don't want social services getting their hands on them. They are material witnesses."

He watched the boys being walked out to the police car.

"Okay, let's get to work."

Three

Dr. William Russo, FBI Special Agent, behavioral scientist and child psychologist, automatically reached for his cell phone as it rang, but then thought better of it. It was sitting on the console of his car between him and his seventeen-year-old son, Andrew. They made eye contact. Andrew rolled his eyes and shook his head, knowing he was being given a lesson by example. It rang again.

Andrew glanced at the screen of the iPhone. "It's Uncle Ed."

"Answer it."

"Hey, it's Andrew. My dad's right here. He's driving me to school." He nodded and smiled. "I'm good." More nods.

"Put it on speaker phone."

Andrew held the phone for Bill.

"Hi Ed," he called out.

"Hey Bill. We caught a bad one. Two dead. Plus, I had a couple of tender-age boys left here."

"Alive?"

"Yeah."

"How old are they?"

"My guess, seven and nine. I'd like you in on this with me. This is turning out to be a serial murder case, and we're going to have a jurisdictional issue. Henson said he found another case, same M.O. in San Diego..."

"Any out of state?"

"Maybe, but right now these two and another in LA. One for sure in Santa Monica, one in San Diego and a possible in Malibu...and you're good with kids. I had them sent to Children's Hospital. I don't want Child

Services getting their hands on them just yet and I need your backing on that. My gut says they've got information."

"Okay. I'll clear my calendar."

"I'll text you the address."

Bill stared at the phone.

"Ah, the light doesn't get any greener," Andrew said in a tone. Bill raised his eyebrows as he stared at his son, then looked forward and accelerated.

Still on the call, Ed congratulated Andrew on his acceptance to Stanford. "Justin told me."

"Thanks. He's coming to the game after school." Andrew, a North Hollywood High School senior, played varsity basketball. "He's invited to my grandparents for dinner after the game. Can you pick him up there?"

"Sure. Sounds good."

Andrew ended the call and put his father's phone back on the console.

Bill pulled up in front of the high school and stopped curbside under the umbrella-like magnolia trees that provided shade to its entrance. Andrew stepped out of the car and turned to look at his father. "Please try to come to the game."

"I'll try, but you know how this goes."

"Dad, it would really mean a lot to me if you came to at least one."

"I'll do everything I can, I promise."

Andrew stared at his father with his steely grey-blue eyes for a moment, nodded, and closed the car door. Bill watched him join his friends, of which now there were many. He admired his son. Like other teenage boys, Andrew could be mercurial, obstinate, and at times a tester of limits. Still, he was also thoughtful, generous, and kind. Bill appreciated the man he was becoming.

Andrew had been what was called a "crack baby." He was born early, underweight, and addicted to cocaine. The image of his pink emaciated body, lying in an incubator, going through withdrawal, was permanently etched into Bill's mind. Eventually, he was able to hold him in his arms and bring him home.

A gay man, he applied and received permission to adopt from the state of California as a single parent. Andrew's mother signed papers giving him up upon his birth. The doctors told Bill that he might find Andrew to be developmentally delayed. One year later, Andrew was officially his son and on schedule for all developmental stages.

Living a few miles from his parent's home, Bill had been able to both raise Andrew and further his own career. As is true with most Italian families, grandparents did all extra-parental childrearing and babysitting. Andrew received love and guidance from his grandfather and nurturing from his grandmother. And living within walking distance of his lifelong friend Kristin and her husband, Ed Coyne, had been an added bonus.

Bill entered the address Coyne had texted him into his navigation system. Then following the prompts, he turned onto Coldwater Canyon Boulevard and fell into a long line of cars heading over the hills to West Los Angeles. He turned on his car stereo and turned up the volume—Puccini's *La Bohème*.

Bill had started his career as a Ph.D. psychologist, working at USC/LA County Psychiatric Hospital with children and adolescents, most of whom had been sexually or physically abused. At the same time, in private practice, he specialized in treating court-referred individuals who were child molesters or incest perpetrators. Several years later, he felt psychically exhausted and concerned that he had little emotional energy left for his newly adopted son and personal life. Taking advantage of the connections he had established in the justice system he moved into criminal behavioral science. This led to a job with the FBI and his training as a profiler, after which he was made a Special Agent and did fieldwork. Ultimately, he traded a career that was emotionally draining for one that put him in physical danger.

He traveled farther on Sunset and then turned right onto Sunset Plaza Drive, heading back into the hills. It was early spring, mid-morning, and already over 90 degrees. The hillsides were brown. Bill tried to remember the last time it rained.

And this is supposed to be our rainy season.

He drove until he saw parked police cars and a house cordoned off with yellow tape. He parked his BMW X5, unlocked his glove compartment, removed his Glock, and holstered it. To his belt, he clipped his FBI badge. He stepped out and surveyed the area. The air was hot and heavy with the smell of car exhaust wafting up the hillside from the traffic below.

This is where the lower end of the upper one percent live.

Without thinking, he reached into the backseat and grabbed his suit jacket. As he was about to put it on, he felt a gust of hot air. He tossed the jacket into the backseat and closed the door. Walking up the hill, he pressed the lock button on the key fob and listened for the BMW to chirp.

An unusually large number of police vehicles were parked on the street. A uniformed Los Angeles policewoman eyed him as he approached the yellow tape. "Sir?"

He took out his ID. She scrutinized it and nodded as she lifted the yellow tape.

"Where is Detective Coyne?"

"Inside, Agent Russo. But first you'll have to sign in." She pointed him in the direction of an officer sitting in the passenger seat of a police car.

Bill recognized the officer. "Hey, Ron. Looks like it's brought out the whole police force."

"Dr. Bill. How are you? Yeah, this has got their attention for sure. They brought Detective Coyne in from Major Crimes." He handed a clipboard to Bill.

The hacienda-style house sat tucked away at the side of a hill: one story with cream-colored stucco and Spanish tile roof. The ornate landscape gave the owners, and any intruders, the privacy they desired. Large, flowering bougainvillea arched over the front porch, dripping bright blood-red blossoms. Bill glanced at the lush green front lawn.

I'd hate to have to pay their water bill.

An officer at the door handed Bill gloves and booties as he entered the house. Slipping them on, Bill asked for Coyne.

"To the left, bedroom at the end of the hall."

"Do they know where this guy got in?"

The officer pointed toward the living room. "French doors."

Bill stepped to his right, into the spacious living room and glanced around: open floor plan, white rugs on dark wood floors, chrome and leather couches, art on the walls. In the dining room stood a large dark-wood mahogany table studded with large-headed bronze nails and chairs. He noticed a chair at each end of the table, three on one side but only one on the other. *Odd.* He took several more steps. Gourmet kitchen. Wolf stove, subzero refrigerator, and freezer. Clearly, a recent and expensive renovation. The house had been tossed. *I wonder if they found what they were looking for.* He stepped into the family room and noticed the French doors ajar. *No broken glass.* He bent down and examined the locks. *Looks like it hasn't been forced. Did he enter through here or just exit? Lucky break for him if he found it unlocked, or did he know?* He glanced around and noticed the doors were wired for an alarm. He stepped outside onto the patio, which was covered with a pergola from which clematis draped in full bloom. Swimming pool. *These people had money, and a lot of it.* He watched a CSI studying an area under an open window. "Find anything?"

"A shoeprint."

He re-entered the house and walked back toward the front door as the suspect might have. *One could easily make their way through the house without being heard.* "The alarm wasn't set?" he asked the officer.

"Doesn't seem so. From what I've heard, it's in working order."

Bill turned and walked down the hallway. As he passed the first room, he glanced in. *A child's bedroom?* Two children's desks, one queen size bed.

The next room was an office. Desk, chair, large leather sofa, armchair, and modern art on the walls. A policewoman was going through the desk.

As Bill walked toward the master bedroom, he noticed what was penned on the French doors. He gave a nod to Ed and Mark and surveyed the bedroom: king-sized bed, two dark wood nightstands with glass and chrome lamps, large black-and-white framed full-body nude photographs of a man and a woman, a white rug soaked with blood, and the two missing dining room chairs. A naked man was tied to one facing a woman in bedclothes tied to the other.

Ed stared at Bill and shook his head. His face was hard and stoic.

"This is an execution," Bill said.

Four

Bill thought that Ed was strikingly handsome. Ed, like Bill, was in his mid-forties, six feet tall, broad shoulders, and absent the often-present potbelly that came with years of police work and age. He had always worked to stay in shape and carried himself with an assertive demeanor that said *Best take me seriously*. To his friends, like Bill, his smile was warm and welcoming. But since Kristin's death, Ed seldom smiled and looked tired of life. His dark brown hair was greying, and the lines around his eyes had deepened.

He turned now to Bill. "We're waiting for the coroner."

The heat of the day was exacerbating the pungent smells of murder—blood, urine, and excrement.

"You weren't kidding." Bill looked at the two slumped-over bodies. "This is bad."

The two were bound and gagged, each tied to a dining room chair and positioned so that they faced each other. The female wore men's boxers and a tee shirt. She had a carving knife stuck into the left side of her chest. Her head hung down, but Bill could see that her face and tee shirt were covered in blood. The male was naked and a bloody mess from the waist down.

"Who are they?" Bill asked.

"Romeo and DeeDee Tremway."

"Clearly they're affluent. What did they do?"

"Don't know."

"Castration?"

"Cock and balls." Ed shook his head. "And he wasn't just cut and left to bleed out." He pointed to the many shallow lacerations on the victim's legs and chest.

Mark walked toward the male's body taking care not to step in the blood. Squatting down with a pen in hand, he pointed to the empty scrotum, which was still attached. There looked to be two cuts. Bill looked around and saw one testicle that had been tossed onto the bed. Mark pointed to the bloody mess on the floor where the other testicle lay. There it sat, the size of an egg.

"It looks surgical." Mark gazed at Bill. "My guess is that he started with these cuts to the legs." Bill looked at the male's bloody thighs. "Then he removed each testicle, which wouldn't have caused all this bleeding. Then he sliced off the guy's shlong, cutting the Helicine artery of the penis. That caused the bleed out. Probably bled out in about four or five minutes." Standing, he said, "The penis is in the bathroom. He used it to leave a message on the mirror."

"Jesus H. Christ. He used his penis?" Bill stepped away from the body. "Did anyone hear anything?"

"We haven't interviewed the neighbors yet."

"They must have been screaming bloody murder. Or were their mouths taped?"

"I gave a quick look to both of them. I don't see any signs of tape residue or red marks. I'll ask the coroner to check closer."

"Maybe they passed out?" Bill asked.

Ed pointed to snap-packets on the floor. "Smelling salts. My guess is that he took his time with him."

Bill stared at the female body. "So, this is his wife. Made to watch this and then killed."

"Made to watch," Ed repeated. "Then he removed her eyes and stabbed her is my guess."

Bill tried to imagine how one person could possibly subdue two adults and tie them to a heavy wooden dining room chair, especially this male, who was in exceptional shape. Both looked to be in their mid-thirties. He noticed the matching patterns of knots of the ropes. "Unless this guy wore gloves, there should be DNA on the ropes." He glanced around the room, trying to remember if he had seen something so macabre. "What's the message he left?"

Ed pointed Bill in the direction of the bathroom. He carefully crossed the room, following Mark. A bloody penis sat on the counter. Written on the mirror: MW 18: 9.

"Bible?" Bill guessed.

"Gospel of Matthew. If your eye causes you to stumble, gouge it out and throw it away."

"This is about her specifically, then."

"Matthew 8 would have been more in line with what was done to him."

"You're quite erudite. Helicine artery...not many people know the name of the artery in the penis. And you know your Bible."

Mark smiled. "Bing."

"Bing?"

"Microsoft Bing. Their search engine."

Bill chuckled.

Dr. Sandra Boudoir from the LA Coroner's office entered the bedroom. A tall, attractive woman from the Caribbean Islands, she greeted Ed and then nodded at Bill. She shook her head as she stared at the male victim's body.

"Damn, what mayhem. Will I ever not be surprised at the level of cruelty and violence one person can inflict on another?"

Bill and Ed stepped toward Sandra as she began to examine the bodies.

"He's gone into rigor. Cause of death seems obvious on both of them. The amount of blood—I'd say he bled out. Time of death..." She removed a probe from the male's torso and looked at her watch. "My guess, between midnight and two a.m." She then turned to the female's body.

A policewoman stepped through the doorway. "I found her purse in the office. It doesn't look like they went through it. Three hundred and twenty-three dollars and credit cards. His wallet was in his pants. There were two diamond rings in her jewelry case."

"Let's find out if they insured this stuff," Ed said.

As Mark began to untie the male body, the coroner examined it more closely. "Did you notice this?"

"What?" Ed and Bill leaned in.

Sandra pointed to one of the shallow cuts on the male's thighs. "See all the bleeding? These were done antemortem. These," she pointed to the cuts on his upper torso. "I'd say that these were done postmortem because there's almost no bleeding. But look here." She used her gloved fingers to put pressure on the cut. "These cover a puncture wound." She looked up at Ed. "I'll check it out and let you know. It could be an injection site."

Ed turned to the female's clothed body. "You'll check her out for the same kind of wound?"

The coroner lifted the female's head. "Where are her eyes?"

Ed pointed to where they had been tossed—behind her chair.

Bill stared at the female's face, thinking how strange it was that even though the sockets of her head were empty, she seemed to be staring at him. He imagined that before her mutilation, she was quite attractive. He then looked back at the black-and-white nudes on the wall, as did the coroner. "Better days," Bill said.

"You notice the doors?" Ed asked.

"Locked from the inside, right?"

"I guess he didn't want the kids to stumble onto the bodies. So, he..."

"...went out the bedroom window."

Bill nodded. "So you have a sadist with a conscience who tortures but worries about traumatizing the kids."

"I'll leave that to you."

"But is this about them? Where were they?"

Ed pointed Bill toward the boy's bedroom as they left the master bedroom. The oldest boy, nine-year-old Connor, had awakened, saw the writing on the door, and called the police. When they'd arrived, he was naked and asleep in bed with his seven-year-old brother Dylan.

"They seemed drugged." Ed pointed at the one bed. "Sharing a bed and naked. Doesn't that seem a bit odd to you? Like you said, they certainly could afford another bed and this room is big enough..."

"Yes, a bit odd." Bill looked around the room. "You said they were asleep when you got here. If they were drugged, any idea how?"

Ed shrugged. "Hopefully, they can tell us."

They walked through the rest of the house. "It seems obvious that someone was looking for something. Is there a safe?"

"No."

When they entered the kitchen, Ed pointed to the knife holder. "He brought rope and whatever else he needed but used the vic's knife."

"On her. But he used something else on him. Like Mark said, it looked surgical."

They stepped into the backyard. Ed pointed to the footprints left outside the bedroom window marked for photographing and casting. Then they walked through the living room and stepped through the front doorway.

"Can you believe this fucking weather?" Ed said. "90 degrees and it's not even noon."

Several people were gathered across the street. They questioned two women who knew nothing about the Tremways. Then they approached an attractive woman, casually well-dressed and fit. "I'm Detective Coyne and this is Doctor Russo, he's FBI. You are...?"

"Carol Reed. I live over there." She pointed to the house next door and brushed a fall of hair from her eyes. "I saw them take the boys away. What happened?"

"Do you know the Tremways?" Ed asked.

"I've chatted with DeeDee. You know, over the fence. I have a son and a daughter around their ages."

"Were they friends?"

"No. Never saw those kids out without their parents."

"What about school?"

"She said they home schooled them." She leaned toward them. "They were into porn."

"And how do you know that?"

Carol lifted her iPhone. "Internet. Gotta know who you're neighbors are, right? She owned the company, Dee-licious Productions, and starred in her videos."

"Did you hear or see anything out of the ordinary last night?"

"The street seemed pretty quiet."

Bill thought about the message left on the mirror. "One more question. How did the neighbors take to having porn people living on the street?"

"Here? No one cared. Half the people in this neighborhood are in the entertainment industry, and they're all screwing each other one way or another– just not on film. He also made videos. Gay videos.

Ed chuckled as they began to walk away. "Married guy making gay porn."

"Probably not gay. There's a lot more money in gay porn for guys."

"Let me buy you an early lunch," Ed offered. "And then I'd appreciate it if you'd talk to the kids and find out what you can."

"Sure. Where we going to lunch?"

Five

Ed ordered a cup of minestrone soup and a half of turkey sandwich for Bill, and a turkey and cheese sandwich for himself, while Bill found a table in the hospital cafeteria. He paid for their lunch and, waiting for their order to be filled, thought that even catching such a gruesome case had a silver lining—spending time with Bill. They had been friends for over twenty years and had worked together once before on a kidnapping case that ended with the recovery of the child. Since Kristen's death, Bill had been the only person he trusted enough to talk to about his personal struggles.

Now he sat down beside him. "I hope I didn't pull you off anything important."

"Just paperwork. I've got a couple of people on it. How are you doing?" Ed gazed at him. "Your anniversary."

Ed felt an ache of grief in his stomach as he took in a deep breath and nodded knowingly. "I miss her, but..." He looked away.

"Anniversaries, birthdays, and holidays are always tough. How's Justin doing?"

Not surprisingly, Justin had taken his mother's death badly. He did poorly in school in the months that followed, but with the help of a tutor, he'd been able to turn things around.

Ed shrugged and shook his head. "Ups and downs. Lately, I don't know, he doesn't really talk to me about how he's doing. Seems withdrawn. I need to talk to you about him, but not now." They both nodded.

"You said this is a serial killing."

"Two murders in LA and one in San Diego with a similar M.O.—torture and genital mutilation." Ed retrieved a small notepad from his shirt pocket. "Three men in their fifties. They were found naked, mutilated and left to bleed out. The first was a divorce lawyer; Leland Jay Rheingold, married with three adult children. His youngest daughter was back from college and living at home. His secretary told the police that he had a late first-time appointment that evening. His wife tried to reach him at his office and on his cell phone. Later she called his secretary and said he hadn't arrived home as expected. Then she called the police. They found him tied to his desk chair, sitting in a pool of blood."

"Like the Tremways. Did the secretary know with whom the appointment was with?" Bill asked and then bit into his sandwich.

"No, which she said was unusual. It wasn't an appointment that she'd made. The police first thought that he might have hired a male or female escort and got himself in over his head. Or that it might have been someone who told him that they didn't want anyone knowing he or she was thinking about divorce. He had Hollywood types as clients."

"He was cut like Romeo? Shallow cuts?" Bill asked.

Ed stared at him as if thinking and then nodded. "They thought that the lawyer let himself be tied up, because there was no sign of a struggle. Or perhaps he was overpowered."

"Maybe it's some kind of drug thing. Lawyers, especially Hollywood types, and cocaine. There could have been drugs at the Tremway's home. Lawyers, porn stars – could be cocaine."

"Maybe." Ed put down the notepad and picked up his drink. "Or maybe they called the wrong escort. You can find anything on the Internet."

"He's not staying local."

Ed shook his head. "LA, Santa Monica and San Diego so far. And maybe Malibu. I got a call on my way here. There was a killing there several weeks ago that is similar. I want to check that out."

"If he's killing in a small area, close to where he lives, he'll be easier to find. Geographically transient killers are harder. I'll call in and have them do another statewide search and take it out of state. Did he leave a message written in blood anywhere else?"

"No. Isn't that unusual for a typical serial killer? Don't they usually get set into some kind of pattern?"

Bill nodded. "This is the first female that he's killed. Maybe he was compelled to tell us why. Cut your junk off. That seems to be the pattern. Being so careful with the kids. Now that seems unusual. I mean he seems like the sadistic or sexual type." Bill moved the bowl of soup closer. "What do you know about the Santa Monica guy?"

"Not much. They found his body a couple of days ago."

"Same thing?"

Ed read his notes. "Found tied to a chair, cut and mutilated. Adult male. Brett R. Levin. Lived alone. A CPA, killed the day before the lawyer and found by his cleaning lady almost a week later. Santa Monica isn't part of LA city, so I don't have jurisdiction."

"I'll call them and have it sent over. San Diego too. You know anything about him?"

"Just that he was a divorced businessman, owned some big retail stores. He lived with his fiancé, a flight attendant, and was killed in his home just like Romeo."

"When she was away."

Ed noticed Bill staring off into space. "What?"

"He's been able to get to these guys when they're alone. They're being targeted, studied. I'll bet he watches them."

"Except for Romeo."

"I think that was planned." Bill picked up his spoon and wiped it off with his napkin.

"Does that come from years of working in hospitals."

Bill smiled, "Old habits. So, next step."

"That murder in Malibu took place a couple of months ago. The victim was found tied to the front seat of his car at Zuma. He had been killed the night before. Pants down. He wasn't castrated but his femoral artery was cut. I want to go out there and talk to them in person. The Malibu murder might be his first."

"Might be. Takes a while to work up to what we saw today." Bill sipped his soup and grimaced. "Tastes like they got tomato soup and added yesterday's vegetables to it." He put his spoon down and pushed the bowl aside.

"Why do you order anything Italian when you eat out? Nothing compares to your mother's cooking."

"We're having dinner there tonight. She's making her 'peasant food.'"

"Your mother's pasta and meatballs are my favorite."

"Stop by. You know how she cooks for an army."

Ed shook his head. "It's going to be a late night."

"My place after, then. I'll have her make you a plate."

"Really?"

"Of course. Justin can come home with us."

"I'll call...if it's too late."

"Fine, call." Bill turned his attention back to their case. "A business owner, lawyer, a CPA who owned a house in Santa Monica—that's gotta cost. These guys are all professionals and well off. What kind of doctor was the Malibu guy?"

"Beverly Hills plastic surgeon," Ed said.

"So the doctor is his first and then there's this long period of time and then four murder scenes one right after the other."

"Four that we know of. Let's see what your statewide query brings in."

"Okay, so the similarities are that they're all wealthy," Bill started to build a profile on the killer from the victims. "Age range goes from early thirties to late fifties. They're all men except for DeeDee. I guess we can say they were all straight men. Was the CPA married?"

"Actually, the maid said he was gay."

Bill shook his head. "So, it's not sexual orientation. All I can say is that it's not a delusional type. It can be either a sadistic domineering type who is getting off on being in control and seeing the victims' fear, which is clearly an element in this. Or the sexual type who typically mutilates the breast and genital area. We don't know if these people are being specifically targeted and for a specific reason, or if it's random. What would really help us is if we can find a link between the four cases."

"Maybe five. The Malibu case."

"Maybe five."

Ed sat back and shook his head. "We have a perp mutilating men in their office, at home, and in a car, but this time he kills the wife too, and he leaves a message. Might be some religious nut that finally tipped his hand. Maybe he wasn't getting the attention he wanted."

"Gouging out her eyes meant something. I'd say it had to do with her eye on the camera, filming, but like you said...Maybe they didn't know she starred in films."

"We'll have to find out if the business owner, the lawyer, and the CPA had anything to do with the porn industry. They could all be involved."

"Or they could be investors," Bill added.

"Also, the call I received on my way here. They said that all the computer hard drives were taken from the Tremway's house. They found no laptops or iPads. He obviously knows his way around computers. And that takes time. We'll have to check into that with the other vics."

"Motive?"

"Money, but that's not top of my list."

"Anger toward a subgroup?"

"Possible. Porn industry perhaps or maybe those who are somehow seen as breaking God's law."

"Jealousy," Bill said. "I'd say that's down on our list."

"But not psychotic."

"I doubt it. Too well organized."

Finishing his sandwich, Bill picked up his paper napkin.

Ed sipped his soda and sighed. "Well, let's hope the kids can tell us something.

Six

Bill flashed his identification to the charge nurse who was seated and staring at a computer screen. He patiently waited for her to glance up. She didn't. "The Tremway boys?" he asked.

She studied Bill's identification and then stared at Ed, who showed her his badge. She said, "Fourth floor. Room 426," as she picked up a phone.

"I'd like to see the doctor in charge."

She pointed to the phone.

As they waited for the elevator, Ed said, "I hate that smell. What is it?"

"Disinfectant. Usually a combination of cleaning fluids. Work here and you get used to it."

"Not sure I want to. I want to hold onto these kids for a while before they get lost in the system."

"I can get them admitted to the UCLA Child Psychiatric Hospital for observation. That should give us four or five days."

There was a policeman at the door to room 426.

Ed identified himself and Bill. "This is Dr. Russo with the FBI. What's going on?"

"They were going to call the Department of Child and Family Service. The doc said they looked physically fine. I told him that they were going nowhere until you said so."

A tall elderly man was approaching. "Is that the doctor?"

The officer nodded.

"Gentlemen, I'm Dr. Randell," he said, never taking his hands out of his white lab coat. "I'm in charge here."

"I'm Detective Coyne and this is Dr. Russo with the FBI."

Dr. Randell furrowed his brow, "A doctor with the FBI?"

"Ph.D. behavioral science and child psychologist."

"Oh." Randell dismissed the information. "As you requested, a physical exam was performed, and blood was drawn for a drug screening. We found a recent small puncture wound on both boys' arms. They were asked if they recently received a flu shot or vaccination. The younger one said that he remembered getting a shot but didn't know when. The older boy said nothing. Actually, he remains verbally unresponsive and quite agitated."

Puncture wound. Just like their parents, Bill thought. He glanced at Ed, who looked at him with raised eyebrows.

"Should we call child services?" Dr. Randell asked.

"I'm an adjunct professor at the UCLA and USC medical schools. I have admitting privileges at both psychiatric..."

Staring directly at Bill, Dr. Randell interrupted, "Like I said, *I* don't see why they need to be hospitalized."

"...hospitals," Bill continued. "These boys found their parents murdered and as you said, Connor is showing signs of trauma."

The doctor continued to stare and then shrugged his shoulders, shook his head, and said, "Do what you want," as he walked away.

Ed looked at Bill, and shook his head, and mumbled, "Asshole."

Bill called out, "Excuse me, Doctor."

The doctor turned.

"I'd like to talk to the boys."

"There's a consult room down the hall."

Bill looked at his watch. It was 1:35 p.m.. "I have to be on my way by three," he said to Ed. "I called UCLA. They have beds for them."

"I'm going to head to my office then. I want to dig further into the business guy, the lawyer, and the accountant—see if I can find some kind of link to the Tremways. And I want to get through to the people in Malibu. Let me know if you find out anything." To the officer, he said, "Escort them to UCLA. I don't want anything going wrong. These kids have enough to deal with and they're in my charge. If anyone gives you any shit, you tell them that these kids are material witnesses and in police custody."

"Yes, Sir."

Ed's phone rang. He stepped away and answered it. He looked to be listening intently, nodding. "Okay, let them know we'll be there tomorrow." He looked at Bill. "DeeDee's studio is in Northridge."

"I'll want to check in on the boys first thing in the morning. Then I have a short meeting at 10:00 that I must attend. The rest of the day is clear. I'll come by the precinct around eleven."

Bill stood in the doorway of the consulting room and watched the boys being escorted to him by a nurse and the police officer. Both boys had a full head of hair left hanging over their ears and cut in bangs. Dylan stood tall and talked with the nurse. Connor stared at the floor as he walked.

The nurse had the boys sit on the couch. "This is Dylan and Connor. Boys, this is Dr..." She glanced at Bill.

"Dr. Russo."

"...he wants to talk to you."

"Hi," Dylan said.

Connor continued to stare at the floor until the nurse began to close the door as she left. He glanced at Bill, wrapped his arms around his chest and moaned.

"Please leave the door open," Bill said.

The boys understood that their parents were taken to heaven. Dylan, the younger boy, explained. Connor was clearly agitated: rocking in his chair with his arms tightly wrapped around his torso, swinging his legs, blinking excessively, and never making eye contact. When Bill addressed him directly, he nodded or shook his head. If Bill asked an open-ended question, he shrugged.

Dylan's affect level was flat, but he engaged more. He expressed concern about where and with whom they would be living, but nothing about the parents' death. "We have an aunt, but we hardly see her. She has children, too." He didn't know where they lived, but they could drive to their house and come home the same day.

Bill asked Dylan if their relatives' last name was Tremway. "It's just Aunt Barbara and Uncle Richard and Emma and Hailey."

Connor stared at the floor.

"Do you remember anything from last night: noises, people in the house, receiving an injection in the arm?"

Connor stared at the floor. Dylan responded in the negative.

Bill explained that they would be moved to another hospital where they would be staying until a nice home could be found for them or until their aunt and uncle were located.

"Will you be with us?" Dylan asked.

"At the hospital? Yes. I work there sometimes. I will see you tomorrow."

"At your house?"

"No. At the hospital." Dylan looked downcast, then glanced toward Connor, who continued to stare at the floor. Bill felt his throat tighten with concern. "Hopefully, you'll be staying with relatives soon."

Memories of the children Bill had worked with were never far from recall. At this moment, he thought about his first patient, a ten-year-old boy named Evan, who was admitted to the child psych ward at USC/LA County Hospital and assigned to Bill for treatment. It was reported that Evan was typically withdrawn. However, when he was confronted by peers or adults at school, he went into a violent rage, striking out, flailing his arms, and kicking, imperious to authority figures. Fortunately, he was thin as a rail, just skin stretched over bones and easily held down.

Evan presented as depressed and always greeted Bill with eyes downcast and a frown. His parents were divorced. He and his brother were in the custody of their mother and their father had weekend visitation. His mother reported that Evan never hurt his brother, but that he had struck her while he was in a rage. She reported that starting when Evan was six, his father disciplined him by dragging him into the bathroom, locking the door behind them, stripping him naked, sticking his head into the toilet bowl and flushing.

After two months of daily one-hour therapy sessions with Bill and having to be physically restrained after going into one of his rage states, Evan sobbed as he described being anally raped by his father while locked in the bathroom.

Now, two orderlies arrived to take Dylan and Connor to UCLA. All the paperwork was done and they were released into Bill's custody. He considered accompanying them, along with the officer, but knew that if he became involved with their intake, he would never make it back in time for Andrew's basketball game.

Seven

After leaving the Tremway house, John rode his motorcycle down Sunset Boulevard to Highway 1 and then west along the beach through Malibu. The night ocean air felt cleansing. When he passed Zuma Beach, he thought about Dr. Adams.

I shouldn't have killed him. That was not part of my plan. I could have pushed for more information. I was sure he gave me all he had. I let my anger dictate my actions. I can't let that happen again.

He glanced toward the parking area where he had left Adams in his car. The doctor's hands had been tied to the steering wheel and his pants and boxers pulled down to his ankles.

"You said if I gave you the information you'd let me go. Everything I know is in that journal. I'm sorry. Really, I am."

"I'm not done with you, Doc."

"What more do you want?"

He'd sat thumbing through the journal. "This is all meaningless to me."

"It's meaningless to me, too."

"Don't bullshit me. You said all the information I wanted was in this journal."

"I was given a list of first names. But they're all fake."

"I see the names."

"Then there are addresses."

"I see twenty-one names but only four different addresses."

"Those are banks. The numbers are safe deposit box numbers."

"So, how do you know who these people are?"

"I don't. Everything is kept by code names and that's what everyone uses. Never their real name."

"And the rest of this stuff. Pages for each of these guys. What's that?"

"Amounts of money."

He scanned the pages. Each name was followed by dates and numbers. "What are these?"

"I don't know. I was given that."

He'd slammed the book closed. "Here's the thing, Doc. You were at the house I was at. The guy's name was Leo and I see a Leo here. So, that was not his real name." Adams shook his head. "What is his real name?" He pressed a scalpel against the doctor's inner thigh and made a shallow cut.

The doctor tensed and screamed, "Please, don't."

"No one can hear you. Besides, you're hardly bleeding. Just a nick. You lie to me and I cut deep. What is Leo's real name."

The doctor had looked at him and pleaded, "If I tell you, he'll kill me."

"I remember you, Doc. I remember everything about you. And I remember you and Leo driving me into the hills, wrapping me in that white sheet, the smell of bleach, putting me in a hole, striking me on the head and leaving me to die. You're going to be left to die tonight, Doc, unless you give me what I want. Leo's real name."

"You're going to kill me whether I give you his name or not. So why should I?"

"If I get what I want I have no reason to kill you, because if you warn the men I'm looking for, I'll go to the police and expose you. I want the names of two men. Leo's real name and the name of the man who brought me to Leo."

"Do you promise to let me live?

"What I am going to do is leave you here like this tied to the steering wheel. Then in the morning when you are found, you'll have to explain this. I would suggest saying that you're a john who got taken advantage of." He chuckled. "Your wife will know you're a perv, but not what kind of perv you are." He pressed the knife to Adam's leg. "Give me Leo's real name."

"Promise me. I know I don't deserve anything, but..."

"...give me their names and you live."

Adams had wept. "Xavier. Victor Xavier."

"And where does Victor live?"

"Oh God."

He pressed the scalpel against his thigh.

Adams blurted out, "721 Clinton Place in West LA"

He took out his iPhone, entered the address in maps to make sure it was an actual address.

"Good. Now one more name."

Adams shook his head.

"He's tall. He has reddish brown hair and ears that stick out. You know him?

"I don't."

"You're lying. He was there that night you and this Xavier guy set out to kill me. Who is he?"

Adams kept shaking his head. "I don't know his name or where he lives. Maybe I can find that out. I'm sure Victor knows. All I know about him is that he has a boy, a boy like you, that he's passing around and is trying to sell."

John's stomach had roiled, and his face burned with anger. *Of course, this is still going on. Why did I think they would stop.* He opened the journal and turned several pages. "You said this was money collected for access to child porn." He put the scalpel back to Adams' leg. "This money is for time these guys are spending with boys?"

"No. That's separate. I don't have anything to do with that money."

"This is still going on?" His anger broke through his voice in spite of his attempt to maintain his composure. His arms began to shake. They stared at each other.

"I have nothing to do with that anymore. You were my last."

"Your last! Your last! You liar! Remember what I said. If you lie, I cut."

"Okay. Okay. I tried to stop, but they wouldn't let me."

"You've been with this boy?"

Adams shook his head almost violently. "Not that boy."

"But you know the man who has him."

"Xavier does."

"So, not that boy. But you've been with others."

"Xavier also knows who has them."

John looked back at the journal. There was a name at the top of each page that contained amounts of money and the date of payment. "These dates here. These are for this year?"

"Yes, but..."

Remembering the smell of Adams' breath, the weight of his body, and the sounds he made, John had pressed hard into Adams' leg and cut deep, unintentionally cutting the femoral artery. Blood streamed out as he watched Adams' life drain away. Immediately, he'd been filled with regret and then anxiety.

Adams screamed out, "Oh God, no. I don't want to die."

"Fuck! Fuck! Fuck!" John had shouted into the night air. A wave of nausea had run through him. *This was not the plan. I was only going to scare him into giving me the information. How could I think they stopped?* He stared at Adam's dead body. "Fuck!" He had never killed a living creature. He had never even intentionally hurt one.

He'd wiped down everything he touched in the car. His mind raced. *The house. Did I touch anything in the house?* His heart pounded in his chest. *Breathe. Just breathe.* Five deep breaths brought his pulse down slightly.

He'd taken Adams' keys, got on his motorcycle, and rode back to Adam's house. Once inside, he wiped down anything he might have touched. He took off his shoes and then wiped down the floor with several towels, which he put into the washing machine and then turned on. He returned to Adams' car and placed the keys back in the ignition after wiping them clean.

He rode his motorcycle back into town where he had parked his camper, hitched his bike to the camper and drove through the night until he arrived at Sequoia National Park the next morning. After setting up, he crawled into bed in the camper and tried to sleep.

His plan was to find and kill the man he now knew as Victor and the other man who kidnapped him. But actually killing someone was different from fantasizing about it. He began to cry. But crying brought him no relief. Only those who have hope can benefit from tears. He was without hope. He had only tortured memories, and crying changed nothing.

There he spent the next two nights. His sleep was fitful. He woke soaked in sweat. Waves of anxiety and guilt pulsed through his body. *This was not my plan. But he deserved to die,* he assured himself. He recited one of his favorite quotations over and over to himself until he calmed. This one was by Leonardo da Vinci. *He who does not punish evil commands it to be done.*

Remembering that night, he chided himself as he rode past Zuma Beach toward Point Mugu State Park, where he had left his camper. *He knew a lot more than he told me. He had to have known about Romeo. He said he signed into their safe deposit boxes. That means that he and each of the twenty-one men had to show identification and sign the sign-in card along with Adams. He had to have known each of their real names. I could have made him talk.*

He stopped and turned off the motorcycle when he was one hundred yards outside the entrance of the camp. He checked his watch—3:46 a.m. When he'd left the campgrounds two days earlier, it was empty. Not unusual for the beginning of April, he was told. He walked his bike through the entrance across the campsite to the most distant site where he'd parked. Beside it was his tall, walk-in tent. He removed the padlock from the zipper, rolled his bike in, and chained the wheels. Taking his duffle, he locked the tent and quietly entered his camper. There, he gathered what he needed and walked out of the still-empty camp to the head of the trail leading into the hills. Once out of sight, he turned on his flashlight and made his way to where he had set up a pup tent.

The next morning, he hiked further off the trail and buried everything he had used the night before to kill the Tremways. He thought about the boys and hoped they were safe. After covering the disturbed ground with leaves and brush, he returned to his pup tent and ate granola, dried fruit, and powdered milk for breakfast.

Later, he hiked off trail, climbing to the top of the hills where he found a large boulder, stripped naked, tucked his stuff away, and went for a walk to explore. California buckwheat covered the hillside with pink and white blooms. Butterflies abound. He spotted Laurel Sumac with its taco-shaped leaves. Nature had a calming effect on him. He again thought of the two boys he left behind and tried to convince himself that by killing their parents, he had rescued them.

Had he saved them from memories that would haunt them forever, like his did him? Memories that he could no longer live with. His life would end soon by suicide or being killed by one of his intended targets or the police.

He returned to his boulder. To occupy his mind, he had decided to learn French before his imminent death. He entered his password into his iPad, found where he had left off, and started on lesson ten.

Later that afternoon, after finishing his peanut butter and jelly sandwich, he gathered his remaining food, utensils, and tin plates and put them into his backpack. He tied his tent and sleeping bag to it and hiked to the trail. Stopping, he stared at the view of the sun arching its way toward the ocean. *While God creates such beauty, men create such evil.* He took a deep breath, appreciating the smell of salt air. Then noticing a shadow pass quickly over the ground, he looked up. It was a red-tailed hawk circling above. The hawk was on the hunt. He glanced around for what might be its prey and spotted a young wild jackrabbit. He glanced up again. The bird was circling the rabbit.

He bent down and picked up a stone. The hawk began its descent with its claws extended. "Sorry Mister Hawk," he mumbled as he tossed the stone at the jackrabbit. The rabbit scurried off and hid.

The hawk broke its decsent and made a hoarse, rasping scream as it flew off. "Live another day, Mister Rabbit."

He continued his walk to the campsite admiring the ocean view. When he arrived, he called out. "Hi, Mrs. Caputo!" He waved to the wife of the park ranger who ran the campsite.

"John. The Mr. and I began to worry about you, two nights sleeping up in those hills. You've got such a nice camper, why go up there and sleep on the hard ground?"

"Like to get away from it all. Clear my mind. Do some nude sunbathing."

"You can do it here on the beach. We won't have you arrested." She winked and smiled.

He chuckled. "I think I burned my butt this time. Should not have put it in the sun the second day."

"Well, if you can sit. Why don't you join the mister and me for dinner. Nothing fancy. Just chicken, veggie stir fry on brown rice."

"I'd love to. Can I bring something? I can get my bike and run into town. How about a bottle of wine."

"That would be great. See you at about 7."

"Vous voir a sept ans."

"Tres bien. Tu francais s'ameliore."

Eight

Sitting in the parking lot of the North Hollywood High School gymnasium, Bill called the head psychiatrist, Dr. Moran, in charge of the child and adolescent wards at UCLA Psychiatric Hospital. She had been informed of the arrival of the Tremway boys. He recounted all that he knew and asked if Dr. Bellows, a Ph.D. post-doctoral fellow whose area of specialization was children surviving abuse, could be assigned as the boy's therapist. Dr. Moran agreed as long as he met with her weekly for supervision.

He then called Dr. Bellows and informed her of the Tremway boys' arrival. He gave her background on the case and the little he gleaned from his time with them. "I wouldn't push right now. Just make them as comfortable as possible. I have no clear-cut evidence at this point, but my gut is saying that they've been abused."

Bill scanned the crowd of cheering students and spotted Justin waving from the top row of the bleachers. He waved back and then made his way to where they were sitting.

"Justin. How are you?"

"Hi, Uncle Bill. I'm good." Justin moved, making room beside Bill's father.

"Hi Dad."

"I saw the boy earlier. He's hoping you'd make it." Joseph Russo, a proud third-generation Italian, was known to boast that his family could trace their lineage to the time of the Medici family. A tall, slender man with a thick head of mostly grey hair, retired from the LAPD, he attended all of Andrew's sporting events. He was proud of his grandson and his son for all that they had achieved. "They've been out already for their warmups. He saw that you weren't here."

"But now I am."

"I heard you're working with my dad," Justin said.

"Yeah. His partner is out on her honeymoon, so I'll be working this one with him." Bill avoided the details.

"Cool. Last time you two worked together he told my mom that he wished you were partners."

Bill was pleased. "He has a great partner."

"I think he just feels more comfortable with you. I mean you two are best friends. Like Andrew and me."

"Andrew got into it with Gavin," Mr. Russo said. Bill looked at him.

Gavin Greenspan, M.D. had been life partners with Bill since Andrew was six years old. That ended two years earlier, soon after Kristin's death, when Gavin left Bill for a much younger man, David.

"Over what?"

"He asked him not to come today with his boyfriend because you would be here. Gavin got angry, said stuff. Andrew got nasty and hung up."

Bill thought of a call he received from Gavin earlier in the day that he'd let go to voicemail and hadn't listened to.

"He wants you to enjoy the game."

"I understand, Dad."

The teams re-entered the gym, the national anthem played, and each team member was introduced. Bill warmed when they called out his son's name—team captain Andrew Russo. Andrew scanned the bleaches, spotted his father, and smiled.

But Andrew's smile turned into a glare. Bill leaned forward, followed Andrew's line of sight, and spotted Gavin. His jaw tightened.

Justin said, "Should be a great game."

"Isn't that Kelly?" Bill asked, nodding toward the back of the head of a blond girl seated a few rows in front of them. Kelly was Andrew's most recent ex-girlfriend.

Justin followed his gaze. "Yes."

"He hasn't said much to me about their breakup. How's he doing?"

"She's going to the east coast for college, so it had to happen. He's okay."

North Hollywood won, and Andrew played well. Bill, Mr. Russo, and Justin waited for Andrew outside the gym. Bill watched as Andrew's coach walked toward them.

"Dr. Russo," he said, extending his hand.

"Coach Becker."

"I've talked to most of the boys' parents at one time or another, but we've missed each other."

"It's hard for me..."

"It is for most parents. I get it, really. I just wanted to take the opportunity to tell you that Andrew is one of my best players. He holds this team together."

"Really?"

"There isn't a boy on that team that doesn't look up to him and isn't his friend. They all confide in him."

"I'm very proud of him."

"He says the same of you."

Andrew made no secret about having a gay father, telling friends how Bill had wanted and adopted him. The coach explained that rather than that exposing him to rejection, his peers befriended him. "And now Stanford."

"He's earned it."

"I'm glad I got to meet you Dr. Russo."

"Yes, same here. Thank you for all you've done for Andrew. I've noticed a real change in his level of maturity since he started playing varsity. He's a lot more focused and assertive."

"Thank you. You'd be surprised by how few compliments we get."

"Actually, I wouldn't."

The coach joined the other parents.

Several basketball players exited the gym. One walked toward Justin.

"Hey," Justin said. "Good game."

"Yeah, glad we won. But I didn't get to play much."

"Next year."

"See you in algebra."

Bill noticed Justin blush. "Who's that?"

"Luke. He's a junior."

"What's up with you and him."

Justin stepped closer to Bill while Mr. Russo talked with another parent. "Andrew said that Luke is attracted to me and wants to know if I'm interested."

"Are you?"

"I am but..." he hesitated and shook his head. "I don't think my dad wants me to date. I mean I'm not really out at school, but neither is Luke. I don't know. My dad and I don't talk much lately. He seems depressed and into himself."

"I think you should still ask your father." He perused the crowd for Andrew and saw him arguing with Gavin. It looked heated. Bill started walking toward them when his father called out.

"Billy!"

Bill looked back.

"Leave it alone."

He shook his head and continued on. It was important to Bill that Andrew respect Gavin. He saw Andrew glance his way while Gavin continued speaking. Andrew put up his hand and said, "Enough."

"Hi Gavin," Bill said. "What's going on?"

"Did you put him up to this?" Gavin said to Bill in an accusatory tone that Bill hated.

"You're kidding, right?" Andrew glared at Gavin. "Are you serious?"

"Did I put him up to what?"

"Did you listen to my voicemail?"

"It's been a busy day."

Gavin glared at Bill in a huff. "Figures..."

Bill's jaw clenched.

"...he insisted that I not bring David to the game." Gavin nodded toward David, standing a few feet away.

Bill took a breath and looked at Andrew. "Insisted?"

"First, I asked nicely and then he gave me attitude. You know how he gets when he doesn't get his way."

Bill smiled to himself, knowing full well what Andrew meant but held to his stern demeanor.

"So then I just told him. And you can see what good that did."

"Your grandfather and Justin are waiting for you." Bill gave him the look that meant, *There'll be a high price to pay if you don't listen to me.*

Andrew sighed, glared once more at Gavin, and left.

Gavin said, "I don't like being told what to do by him."

"Or anyone else."

"I'm just as much a father-figure to that boy as..."

"Careful." Bill tried to control his anger. "It's important to me that he respect you, but come on... a father-figure. You're kidding. Having you there was like having two children: each of you were as impudent, obstinate, and petulant as the other. The only difference between you two was that for him it was age appropriate and he's outgrown it."

"Well, at least I know where he gets his attitude toward me."

"That and a lot more." Bill walked away.

When he joined his father, he told Andrew, "I've taught you better than to get into it with Gavin."

"I'm sorry, but..."

"No buts. Remind me to ground you when we get home."

"Really! And for how long?"

"'Til morning."

Justin and Andrew walked ahead of Bill and his father. Bill heard Justin say, "That's funny. You're grounded after you get home tonight until tomorrow morning."

Mr. Russo said to Bill. "He's just protecting someone he loves. It's a good thing."

"I know, Dad. And I love him for it."

Ed arrived at Bill's house at 9:30 p.m. Bill poured him a glass of wine as he dug into his dinner.

"I heard the boys made it to UCLA." He put a forkful of pasta into his mouth.

"What did you find out?"

"So far no prints, fibers, or anything else that didn't belong to the Tremways and it's the same with the CPA and lawyer. As I told you, the hard drives were taken out of their computers. We checked their financials. The Tremways had accounts at a Bank of America in Northridge—one business and one personal. They also had an account at a USA bank in Culver City, which is miles from where they lived. I mean there are dozens of banks closer and certainly several B of A's in their area."

"That's odd."

"They also found a safe deposit key at the Tremway home. I have the number. I'm not sure what bank. But we'll find out."

Bill readied himself for bed. He thought about the Tremway boys and the loss of their parents. And then he thought again about Evan, his first young patient, abused and frightened. *Why Evan, and why now?* He sighed.

Porn stars, a doctor, maybe a surgeon who performed abortions? Could this be a religious nut posing as an escort, acting out some kind of anti-abortion anti-gay apocalyptic fantasy? But then there's the lawyer and accountant. How are they tied to this?

We're going to need more information and perhaps, unfortunately, more bodies.

Then he thought of Gavin. *Asshole.*

Lying in bed, he wondered what it was that he saw in Gavin in the first place. Kirsten said Gavin's playful, break-all-the-rules, Peter Pan attitude balanced out his cautious, old-soul way of being in the world.

Nine

Bill met with Dr. Bellows and the head psychiatrist to discuss the case management of the Tremway boys. Then he entered the locked ward and made his way to the nursing staff's office.

"Dr. Russo." The charge nurse smiled at him. "You want both Connor and Dylan's chart."

"Yes, please." He sat at the desk and read through what had been reported since their arrival. "I don't see any results from the blood tests taken at Children's Hospital."

"We called last night. They had nothing. I'll call later today."

"Please call me with anything you get." He read a note from the night nurse. Connor and Dylan were found sleeping together naked. "Did you read this?"

The nurse glanced at the chart. "He told me about it."

"Do you know who moved to whose bed?"

The night nurse had awakened Connor, redressed him in his pajamas, and put him in his own bed. He decided not to wake Dylan.

"Do you think we should separate them?"

Bill shook his head. "I think it would be too traumatic right now. Have the night nurse talk to them and keep an eye on Connor. It will probably happen again. Where are they now?"

"They've just finished breakfast. They're in the group room."

"I'll be in the playroom. Can you have them brought to me?" He handed the charts back.

The playroom was a large room where families could meet. It had several comfortable chairs, a table with small chairs, and shelves of toys—tea sets, doll houses and dolls, toy guns and rubber knives, Legos and games, and crayons and pads of paper.

Connor stood in the doorway and then entered, shyly glancing around the room. Then his big brown eyes fell on Bill. Immediately, he looked away.

Dylan looked at Bill and smiled. "Hi."

"Hello Dylan."

He scanned the room and walked to the one shelf that held toy weapons. He ran his fingers over a Jedi lightsaber.

"Hello Connor," Bill said.

Connor gave Bill a quick glance and then looked back at the door as the nurse closed it. Dylan continued to peruse the room. His eyes fell upon a large box of crayons and several pads of paper.

"Can we draw?" Dylan asked, glancing from Connor to Bill.

"Yes, you may."

Bill watched as Dylan moved the box of crayons and two pads of paper to the table. Connor followed him. Bill sat beside the table as Dylan picked a blue crayon and drew three stick figures. He then drew what looked like a swimming pool. Connor stood beside him and stared at the drawing. Dylan said to Connor, "That's us at our house."

"Who are the people?" Bill asked.

"Daddy, me and Connor."

Dylan then drew a penis on each of them. One of the figures had a larger penis than the other figures. "That's Daddy," Dylan volunteered.

Connor stared at Dylan's picture and then picked up a red crayon and began making rapid strokes at the bottom of the page. Scribbling, he worked his way upward and to the sides. As before, he did not respond to questions. Dylan stopped drawing and watched as Connor's strokes became frenetic, often marking the table. Then he stopped and stared at what he had created. Carefully, he drew a small stick figure with horns on its head.

"It's the devil," Dylan nodded his head. "Connor saw the devil and showed me."

Had they seen the killer? Bill wondered. "When?"

"This morning."

Was Connor hallucinating? "Connor saw the devil this morning?"

"We both did." He went back to his drawing.

This concerned Bill. Seldom does one see a shared hallucination. "Where?"

Connor pointed toward the door.

Dylan said, "In the hall."

"Outside this door?"

Dylan nodded.

Bill rubbed his brow. "How about taking me to where you saw him so I can see him too."

Connor remained frozen where he stood. Dylan walked toward the door. Leaving the door open, Bill followed Dylan. Halfway down the hallway, Dylan stopped and pointed to the door of the cabinet that housed the fire hose and extinguisher. The glass within the door had a red decal that read 'fire hose' in big block letters with a cartoon figure in red clothing and a pitchfork in hand between the words fire and hose.

"See," Dylan said.

"Yes, I do."

Bill had walked down that hallway hundreds of times, had seen the fire hose cabinet but had never noticed the little devil. But Connor had in just one pass.

Hypervigilance.

Bill explained to them that it was a cartoon character, that they were on a locked ward, and that there were guards at the hospital that wouldn't allow anyone to enter. He noticed that Connor had used Dylan's blue crayon to draw a stick figure in the flames of hell.

"That's me?" Dylan said to Connor.

Connor nodded.

"You? Why you?" Bill asked Dylan.

"My dad says that he's the only one who can protect us from the devil and that if we ever talk to people and tell stuff, the devil will come and take us to burn in hell. That's why Connor won't talk."

Abuse. Probably sexual, Bill noted to himself.

Connor began breaking the crayons, one by one, and throwing them. Dylan and Bill watched while Bill considered whether to question Dylan any further.

"I know you are both very frightened. Have you ever been someplace without one of your parents?"

Connor stared, terrified. He began moving away from Bill, his anxiety palpable.

"I want you to know that no one here is going to hurt you and that there is no devil here, and you're not going to burn in hell."

Connor looked too fragile to continue. If the boys had any information about the killers, it would have to wait. He escorted them back to the group room, then returned to the nurse's station, sat at the desk, and charted, leaving a note for Dr. Bellows.

"What are you thinking?" The charge nurse asked.

"My gut says sexual abuse." Although he had no actual evidence, the threat of the devil and hell if they spoke, their isolation, and his recall of Evan, was enough for him to consider the possibility. "My guess is that at least Connor was abused."

She nodded. "That's usually what brings them here."

Bill knew that the nursing staff, who spent the entire day with the children, had a wealth of information and insights and appreciated being asked their opinion. "Do you have a read on them yet?" He sat back in his chair.

"Behind Connor's anxiety and silence is a very loud scream."

Bill opened Dylan's chart. "I agree, and although Dylan presents as affable, I'm concerned about him also."

She nodded. "Dylan is a little talker, makes friends with all the staff."

"Quite precocious, isn't he."

"I think he's trying to create a safe place for himself and maybe for his brother. Or from his brother."

Bill had started making a note in Dylan's chart and stopped. "From his brother."

The nurse nodded.

"Interesting. Thank you. If you see anything that might suggest that, please let me or Dr. Bellows know."

He left instructions for Dr. Bellows to spend time with them, but only to do what she could to make them feel safe. He included the drawings for her to see and made notes regarding the drawn penis, the devil, and hell. Finally, he suggested that she schedule a full physical examination for both the boys with an eye toward possible sexual abuse.

Ten

"I saw the boys this morning," Bill told Ed as they left the precinct. He explained what happened and what he thought was possible. They were heading to Northridge to the Dee-licious Production studio.

"Odd that their parents talk to them about the devil. I can't imagine they were religious," Ed said.

"I've seen this before. Children have very powerful fantasy lives. Boys dream of monsters and in their waking hours have an affinity for superheroes. They identify with the superhero and feel empowered. It also can be their first exposure to problem solving and helps organize their fantasy life. 'The superhero in me can control the monster in me and save my world.' Take all the energy of a boy's fantasy life and give him the devil to fear and then add parents telling him that Dad is the only one who can save him, and you have a dependent and terrified child. Instead of the superhero saving him, his parent has all the power. In Connor's case, he wants to scream something out, but it will send him to hell."

"But Dylan is younger. You'd think he'd be the one terrified into silence."

"Part of the puzzle."

They entered a parking lot surrounded by warehouses. One housed an antique car restoration business. Bill could see men working on sheet metal. Another was a motorcycle repair shop.

Ed parked in front of the Dee-licious Production Studio. He rang the bell and a female voice asked them to identify themselves. Ed held his badge up to the camera. A grey steel door opened.

"Detective Coyne. I'm Donna. Your sergeant and I spoke."

She was tall, slim, and dressed, wearing sandals, jeans, and a tee shirt. To Bill, she looked to be in her fifties. Her greying dark brown hair was worn short.

They entered what looked like a showroom with shelves of boxed DVDs and posters of male and female porn stars on the walls. They exited and walked toward a windowed office. Bill noticed various sets: several bedrooms, a kitchen, what looked to be a men's bathroom, a barn with hay, and a classroom. On one set, lights and three cameras surrounded what looked like a cheap motel room.

"DeeDee had a shoot scheduled for today. We cancelled it," Donna said.

They followed her into an office.

An attractive, sharp-featured, slender but fit male who looked to be in his late twenties was seated behind a desk. He stood and extended his hand. "I'm Tristan. Tristan McGuire. Do you have any idea who did this?"

"Not yet," Ed said. "This is Dr. Russo with the FBI."

Tristan told them he oversaw casting men for gay videos. Under another label, the Tremways produced gay porn, which Romeo directed. DeeDee produced any video that included a female actor.

"Were they sole owners?" Ed asked Donna.

"Yes." The business was doing well—a record year, even in a down economy. There were always competitors, and the industry was replete with all kinds of unsavory characters, but the Tremways had not had any trouble.

"There are no outside investors or anyone with a financial stake in the company?"

"None. Not only does she own Dee-licious, but she owns and rents out all the warehouses around us and the land they sit on.

"Really." Ed sounded surprised. "This business is that successful?"

"They own several on-line porn sites, also," Tristan added.

"Any recent trouble with fired actors or neighbors?"

Donna glanced at Tristan. "Nothing really. There was trouble with a male actor that was under exclusive contract. He missed a shoot. When he did show the next day, he was high. DeeDee demanded that he be fired. Under his contract they were within their rights. But it was Romeo who was left to deal with him. They argued, but I can't imagine..."

"I need his name and address and any other information you have on him. You hassled by any extreme religious types?"

"Extreme?" Tristan opened his desk drawer and pulled out a three-inch stack of papers. "They don't have to be extreme to hate us. This is only the last six months."

"Your actors. Any trouble with STDs?"

"DeeDee was very careful," Donna said. "All the actors had to be tested before they could work on a film, and they used protection."

"Always?" Bill doubted that. "Those tests have a recent-exposure window."

Tristan said, "No, they didn't always use protection. But Romeo had a deal with a lab." He reached across the desk and handed Ed a card. "They do viral screening. No lag time like with the antibody test. It's expensive but he insisted."

Ed began asking for lists of their employees, their lawyer, personal money manager.

"Can I look around?" Bill asked. He wanted to do some exploring before he expressed his concerns.

Tristan volunteered to show him the studio. They walked through the warehouse. There were other sets sitting in the dark. Bill followed Tristan, taking in his demeanor. He walked with his shoulders slouched, and his arms crossed over his chest. He looked to be inches shorter than Bill, making him no taller than five foot ten inches. "Tristan your real name?"

"Yeah. I worked under the name Sean Williams."

"You're a porn star?"

"There's a difference between a person who acts in porn and a porn star. Romeo was a star." Bill glanced at him questioningly. "Equipment. Stamina. Looks. Buff body. Large load. In gay porn, most of the big stars are tops. Romeo was a top. I'm not at all hung the way he is. I bottomed for him in several films. He and many others."

Bill asked if Romeo was heterosexual and monogamous.

"In his personal life, yes." Once Romeo was married, Tristan never knew him to be with a man or anyone else other than when he did scenes. "You find that hard to believe?"

"No."

"Doing scenes really isn't about having sex. It really is work."

"I understand."

"I admired them. It's hard to have a real relationship and be in this business. Believe me, I've tried."

"You still work scenes?"

"I quit doing scenes a year ago when I started dating a man I thought I could marry. I knew I would lose him if I kept working."

Bill noticed Tristan staring off into the distance. "What were you thinking just then?"

Tristan glanced at Bill and nodded. "When I told Romeo, he asked that we do one last video together. Romeo had never been topped on film, that means fucked…"

"I know what it means."

"We shot four scenes. Romeo wanted all the scenes to be bareback. We shot at night when no one was at the studio. One was going to be a slave/master scene with me as the bottom. The second night Romeo wanted a pick-up impersonal scene. The third night was going to be me as the master. Him tied up."

Bill noticed Tristan's face blush. "He wanted it rough?"

"Very. I never thought he'd be into anything like that. The last night was a romantic type of thing. You know, kissing… lots of kissing, really intense and passionate. Again, I topped him."

"What do you think that was about?"

Tristan stopped walking and looked at Bill. "Romeo was pretty fucked up in the head I guess…not that I'm not. He was always kind to me, but never…I don't know, affectionate or said stuff… you know, that he liked me or…I think…" His mouth pulled into a frown.

"You think he was expressing affection through having sex with you?"

"It's like the only way he knew how to show feelings. Mostly, when he did scenes, he treated the guys like meat. That was his thing…angry…aggressive…" Tristan sighed. "I really shouldn't…"

"You said the scene where he was tied up was out of character?" Tristan nodded. "Look, anything you can tell me about him may help me find who did this."

Tears filled Tristan's eyes as he recounted a slave/master scene he and Romeo had shot several years ago. He was bottoming for Romeo. "I mean it was all acting stuff. You know, make believe violence. But…"

"He got into it?"

"While he was topping me...I was tied up...had a ball gag in my mouth so I couldn't talk, but we had these safe signals. You know, hand signals not noticeable on camera...if I wanted a break or whatever. He ignored my signals and became...He was choking me and hitting me, and it wasn't like acting. He was really hitting me while he fucked me."

"He hurt you?"

"Yeah, it was like he was possessed. But mostly, it scared me."

The videographer filming with the handheld camera had seen Tristan's hand signals. He stopped filming and told Romeo to stop. Romeo wouldn't stop. Romeo was pulled off of Tristan. He stormed off the set. Later he said he misread the signals and thought Tristan wanted more.

Bill studied Tristan.

"The scene that first night was like that but not as bad...I mean I wouldn't let him tie me up and no ball gag. The last..."

"You said there was a scene where you tied him up." Tristan looked away. "It was like the scene he got carried away, only you were topping him."

"Yeah."

"Tristan, I know this is tough, but you really need to be honest with me."

"He wanted it rough. It surprised me. I've seen all his work and he never allowed anyone to be the aggressor with him. He wore a gag, so we had two signs—one for more and one for stop. He wanted to be hit and fucked." Tristan quickly glanced at Bill and then looked away. "He only used the sign for more. Never stop."

Bill wondered if the scene was being played out again at the Tremway's home. "What did you think?"

"I don't know, but..." Tristan wiped tears from his eyes. "He trusted me. It's weird to say this, but the next night was very loving and passionate."

Tears fell.

"He loved you," Bill said with compassion.

"He was good to me—very good. I was a fourteen-year-old runaway who was selling myself on the streets of Los Angeles. Then this guy, Carl, housed me, provided drugs and pimped me out for more than three years. I had lied to Carl about my age, but after three years Carl said that I was too old for his clients, and he sent me to Romeo."

"Romeo had connections to someone like that?"

"A pimp? Yes. Carl ran boys to houses in the Hollywood Hills and Beverly Hills until they looked worn out, then he threw them out or sold them to people who might hire them. Romeo got some of his actors from him. But Romeo demanded real ID, with a legal name and age. Eventually, he discovered that I was really seventeen, which is too young to work porn. I begged for a job. I would have done anything with anyone, safe or unsafe. He helped me get clean and hired me to clean up the studio, prepare sets and do stuff like that. He allowed me to live here until I could afford my own apartment. And I know you'll probably think he did me no big favor, but when I turned eighteen, he let me do scenes with him and only him, but I had to stay clean. Then, a couple of years later, he let me do scenes with other guys."

"Did Romeo regularly take interest in the welfare of underage boys?"

Tristan looked away from Bill and shook his head. "I don't know what he did before me, but no."

"Why you?"

Tears filled Tristan's eyes. "He said I reminded him of someone he knew when he was a kid."

Bill nodded.

Silence.

"Did he release the videos he made with you?"

"No. I think he never planned on using them. You just had to know him. He never showed emotion. He was almost cold, matter-of-fact. Even with the boys. But at least he gave them attention."

Bill noticed Tristan's lower lip trembling. "You loved him."

They began walking but not speaking.

"Romeo was tied to a chair. Chances are that he was kept silent with a ball gag. DeeDee was tied up and made to watch. Before he was killed, he was cut, shallow cuts, but I'm sure painful. Do you think Romeo had...might he have arranged for some type of sadomasochistic play?"

Tristan shook his head. "I can't imagine he'd do that...he did that once with me, but like I said I never saw anything like that before...he'd never let anyone touch DeeDee and she'd never let herself be tied up. Never."

Silence until Bill went on. "Okay. So now you do casting? Did you hire this guy that was fired?"

"Randy? No. DeeDee does all the hiring for the straight porn. I did the gay porn casting. I guess I'm out of a job...About this Randy thing. It was pretty bad. Romeo had it out with him and then Randy went after DeeDee. You don't do that in front of Romeo. There were punches thrown. And then about a week ago, Randy was pounding at the door demanding money he thought he was owed. They called the cops on him."

They made their way across the warehouse. "It's my understanding that Romeo and DeeDee never went anywhere without their boys and that they home schooled them."

"I was so relieved to hear that the boys weren't hurt. How are they?"

"As good as can be expected."

"Do you think I could see them?"

"They're at UCLA hospital for observation, but no visitors right now."

"DeeDee had this built for them." Tristan pointed to a doorway, and they entered a room that looked like a small studio apartment: kitchenette, table and chairs, a bed, TV The room had no windows, and the only door was the one they entered through.

"So the boys walked the length of the warehouse to get here..."

"All filming stopped. Everyone was robed any time the boys were around. They were never exposed..."

"But they must have known what was going on. At least Connor was old enough..."

"They never hid what they did from the boys. They never saw anything happening, but they knew sex was being filmed." He looked away from Bill, uncomfortable.

They left the room and started back to the office.

"You understand that my concern now is with the children."

Tristan nodded.

"What kind of parents were they?"

"She should never have been a mother. Actually, she never was. Those boys were just props to her. Romeo spent time with them. He did the home schooling, although he was no bright light bulb. Not that I am either," he added. "What's going to happen to the boys?"

"I understand she had a sister. Do you know if he had family?"

"Him? Ah..." Tristan stammered. "No, no family that I know of. I don't know anything about hers. Those boys are going to be lost without him."

He looked around as if someone might hear and lowered his voice when he explained that Romeo gave the boys drugs—tranquilizers for kids—to make them sleep when they had long days, and Romeo would be working a scene, and Dee Dee would be directing and filming. "He'd give them these pills. Five minutes later, they'd be out."

"Do you know what they were?"

"Twenty-five milligrams of Xanax."

"You mean, point two five. They were white, oval shaped, right?"

"Yeah, right."

"You saw the bottle?"

"Yes. Fuck, I really like those boys. Good kids. Dylan was a tough kid, but Connor." He shook his head. "Connor was a mess. I saw on the bottle that the pills were prescribed for the boys. I wouldn't have given it to them if they weren't." Again, he looked around. "They'd be so out of it sometimes. I started to break the pill in half and give them each a half and throw one away so that Romeo wouldn't know."

"Did you see the prescribing doctor's name?"

"Adams. I remember it because it's my boyfriend's name. Christopher Adams."

"The doctor's name?"

"My boyfriend's name is Christopher Adams. The doctor's first name was Ralph. I remember it because I thought it was weird. I mean why would parents call their kid Ralph."

Bill looked at him questioningly.

"You know when you throw up."

Bill nodded. "So, Dr. Ralph Adams?"

"Yeah there was a letter in their like a X or a Z in the middle. I don't remember."

"How was your tour?" Ed asked as they entered the car.

Bill recounted what Tristan said about Randy and about Romeo drugging the boys.

"Romeo gave the kids his Xanax?"

"Prescribed for the kids by a Dr. Ralph Adams."

"Adams! Fuck."

"What?"

"The Malibu doctor's name is Adams."

"This might be our first break," Bill said as he took out his phone. Into it, he said, "Yeah, this is Russo again. I want to find a Dr. Ralph Adams. He has a middle initial like an X or a Z. He's either a plastic surgeon or a pediatrician and lives...Damn, okay, thank you."

"Ralph Q. Adams," Bill said to Ed. "Beverly Hills practice, lived in Malibu and murdered."

"Bingo." Ed called his office. "I'd like to talk to someone in-charge on the Adams case in Malibu...Tell them it's important."

"Where to now?" Bill asked.

"I've got this Randy guy's address. I thought we'd drop in on him unexpectedly. What's your take on this Tristan kid? You think he could be our guy?"

"Ah." Bill realized that he also thought of Tristan as a kid in many ways. "I doubt it. He seems pretty fragile and I think he really cared for Romeo. But I wouldn't rule him out." They entered the freeway. "Did you find out anything interesting?"

Ed told him Donna handled all the Tremways' financial matters, including their personal account at Bank of America. She wrote the checks and Romeo signed them. They had a large safe deposit box in Northridge for their legal papers, deeds, insurance policies, and their wills. "The number of the box is 149. But the safe deposit key we found at their house was for a Box 406."

"It's probably for the box at the USA Bank," Bill said. "I guess it's not strange to have an account and box that your businesspeople don't know about. But, like you said, why so far from where they lived?"

They exited the freeway turning onto Laurel Canyon Boulevard, then onto Magnolia Boulevard and parked in front of a building. It was a typical apartment complex built in the mid-1950s—two stories, open courtyard, small pool. It was now rundown.

They climbed the steps to 204. Ed knocked. They waited. A man, who looked to be in his early twenties wearing nothing but a pair of boxer briefs, opened the door. Ed showed him his badge and asked if they could come in.

He stared at them. "I want to talk to you about Romeo and DeeDee Tremway."

Randy shook his head. "Look, I just went out there to get what was owed me."

"Can we come in?" Ed repeated. Randy stepped aside. They entered. Bill noticed Ed's hand poised on his sidearm. He looked around the room.

Bill heard the shower running. "You have company?"

"My girlfriend. I know I shouldn'ta gone out there, and maybe I shoulda waited for the police, but..."

"Where were you last night?" Ed asked.

"Why?"

They stared at each other.

"My girlfriend and me had friends over."

"Friends?"

"What's this about?" He glanced toward the bathroom door. The sound of running water had stopped. "Ah, she's gonna come out here bare assed. Let me..."

"Just tell her we're here. Nothing else."

Randy walked to the bathroom door and shouted that the police were in the living room. "Use a towel."

The bathroom door opened and an attractive woman, wrapped in a towel, hurried into the bedroom. Randy explained that a couple they'd entertained, spent the night and had just left. He gave Ed their names. "Look if something happened at the studio last night, it wasn't me. You should talk to Tristan."

"And why is that?"

"He uses that place at night. I'm sure Romeo knows it, but they keep it off the books and...Look, I was here. You can ask my girlfriend."

She joined them and gave the same information Randy had.

"DeeDee doesn't know about Randy and me. Is there any way you can not tell her? I'm not under contract and I need the work."

Bill studied them as Ed spoke about the incident at the studio. Randy admitted to the fight. "I know I fucked up. I want to let things cool down and then I'll call and apologize."

"The Tremways were murdered last night," Ed said.

They both looked stunned.

"The boys?" Randy's girlfriend asked.

"They weren't harmed."

"You think I did it?" Randy asked. "My God. No, I promise. I mean I was angry, but..."

Ed stood. "We'll check this all out with your friends."

Eleven

"Did this Tristan guy say anything about stuff going on at the studio at night?" Ed asked as they pulled into traffic.

"No."

Ed called the studio and was told Tristan had left for the day.

Bill looked through the information that Donna had given Ed on their employees. "Tristan McGuire lives in West Hollywood."

"Good. We can stop there on the way back."

"Let's go to Henry's. I'm starved. My treat."

Henry's taco stand was well known throughout this area of the San Fernando Valley. It had been a high school hangout since the early sixties, still owned by the same family, and the food was as good as ever. Bill, Ed, and Kristen had passed their love of Henry's on to Andrew and Justin. They ordered tacos and soft drinks. After receiving their food, they sat alone at an outdoor table.

"I want to talk to you about Justin," Ed said as they sat. "He seems depressed and withdrawn, preoccupied. I'm worried. Maybe he's having trouble at school. You know, being bullied. I'm pretty sure he's not out to his teammates or his friends at school."

"You don't know?"

Ed picked up his taco and shook his head.

Silence.

"You're still not comfortable talking to him about how he's dealing with being gay?"

"He talked to Kristen about all this stuff. I mean everything, not just gay issues. He and I don't talk much about anything." Ed looked at Bill. "No one ever talked to me about my issues and you know I had plenty."

"What stops you from sitting down with him and just asking how he's doing?"

"I do that, and he says fine and that's it."

"There's a lot going on in that boy's life, Ed. He talks to Andrew. What they talk about, I don't know, but he needs to be talking to you."

"He's doing well in school, but... Ed took another bite out of his taco and sat staring into space. "I worry that maybe kids at school know and they're giving him grief. But he hangs out with Andrew and his friends and there's no way..."

"Andrew would never put up with shit like that and from what I hear neither would any of his friends."

Andrew and Justin had always been close, but after Justin's mother's death, Andrew made an effort to draw Justin even closer. After Andrew received his driver's license, he always included Justin whenever he and his friends took off to one of the beaches, a movie, or sporting event. At the end of the previous summer, they both attended a two-week sleepover camp in Simi Valley. The focus of the camp was team sports, but they also had a pool.

"I've noticed his moods," Bill finished his taco and sipped his drink.

Ed nodded. He picked up his paper napkin and started nervously pulling at it. "I don't know how to talk to him. I know it's me. He and his mother could talk about anything."

"Look. You know adolescents, adolescent boys in particular, are not communicative. It's going to be up to you to reach out to him. It's work to get Andrew to open up. Each time I asked him about one of his girlfriends and what they are up to, he gives me that teenage eye roll and head shake."

"I should have retired when Kristin died." He tore the paper napkin in half, tossed it aside, and looked up at Bill. "I can't tell you how grateful I am for Andrew and for you and your parents."

"We love having him over."

"He deserves a parent."

"You're his parent."

"It's gotten like we both live in the same house..."

"For the sake of your son if for no other reason, do what you have to do to get your emotional house in order. He believes you're depressed and still grieving. That boy needs you."

Ed felt his mouth pull into a frown. "I know you're right. I want us to be able to talk to each other." His voice felt heavy.

"Maybe you should start doing stuff with him. Is there anything that you two both enjoy? Some kind of activity, so that you're both occupied and then you can work your way into talking."

He shook his head. "I don't know." Ed continued staring down at the table. "I just feel like my life is over. I am forty-six years old, have a sixteen-year-old son who will be off to college in a year, my job doesn't have the same meaning," he sighed. "Nothing does. You know my history. I don't do well being left and being alone."

"Then start dating."

Ed stared at Bill and shook his head. Their conversation continued at length. As they got up to leave, Bill said, "Ed." Ed turned. "Surfing. You spent years surfing. Teach him to surf. He's a great swimmer. He loves the beach. He'd love that."

Ed smiled and nodded. "Good idea."

Bill did know Ed's history and how it affected him. Ed was not a man of words, or more precisely, words that were used to express intimacy. There were only two adults Ed allowed himself to trust and love, Kristin and Bill.

Sherwood Drive was in the middle of what people called 'Boys Town' in West Hollywood. "1640," Bill said as they drove up Sherwood Drive. "There it is." They parked. The building was a two-story garden apartment building with twenty units. Bill pointed. "Apartment 6."

"Detective Coyne." Tristan closed the door, removed the chain, and opened it.

"I have a few more questions."

"Come in."

It was a small, clean one-bedroom apartment. "Anyone else here?" Ed glanced around again with his hand poised on his sidearm.

"No. Christopher is at work. Sit down," Tristan said, pointing to his sofa. He noticed Bill sniffing the air. "Incense. The aroma is frankincense. Our neighbors cook everything with garlic. It comes through the vents."

"I thought it smelled like the Catholic church I went to when I was a kid."

Tristan smiled.

"I understand you use the studio at night," Ed said.

Tristan hesitated and then nodded. "I suppose it doesn't matter now." He explained that several years ago, Romeo started renting out the studio to private parties since the sets sat idle most nights.

"For what?" Ed asked.

"Real people, couples, friends or whatever, book the place for a night. They tell us what set they'd like to use. We set up and provide a videographer or they bring their own camera and have their privacy. We can cut and edit, make it professional looking or they keep what they've recorded. Also male actors—straight and gay—are available if they're interested. DeeDee wouldn't let any of her girls work with non-professionals. A guard is present for insurance purposes, but stays in the business office."

"Romeo ran this?"

"It was his idea and he... I actually ran it and sometimes directed and filmed it. Guys... a gay guy might call and ask to have a filmed session with his favorite star. We'd contact him and if he was interested, we'd set it up. A couple of times I was also asked to participate. You know, be in the video with these guys. It's good money...was good money."

Ed notices Tristan's reluctance to speak about this. "And?"

"I got paid on the books, but..."

"We're not the IRS. So, this was off the books?"

Tristan nodded.

"No records were kept of when these private sessions were booked, or who booked them?

Tristan shook his head. "No records."

They got up to leave, then Bill turned. "Earlier today, you said that Romeo wanted valid ID." Tristan nodded. "I assume you didn't have a driver's license. What did you use?"

"While I was getting clean, I finally told Romeo that I was seventeen and he sent for my birth certificate—copy from the state."

Bill stared at him.

"He had to have proof, especially when he used young looking guys like me. So he'd done it before."

Bill nodded.

Driving back to the precinct, Bill and Ed tried to come up with a feasible motive which would help them with a profile. Ed's phone chimed. He listened and then nodded. "We have an appointment tomorrow at one in Malibu to talk to them about the Adams' murder."

"Saturday?"

Ed sighed. "I know, less time with Justin, but we've gotta catch this guy before he kills again." He parked the car in front of the police station and looked at Bill. "Two months between him and these latest murders and then one right after the other. There has to be others."

"That's what I was thinking."

They stood beside Bill's car. "Plastic surgeons don't do abortions, do they?" Ed said.

"I guess they could, but not really."

"I wonder what the hell the connection is between this guy and Romeo?"

"One of the Tremways could have had work done. We'll know more tomorrow."

"I can pick you up."

"Sounds good." Bill got into his car and then called out. "How about this? There's this great breakfast place on Pacific Coast Highway. It's a shack..."

"Smithy's. I know it."

"Andrew and I will drive out in my car and meet you and Justin there. Let's say around ten. That will give the two of you time together. Then they can take my car, head back home and you and I can drive up to Malibu."

Ed smiled and nodded. "Sounds good."

Twelve

"This is Coyne." Ed sat in his car with his phone instead of heading to his office, where he knew he'd be delayed for hours. "Did we hear from the coroner yet?... I'll hold." He watched Bill pull into traffic. He had always been drawn to Bill as a confidant and good friend—he enjoyed them spending time together. He wondered if there could be more there.

"This is Coyne." Ed sat in his car with his phone instead of heading to his office, where he knew he'd be delayed for hours. "Did we hear from the coroner yet?... I'll hold." He watched Bill pull into traffic. He had always been drawn to Bill as a confidant and good friend—he enjoyed them spending time together. He wondered if there could be more there.

"No. Okay, I'm heading there now and then I'm heading home."

It was a thirty-minute drive through downtown Los Angeles to the coroner's office on North Mission Road. Ed took the freeway and tried calling Justin, who might be done with his afternoon swim practice.

"Hey, Dad. I'm just getting home. What's up?"

"I have to make a stop and then I'll be on my way home. How about we order out?"

"I could go to Henry's and get Tacos."

"Bill and I ate there this afternoon. Do you have plans for tonight?"

"No."

"Let's hang out."

"Sure. How about we go out and get dinner. I heard about this great Thai place on Ventura Boulevard."

Ed smiled. "You're on."

"Love you, Dad."

"Love you, Son."

Ed took notice of how eagerly Justin responded to his reaching out. He saw so much of Kristen in his son—his comfort with expressing his emotions, his warmth, his gift for words both spoken and written, and his intellect. Since her death, so much of that spark had dimmed. Ed had attended most of Justin's swim meets and cheered loudly. Everyone on Justin's team knew when Ed was in the bleachers. But words like 'proud and love' were not available to him other than as a response. They were triggers to his loveless childhood.

Ed parked in front of the coroner's office, which was a two-story, non-descript beige stucco building. He climbed the four steps from the sidewalk and entered the double glass doors. A security guard glanced his way and asked him to sign-in. Ed walked the long hallway to Dr. Boudoir's office.

"Hey, Ed." She glanced up from her desk.

"Hi, Doc. I really could use..."

"Just got this in." She shuffled papers but didn't find what she was looking for. "Come with me."

Ed followed her into the laboratory, where a male body lay naked on a table. Dr. Boudoir walked to a row of large stainless-steel doors and opened one and then another. She pulled the drawers out. On metal shelves lay the bodies of DeeDee and Romeo Tremway.

Boudoir pulled a sheet back. "A puncture wound. It's like the one her husband had."

Ed was focused on the greenish gel-like substance that had oozed from her empty eye sockets.

"Before last night," Boudoir said, "she must have been a very attractive woman." Her lips were full, her nose angular and proportional to her face, and her hair was thick and dark brown.

"I usually don't see them cleaned up like this... except for that green stuff." He then examined the puncture wound in DeeDee's chest.

"This is not an injection site," Boudoir said. "This is done with a large gauge needle." She then turned to Romeo's body and pulled the sheet back.

Again, Ed was struck by Romeo's appearance. He looked peaceful. Seeing him tied to the chair and covered in blood, Ed could almost hear him screaming from pain. "How does this guy inject two people lying in bed asleep? You would think that Romeo would react in some way before this guy could get to DeeDee?"

"Dart gun. He darts Romeo first, who must have been asleep on his back. They're awakened by the sound of the gun. It's just a pop like a BB gun. Then while Romeo is struggling against the drug, he reloads and shoots DeeDee who maybe sat up and faced your guy. Very quickly they're out cold."

Ed turned from the body as he was reminded of Kristen. "Do you know what the drug is?"

"Ketamine. It's an animal tranquilizer. It would easily put them down for long enough for him to get them into a chair and tie them up." She slid DeeDee's body back into the wall.

"Special K is what they call it on the street," Ed said.

"Exactly, so you're not going to be able to trace the sale." She closed the metal door.

"He's got to be pretty strong. I mean they're dead weight."

She nodded.

They headed back to her office. Again, she searched her desk for the paper she was looking for. "Found it. I've got the report on the lawyer. Ketamine. You better get this guy soon. I think he's just getting started."

"I'm afraid you're right." Ed walked toward the door. "We'll probably be seeing more of each other. You'll be getting a report from Santa Monica and San Diego. Let me know."

Driving home, Ed thought about how best to open a serious dialogue with Justin. He felt queasy—hungry, he decided.

Thirteen

It was a beautiful day for a drive to the beach. Bill roused Andrew early and was on the road by nine. A twenty-mile drive took them an hour. Smithy's, a small shack on the Pacific Coast Highway, had been there since the 1950s. It was said by some to serve the best pancakes and waffles in LA.

They met outside the restaurant. Justin and Andrew stepped away from them and became fully engrossed in their own conversation. The headwaiter said they would have a ten-minute wait before they would be seated.

"Did you talk to Justin?"

"I'm going to take two weeks off at the beginning of the summer. I told him we'd go down to San Diego and I'll teach him how to surf."

"How did he respond?"

"He suggested we rent a small RV and start there and head up the coast."

"Sounds good. Did you talk about anything else?"

"School, swimming. That's it mostly."

The waiter sat them at a table by a window. The view was spectacular—the coastline curving to the east, white sands, and the blue of the ocean. Bill and Ed ordered a coffee and a stack of pancakes. Andrew and Justin ordered waffles, a side of bacon, and two eggs over easy.

"Didn't you boys eat yesterday?" Bill said.

"Athlete's diet," Andrew said.

"We have to balance carbs and protein and have some fat," Justin said.

"Gotta have the bacon," Andrew said.

"Do you guys always order the same thing?" Ed asked Justin.

"He usually orders more, but yeah."

Bill shook his head. "So, Justin. How's school?"

"Good. My grades are great and I made varsity. I'm excited."

At Bill's urging, Justin spoke about workouts and races. "Free style is my best."

"He's the best free styler on the team," Andrew said.

"I'm pretty good at the backstroke and the breaststroke, but I really struggle with the butterfly."

"How's advance algebra going?" Bill asked, hoping Justin would use the opportunity to mention the possibility of dating Luke.

"It's my hardest subject. But Andrew helps me."

"If Justin and I could put our brains in one body, we'd be a genius."

"And we'd be bisexual," Justin said. The boys fist-bumped and finger-waved at each other. Bill and Ed looked at each other and shook their heads.

"He's going to apply to Stanford," Andrew said as the waiter placed their order in front of them.

"Is that okay, Dad?"

"Sure. That would be great."

Bill noticed the smile disappear from Justin's face.

"Uncle Ed. Justin told me you're going to teach him to surf." Ed nodded as he chewed. "I didn't know you surfed. Did you know your dad surfed?"

With a mouthful, Justin nodded and then swallowed. "His boards are in the attic. And Mom told me."

"When did you learn?" Andrew asked, cutting into his waffles.

"High school. So, are you ready for Stanford?"

The rest of the breakfast talk was about the boys going to college. Walking to the car, Andrew asked if he and Justin could go to the Venice boardwalk. When Bill and Ed agreed they asked for money.

Once on their way to Malibu, Ed told Bill what he had learned from the coroner. "And she said that the puncture wound was the type that would be left by a large gage needle, like in a dart gun."

"Ketamine. Interesting. If he keeps the dosage low enough it would just knock them out for a while. But if the dosage is too high they can die of respiratory failure or when they come to, they might hallucinate."

Bill called UCLA and asked to speak to the head nurse. "This is Dr. Russo. Did you get the tox-screen for the Tremway boys." He listened and then hung up. "Interesting."

Ed glanced at him.

"They found Versed. It's an anesthesia medication. A sedative. Causes sleepiness and impairs short-term memory. You found Dylan asleep?"

"Yes, in his bed."

"How was he positioned?"

"You know. I thought that was strange. He was lying on his back, but propped up with pillows, almost at a forty-five-degree angle. I've never seen a kid sleep like that."

"Wow, this guy knows what he's doing. Versed can cause respiratory problems. If Dylan was put on his stomach, he could have suffocated."

"This isn't just some street drug?"

"No. Maybe he knew the boys, and was doing something to try to protect them. Connor was terrified to talk because he was threatened not to tell, and this killer seemed to be very protective. Maybe they weren't always tucked away in that back room at the studio. Maybe someone thought they had to be rescued." Bill mentioned the large penis on Dylan's drawing.

Ed listened and shook his head.

"I mean they could have just called child protection and filed a complaint rather than committing murder. But there is something sexual in all of this regarding those kids."

"You're thinking that they were molested?"

Bill nodded. "Probably, but...those boys were always under the watchful eye of Romeo and Tristan."

"You think Tristan could have molested them?"

Bill shook his head. "I guess anything is possible. I wouldn't rule it out. But right now, I doubt it."

"So, he darts the parents, injects the kids, ties up Romeo, then DeeDee." Ed glanced from the road to Bill and then back to the road. "He could have done his work on them and then hunted for whatever he was looking for, cleaned up and left before morning."

"It would really help if we knew what he was looking for."

"Maybe we'll find that in the safe deposit box. We're getting a warrant and we'll go to the bank on Monday."

"Okay. This is making more sense. My guess is that our guy knows the victims. It could be about drugs...it could very well be about drugs. This guy knows these people and knows the boys."

They arrived at the Malibu Sheriff's Department and asked for Deputy Goodman. "I'm Goodman," a man dressed in civilian clothing called out. "Excuse the civies. It's my day off."

"Sorry to bring you out," Ed said.

"Not a problem."

"This is Deputy Mary Frasier. She's been working the case also." Goodman asked about the Tremway crime scene, then he told them about Dr. Adams. "At first we weren't sure if the suspect was male or female."

He took them through all the evidence they'd gathered. Dr. Ralph Quincy Adams was a fit fifty-six-year-old man who lived in Malibu with an office in Beverly Hills. Married and the father of two adult females. He was found in his Mercedes, sitting in a pool of his own blood. It was assumed he was having a sexual liaison and was cut while receiving oral sex. However, they tested and found no foreign DNA anywhere on his body.

"And he wasn't castrated," Ed said.

"No."

Mary Frasier added, "His briefcase and wallet were gone through, but it didn't seem as though anything was taken." All of Dr. Adams' credit cards and cash were accounted for. His gold Cartier watch and his wedding ring were left behind. And, of course, there was his car. That morning, upon her return, they interviewed Mrs. Adams. She said that she was sure someone had been in her house. Their safe was left open, but she did not think anything had been taken except maybe a leather journal/address book with the list of Dr. Adams' old college friends. Since his death, she couldn't locate it.

Ed thumbed through the pictures of the scene and then handed them to Bill.

"You have the autopsy report?" Bill asked. Goodman pushed it toward him. "Any puncture wounds? Did you do a tox-screen?"

"Yes. We found Ketamine. Our coroner said she can't believe he was injected with Ketamine and then drove his car. He had to have been injected in Beverly Hills. The perp drives him home and to the beach and then ties him up behind the wheel. We went over that car with a fine-tooth comb and found nothing that belonged to this guy."

"We're not finding anything either," Ed said. "Do you know if he took the hard drives of their computers, or laptops?"

"Nothing other than the journal was missing."

Bill looked at Ed. "It *is* our guy. Now, we are sure there's a connection, but we don't know the motive."

"He had partners in his medical practice," Goodman said. "You can talk to them, but we checked them out. I'll give you the address."

"They'd certainly have the ability to cut someone like we've seen," Bill said. "And a knowledge of anesthetics."

Goodman said, "That's what we thought. They all had solid alibis. We figured that if it was a sexual hook up, he picked her or him up on the way home. When we got the autopsy, we had to figure out where and when he was poked."

"What did you find?" Ed asked.

"Adams' office building had security cameras for the parking structure. However, the backside exit was for only tenants. No camera. At the end of his day, 6:43 p.m., he took the elevator to the parking structure. Ten minutes later he returned to his office."

"How do you know that?"

"After 6:30, you can't enter the building from the parking lot. Doctors can, but they have to punch in a code or use their key card and there's a camera. Adams punched in his code. But interestingly, he didn't take the elevator up or down. He must have used the stairs."

"No cameras in the stairwells?" Bill asked.

"No. Anyway, he didn't leave the structure until 7:22 p.m."

In his desk at his office, Goodman and Frasier found a safe deposit box key that his wife knew nothing about. They couldn't find the bank that issued it.

She thought it might be a key to an old box they'd closed. "A week later, during the funeral services, there was another break in at the Adams home. By then the news had covered his death and the funeral was well publicized, at least here in Malibu. Mrs. Adams was pretty shaken by the whole thing and her daughters insisted that she move her valuables out of the house. But again, nothing of note was taken, or so we thought at first."

"He hit her while she was burying her husband... damn," Ed said.

"Her house was wired for security," Goodman said. "The alarm company said someone disarmed the system with a code that she did not recognize, then went through everything in his office. Later that night, his Beverly Hills office was broken into and tossed."

"So, you're thinking the killer didn't get what he was looking for when he abducted Dr. Adams. He came back to the house a few days later and didn't find it and then went back to the office."

"Maybe the key?" Bill suggested.

"Which we already had," Goodman said.

"You said the office building had cameras."

"That's what's the damnedest thing." Frasier opened a folder. "As I said, the entrance from the parking structure to the building has a camera. After hours, when you slide your card or enter your code, the camera takes your picture."

"Like an ATM."

"Exactly." She handed Ed the picture. "Here's the suspect when he used Adams' card to enter the building and in the elevator."

"Something wrong with the camera?"

They stared at the pictures. Everything was clearly in view except for the area of the man's head. It was a complete blur.

"What's with this?" Ed said.

"I've seen this," Bill said. "He's wearing head gear that emits a type of microwave noise that interferes with digital imaging."

"And we've checked," Goodman said, "you can't buy a gizmo like that at Radio Shack. This is sophisticated stuff.

Frasier said, "Government issue."

Ed tossed the photos onto Goodman's desk, shaking his head. "This guy is a pro."

"He had Adams' keys. Must have taken them from the house along with his card key. We asked that all his partners inventory their offices. They said they thought they were missing several vials of some drug."

"Ketamine," Ed said.

"No," Frasier said. "It was Versed."

"The Tremway boys were drugged with that. But would he go back for that?"

"He could have been looking for the safe deposit box key and probably came across the Versed," Bill said.

"That's what we're thinking," Frasier said.

"Is it possible to get copies of the images you have? We have software that can at least give us his height, weight..."

"He's at least six-two and about one-eighty pounds they're guessing." Goodman handed Bill the photos from the file. "We have copies."

Fourteen

Bill called Mrs. Adams and expressed hope that she would allow another interview. She agreed. Just a few minutes up the coast from the Malibu Sheriff's Station, the house was on Cliffside Drive, overlooking the Pacific Ocean. Mrs. Adams buzzed them through the community gate.

"We should have been plastic surgeons," Ed said, smiling.

"Imagine...a house on a cliff with a view of the ocean. But who knows? If the 'big one' hits, you and I might end up with beachfront property."

Mrs. Adams was an attractive woman, stylishly dressed. She asked them in and offered coffee, which they declined. She showed them into the living room. From what Bill could see, most of the exterior room walls that faced the ocean were made entirely of glass.

"Magnificent view," Bill said. Sailboats were out with full sail, gliding across choppy waters. The sky was blue, not a cloud in sight. And Jacaranda trees that bordered their property bloomed, head-dressed with pale blue flowers.

She nodded. "On days like this when it's sunny and clear...on grey and dreary days it can be pretty gloomy." Bill heard the heaviness of grief in her voice. They talked about Dr. Adams and his practice.

Ed inquired about the address book.

"He referred to it as a journal. He was president of his fraternity and I thought it held information about his fraternity brothers. He'd had it for years. He usually kept it in the safe here, but sometimes..."

"He kept an address book of college friends in the safe?"

Bill said, "Seems odd to come back here just to get it... unless it had our killer's name in it."

"A clue?" Mrs. Adams asked.

On Thursdays, Dr. Adams had a late night. "I so hated being here alone." She usually used that time to spend the day with her daughter, who lived in Encino, and would have dinner with her, her son-in-law and their children. Sometimes she stayed the night.

When she returned home the next day, she noticed that their bed had not been disturbed. Ralph hadn't made a bed in the thirty-one years they had been married.

"Was there anything else out of the ordinary?"

She nodded. "Yes. A wash had been done—a towel and rags left in the washer. I'm not sure Ralph even knew where the washer was."

"This address book or journal. You never were curious? Never looked to see what was in it?"

"It was one of those very expensive Italian leather books that had a flap with a lock. It was always locked."

"The sheriff found a safe deposit key in his office."

"Yes." She stood, left the room, and returned with her purse. "It's in here. I put it with my keys so I wouldn't lose it. I've become so distracted lately." Her voice cracked. "I've got the house up for sale...Actually, someone is very interested. I want out of here as soon as possible."

"I didn't see a for sale sign," Bill said.

She took her keys from her purse. "Here it is...I've asked them not to put up a sign. Box 182. But I have no idea what bank. I'm sure they'll get in touch with me when the bill is due."

They left the Adams house with more questions than they had answers. What was in that book? Did Adams let the suspect in, open the safe, and then leave with him? Or did he give the suspect the code to the alarm and combination to the safe? If he brought Adams home, why kill him in his car? A safe deposit box that the wife knows nothing about... and a second break-in days later.

"I guess everyone has safe deposit boxes now," Bill said as they pulled out of her driveway. "But it is odd that she didn't know about it. What was Romeo's box number?"

"406." Ed looked at Bill. "Yeah, I had the same thought. We'll check into the box Monday at the bank."

"Goodman said Adams left the parking structure around 7:20. The death occurred around midnight. Where were they for five hours? And if he brought Adams back to get the book, was this guy going to off his wife too?"

"Or did he know her routine..."

"She did say that she went every Thursday."

"We need to find out what his Thursday night meetings were about and who knew about them."

"Washed towel and rags?"

"That's strange. Maybe they had sex."

"The autopsy showed no fluids or foreign DNA on his penis."

"Did they swab his mouth?"

"We'll have to check. If the reason he brought Adams to his house was to get the book, that book has got to be important."

"Maybe he's in it."

"Maybe," Bill said. "And I bet the Tremways and the rest of them...This has to be specific to these people. Now we have to find out why."

They headed back to town on Pacific Coast Highway. The mountainous coastline snaked southeast and disappeared in the brilliant azure of the ocean. The waves were breaking big. "They're out today." Bill pointed to the ocean. Hundreds of surfers were in wetsuits on the beach and in the water. "I thought you learned to surf when you were in the Marines at Pendleton?"

Ed smiled. "Before that. One of my foster homes was in San Diego. I learned to surf there. But I really got into it when I was in the Marines and came back to the states and I was stationed at Pendleton." They glanced at each other. "Joseph loved to surf."

"You ever hear from him?" Bill asked.

Ed shook his head.

"Nice surfing down there, from what I hear."

"How come none of you surfed?" Ed asked.

"We body surfed, but never on a board. Actually, a group of us including Kristin spent many summer days at Zuma beach body surfing."

"Once I married and joined the LAPD I never seemed to have the time anymore."

Bill recalled the many drives from the valley to the beach and then back again on Malibu Canyon Road. "Wait!"

"What?"

"Fuck. How the fuck did he get back to his car?" Ed looked to the road and then back at Bill. "Okay, he's in Beverly Hills. He drugs Adams, drives him in his car to, well let's assume he takes Adams to his house and forces him to open his safe and get the address book."

"Okay."

"Takes him down to Zuma. Why? Maybe he knows the wife might come home, or Adams tells him she might. Adams is worried for his wife. He tells our guy she's coming home. The suspect makes Adams get the book. Then they head down to Zuma, which is deserted at night. They spend time doing who knows what and then he offs him in his car and leaves. How does the suspect get back to Beverly Hills where he must have left his car? Fuck."

"Maybe a cab? No. He'd have blood on him and the book and whatever shit he used to cut and tie up Adams. No way he'd take all that shit into a cab."

Silence.

"He knows he's bringing the doctor back," Bill said. "He drives to Malibu, parks his car, and then takes a cab to Beverly Hills, abducts the doctor, and takes him to Zuma."

"We need to check the cab companies, even car services."

Bill stared at the ocean, thinking about Andrew leaving for Stanford and his empty house. "This is what's beautiful about Southern California, views like this." Then he turned in his seat again. "I noticed something at breakfast. When Andrew asked you when you learned to surf, you told him that it was when you were in high school. When I just brought it up, you said you learned while in one of your foster care homes in San Diego. Does Justin know you were in foster care?"

Ed exhaled loudly. "No."

"Does he know about Joseph?"

"No."

Silence.

Ed glanced at Bill and then back at the road. "What?"

"Do you want to open the door to meaningful conversations with Justin?"

"Of course, I do. But..."

"Yeah, I know, you don't know how. Before I was out, anytime a conversation got serious, or I thought it might lead to questions I dreaded, I changed the subject. I kept everything superficial at best. If at all possible, I would avoid talking about anything personal. And that's what you're doing?"

Ed stared at the road ahead, not speaking.

"Eddie, your son loves you, looks up to you and worries about you. He has a loving and generous soul. If you trust him and are vulnerable, he will respond and open up to you."

Ed frowned and shook his head. "I don't want to burden him with..."

"Your history is a burden to no one but you."

Ed made eye contact with Bill. "Sometimes I hate you," he said tenderheartedly.

"I know."

Silence.

"Especially, when you are right."

"Sometimes I hate myself when I'm right."

Fifteen

John parked his camper several houses north of the address he thought belonged to Wayne Russell. It was a tree-lined street east of N. Fairfax Avenue and south of Santa Monica Boulevard in an area known as the Fairfax District, a neighborhood that he frequented when he lived in Los Angeles as a teenager. And it was the same neighborhood he had scouted a few weeks earlier while planning his attack on Victor Xavier, the man who housed him as a boy.

He sat in his camper and watched the stars disappear as the light of dawn moved across the sky. The air was still—not a leaf on a tree stirred. He moved to the back of the camper, grabbed a bottle of water, and watched the house through the partially drawn shaded window. He heard the call of a blue jay. Its song was loud, combining whistles and vocalizations that sounded like 'Jeey, Jeey.' Another answered, and the birds talked back and forth.

He wondered what his life would have been like if not for these men. *Would I have lived with my mother in a neighborhood like this one? Would I be able to love a man, someone like Ryan, giving myself to him without hesitation?* His eyes welled. *Ryan should have so much more than I can give him. With me in his life, he'll never have the love he deserves.* He swallowed hard as he picked at the paper label on the water bottle.

A burning rage washed over him when he noticed a light in the window of the Russell house come on.

Is this the one who stole me? That night was seared into his memory. He'd been shaken out of a deep sleep. He rubbed his eyes and then noticed the man sitting beside him on the bed. He froze with fear.

"Don't be afraid." The man had smiled.

He glanced around the motel room for his mother. Staring at the man, he slowly rolled away from him. "Where's Mommy?" He and his mother had been on the run for two days, leaving their apartment in Colorado to escape an abusive boyfriend. They were heading for Los Angeles and had stopped in Las Vegas almost out of money.

"You remember me. We met last night in the coffee shop."

John shook his head. "I want my mother." He sat up. He was naked except for a pair of jockey shorts.

"Remember last night, I brought your mom to this motel. And while we were in this room talking, you slept in the car parked out there."

"Is she outside?" He looked toward the window, moving to see through a crack in the curtain. He saw nothing. He pulled a lumpy pillow to his chest and wrapped his arms around it.

"No. She was arrested."

"Arrested? But what about me?" Tears filled his eyes.

"She called me from jail. I'm going to get her out. But she wants me to bring you along. She really wants to see you."

"But she said I should never go anywhere except with her."

"Okay. Well, I can leave you here. But you'll be all alone and if the police come while I'm gone they'll put you in jail too."

"But I'm only six. They don't have jail for kids. Do they?"

He nodded. "If you come with me, we'll get your mother and then you'll be with her. Okay?"

He nodded.

Before we go, I have this for you."

"What?"

"Chocolate milk. I know you love it. Remember you had it at dinner last night." He handed the container with a straw to the boy. "I have to pack all your stuff and then we'll go and get your mother. Come on, drink up."

He sipped and watched the man gathering his shoes and clothing. Then he fell asleep. When he woke, he was naked in a strange room lit only by a nightlight plugged into the wall. He slowly eased himself off the bed. There were no windows in this room. He had stood by the door, hoping to hear his mother's voice. "Mommy," he had called out. There was no answer.

After spending days outside Wayne Russell's house, he learned that Mr. Russell either worked at home or was unemployed. He left only to go for a jog or to the gym soon after his wife left for work. Occasionally, Wayne ran errands in the morning or met his wife for lunch.

He surveilled Mrs. Russell and learned her schedule changed from week to week. He followed her to the Beverly Center Mall and sat on a bench close enough to Milgram's Jewelry store where she worked. She was a woman of poise and beauty. She had long black hair with streaks of silver and a perfect smile with which she greeted each customer. She seemed genuinely pleasant.

On the days she worked, she left the house at 9:40 a.m. and arrived in time for the opening of the store. When she did not meet her husband at the mall for lunch, she returned home at lunchtime. That varied, but once back at the store, she remained there until 6:00 p.m.

John lingered outside Milgram's, waiting for her to leave for lunch. Being a Sunday, the mall was busy. He watched people of different types stroll, window shopping lazily, while others darted into stores. Some loitered, holding what they had purchased, waiting with their back to the store window and staring at everyone who passed.

After Mrs. Russell left for lunch, John called the store and asked for her.

"She just went to lunch. May I help you?"

"I was in a couple of days ago. Mrs. Russell was helping me. I'd really like to come in when she's there."

"She'll be back at two."

"I can't come today. What about tomorrow?"

"This week she's here on Monday and Tuesday from ten when we open, until one when she takes lunch and then she's back at two. She's off Wednesdays and Thursdays this week."

"Great. I'll be in tomorrow or on Tuesday."

He hung up.

He left the parking structure feeling sure he had enough of a window to get to Mr. Russell on Monday. Surveilling Mrs. Russell so closely, he began to regret the pain he would cause her. After all, she had no part in any of this. But Mr. Russell deserved to die. *But I'll go easy on him for her sake.*

He headed across town to continue his reconnaissance on another of his targets—a gay real estate agent.

Sixteen

Monday morning, Bill met with Dr. Bellows at UCLA. She had spent time with Connor and Dylan and found it odd that neither of them seemed to be grieving their parents. "There is nothing to suggest that they miss them or that they're concerned for them. Dylan is worried about what will happen. Connor still hasn't spoken."

Bill explained what he had seen and learned at the studio.

"Trophy children? And the boys knew what was going on there?"

"Not even trophies. They didn't parade them around or put then in private school. The kids never socialize with the neighbor's children. I had the sense that they were just there, like objects."

"If she didn't want them, why not get an abortion." She shook her head.

"Part of the puzzle."

"Something is going on, especially with Connor. And it's not just emotional neglect. Maybe he saw something," Bellows suggested. "Perhaps at the studio."

"Something that he was unable to process. I know if I was put in a room day after day, I would have found a way to satisfy my curiosity."

"I do think that they could have been abused."

"Sexually." Bill nodded. "It sounds like those boys were always with them and at the studio...Tristan was taking care of them if Romeo wasn't."

"You think he might have molested them?"

"I guess it's possible, but my gut says no...Have you set up a physical exam yet?"

"Yes. Later this week with Dr. Cartwright." Ruth Cartwright was a well-known UCLA pediatrician who specialized in the physical detection of sexual abuse of girls and boys.

Bill met Ed outside the USA Bank. Ed showed the warrant to the bank manager who had Craig, the bank employee in charge of safe deposit boxes, escort them into the vault and to Box 406.

Ed asked, "Who are the signatories on this?"

Craig opened a file. "Beside the Tremways?" he asked.

Ed and Bill looked at each other.

"A Victor Xavier."

"Really?" Ed said. "He's a secondary?" Craig nodded. "Can you tell me who beside Dr. Ralph Adams is on Box 182?" Ed played a hunch.

"I'm not sure I can give you the information."

"I can call Dr. Adams' wife or get a warrant to have the box opened. Unfortunately, Dr. Adams was murdered two months ago."

"Really? Okay, let me look."

"Wouldn't it be interesting," Ed said to Bill.

"Uh, 182...Adams, Romeo Tremway and Victor Xavier. The three of them." He looked up from the files. "But Dr. Adams is not the primary. Xavier is."

Ed thought out loud. "The three of them. Does Romeo have another box here?"

Craig hesitated. "I thought you'd ask. Box 4209 which is one of the largest safe deposit boxes we have."

"Anyone else on that box?"

"Victor Xavier." He stared at the computer screen. "Okay, I'm seeing what they've done. Xavier has a box with only Romeo as secondary. That's 4209. Adams had a box with Romeo and Xavier. That's 182. Romeo has a box with DeeDee and Xavier on it. That's the box you have the warrant for, Box 406. And Romeo and DeeDee Tremway have a large box all their own. Box 4220."

"You can have multiple boxes and a box with three keys?" Bill asked.

"If they're available. Mr. Xavier has been a client here for years. And you can have extra keys made. Wait, here's a box that Adams has all by himself. Box 131. It's one of our smallest."

"We never found a key to that one." Ed said. "Maybe our guy did find what he was looking for."

Craig unlocked Box 406 and gave it to Ed. "I can get someone here to drill open the lock on the other one," he said, leaving them. "But you'll have to have a warrant."

Ed called the precinct for the warrant and asked to have it brought to the bank. "I want in it today."

They took Box 406 and went into a private room. "Something strange going on here. It's almost as if they used the boxes as a drop," Ed said.

"Drugs?"

"Let's see." He opened the box. In it, they found dozens of computer flash drives labeled with a number, letters, and a date. "What do you think these are?" He held up one of many small plastic containers that were also numbered and dated.

Bill took one from him and popped it open. "It looks like memory cards from a video camera."

"Okay." Ed sat back. "Tristan said the Tremways were renting the studio to private clients at night. Maybe these are copies. Maybe this was blackmail. Dr. Adams gets his rich clients to the Tremways. They rent the studio and do private porn maybe with porn stars. The Tremways secretly film it and Xavier does the blackmailing."

"That doesn't explain the CPA and lawyer. We have to get to this Victor Xavier guy."

Ed called in for someone to come to the bank to log and collect everything they found in box 406. Two policemen showed up with the additional warrant as the locksmith arrived. They sat and logged in each of the memory cards and flash drives. Then, Ed and Bill opened DeeDee's box.

"Holy shit," Ed said. He took out banded stacks of $100 bills. "That's at least two-hundred and fifty grand." Also in the box was a man's leather toiletry bag. "It's heavy." He unzipped it. "Damn." He said, showing Bill the contents—one-ounce gold coins.

"That's another hundred and fifty grand. Where do you get money like that to just store away?" They looked at each other.

"Drug money."

"Or blackmail. You can't just deposit it, can you."

The two policemen logged in the cash and gold, packed it up, and the four of them headed to their cars.

"Give the flash drives and the memory cards to Brandon in tech," Ed instructed. "Tell him I want a still shot of everyone that is on each of these. I want to be able to see who these people are."

Bill Googled Victor Xavier. 421 Clinton Drive. The neighborhood was one of the older areas established in the 1930s and was referred to as "The Bagel District." Historically, it was the center of the Jewish community in Los Angeles. Restaurants, butchers, bakeries, and kosher delis line nearby Fairfax Avenue, creating a unique place in the heart of the city. It was also the location of Melrose Avenue, known for funky shops, art galleries, and a fashion district similar to SoHo in New York and Haight-Asbury in San Francisco.

The house was single-storied and of a 1930's Art Deco style—clean geometric lines, no arches or tiled roof.

They stepped out of the car. Bill glanced around. The sky was clear and the air hot. A gust of fresh afternoon wind promised a cooler night than the night before.

Ed said, "Looks quiet."

"Dead."

Ed shook his head. "Let's hope not."

The curtains in the front of the house were drawn. No car was parked in the driveway or in front of the house. Ed knocked on the door and rang the bell. No answer. Bill tried to find a gap in the drapes. There was none.

"Can I help you?" A female voice called out from the house next door.

Ed flashed his badge. "We're looking for Mr. Xavier. Victor Xavier."

"I'll be right out." They waited.

An elderly woman limped toward them. "Just had hip surgery," she explained. She looked frail.

"Sorry to bother you," Bill said.

She approached them and introduced herself. "Victor's not here...at least I haven't seen him in a while."

"Do you know where he is or when he'll be back?"

Mrs. Silver shook her head. "No. And it's odd. I haven't seen him for well over two weeks. He usually asks me to collect his newspaper and watch his home. I noticed them piling up, so I picked them up. He typically vacations for four or five weeks but not this time of year."

"You didn't see him leave?"

"No. He always gives me his itinerary and how to reach him in case of an emergency. This time, nothing."

"Does he live alone?" Ed asked.

"Yes. He's a very nice man. Friendly."

"Everything looks to be closed up," Bill said.

"He's very private. I've never been in his house."

"Thank you."

Ed opened the gate, and he and Bill stepped into the backyard. Looking through a sliding glass door, Ed could see into what looked like a den. "It's been tossed." He stepped up to a windowed kitchen door and pounded. Nothing. "Mr. Xavier, this is the LAPD."

"We have cause," Bill said.

Ed put his shoulder to the door. It was solid. He took out his sidearm, smashed the window, stepped back, turned his head, and winced. "Decomp."

He reached in, turned the lock and the door swung open. "LAPD," he shouted. "Deadbolt wasn't on." Holding his sidearm out in front of him, he stepped into the kitchen. Bill did the same and followed.

"Clear," Ed shouted, stepping through the den.

Bill went to the right and into the living room. "Clear!"

They met in the hallway. The stench suffused the entire house. Four closed doors. Ed opened one to a bathroom.

Bill opened another. "Bedroom. Clear."

"I'll never get used to that smell," Ed said.

Ed opened a third door to a pitch-black windowless room. He reached in, found the light switch and turned it on. A body hung by the wrists from a suspension device attached to the ceiling. There were sex toys on shelves, whips and paddles hung from hooks on the wall, and a bed. "Let's get out of here," Ed said. "He's not going anywhere.

A fourth room contained various types of video equipment. A car was in the garage.

They put their guns away.

Cameras flashed. A CSI dusted for prints. The coroner could not determine time of death but guessed ten to twelve days. Mr. Xavier's genitals had been removed like Romeo's.

"There are twenty or thirty shallow cuts on this chest, arms and legs," the coroner observed, examining the body. "These were all done antemortem."

"Torture," Ed replied.

Bill noticed a police baton crusted with blood lying on the bed. "He was beaten?"

"I don't think so," Dr. Boudoir said. "My guess is that it was anally inserted, puncturing the colon from what I can see. Just guessing right now, but I'd say the small cuts, then the anal rape, and then the castration." She looked at Ed. "You better catch this guy."

Mark pointed to remote cameras hidden in the walls. "I think that's one over there. And there in the ceiling. Look, there's another. He had the entire room, every angle covered. His playroom. He videoed whatever was going on in here."

"Maybe we caught this guy on camera," Ed said.

"Those flash drives at the bank?" Bill said.

They watched Mark search the room. "These cameras are remote. They broadcast to a terminal..."

"The room next door," Bill said. "There are computers and other kinds of equipment in there."

Mark left, then returned. "That's where the receiver is, but it's hard drive is gone. Just like the Tremways."

Standing beside Bill, Ed said, "What the fuck is going on here? This guy leaves nothing behind."

"He knows these people," Bill said. "He must. He knows where they work, when they are at home alone, where the cameras are..."

"Seems so. He does Adams first, then Xavier, then the others, and then the Tremways."

"What's odd is a de-escalation of torture after this. The lawyer and the accountant. That's unusual."

Ed agreed.

"We have a safe," Mark shouted. "Opened and empty. And that equipment in the other room is expensive and used for editing videos."

A CSI found several bloody smudges. "Our guy is wearing gloves. Also, at the Tremway house we found footprints outside that were size eleven. Tremway was a size eleven. Here we found bloody footprints where the guy exited. Size ten. Same size as your dead guy."

"Fuck," Ed said. "This asshole is wearing their shoes. I want this guy, and when I get him, I'm going to nail his..."

A CSI, kneeling at the door jam, called out, "I've got prints here..." Mark knelt beside her. "These aren't this guy's prints... they look like..."

"They're a kid's prints." She looked at Mark and nodded.

"Are you sure," Ed said. "A kid in here?"

"Either that or a little person – the size and the location says a kid."

A chill ran through Bill's body. He thought of Connor and Dylan. "Fuck."

Mrs. Silver and other neighbors stood on her lawn, watching people come and go. From them, Bill and Ed found that Mr. Xavier lived in his house before the Silvers moved into the neighborhood five years prior.

"He moved here the same year I did," a neighbor woman said. "Seventeen years ago. From the other side of town, Culver City, I think."

USA Bank, Bill thought.

Mrs. Silver told them Xavier went to Hawaii or London on vacation. He'd spend a few days there and then head to Thailand or Romania. "I never knew anyone who vacationed in Romania. I mean I know people go to Thailand. It's supposed to be beautiful. But Victor said that Romania is beautiful and cheap. Who knew?"

"Did he have visitors?" Bill asked.

"There was this good-looking man. Victor said it was his nephew, so I guess he had family. There was also another man – tall."

"No one else coming and going?"

"Sometimes, on Thursday nights."

"Thursday nights," Ed repeated.

"He had friends over once in a while to play cards."

"The good-looking man..." Ed asked Mrs. Silver while glancing at Bill. "...he came by with two boys?"

"Actually, he used to come by with just one, but the last time he had another one in tow. Cute boys. The other man always had one too—a blond boy."

Bill said, "The two boys, they had brown hair, slender, one about nine-years old, the other about seven."

"Yeah, I guess so. The blond boy was about the same age—eight or nine. They were usually here the same nights." She hesitated. "Sometimes on Thursdays but sometimes on the weekends."

Bill stepped away from them to call the hospital and ask the charge nurse if she had an iPhone and if she could take a photograph of Connor and Dylan and send it to his phone. Then he joined them again. As they watched the bagged body being wheeled out of the house, a rush of cool air shook the surrounding tree branches, and the hush gave way to the swirl of leaves. Mrs. Silver put her hand to her mouth. "Was it a heart attack?"

"We're still trying to determine that," Ed said.

Bill's phone chimed. He checked, then showed it to Mrs. Silver. "Are these the boys?"

She grabbed a pair of glasses that hung from her neck, put them on, and took his phone. "Yes, that's them. Sometimes the older boy spent the night."

"Are you sure?" Bill asked.

"A few months ago, just after the New Year, I think, the three of them showed up. It was around dinnertime. See there's my kitchen. I can see his driveway and the walkway to his front door. That night the man left with just the younger one. I thought it was odd because it was a Thursday night, a school night, and a number of Victor's friends were visiting—you know, card game night. The next morning I saw the nephew drive up and then leave with the older boy. The reason I remember it is that he was carrying him. I mean the boy seemed too old to be carried."

As Bill and Ed walked to their car, a woman called out, "Ashley Cotton, L.A. Times. Detective Coyne, is this another murder..."

"No comment."

"Agent Russo. Is this a serial killing? Is that why you're here?"

"No comment."

She followed them to the car. "I have information that these men have been mutilated. Is that true?"

Coyne closed the car door and started the car. "Shit. We'll see this in the paper tomorrow."

"Fuck," Ed said as they rode back to the precinct where Bill had left his car. "What kind of father would leave his son with a man he thought would sexually abuse him?"

"The worst kind of sociopath."

"I've seen everything, but sociopath or not..."

"Sorry to say this, but I've seen shit like this before. I wonder who this blond boy is?"

Ed called in, asked for a warrant for Xavier's safe deposit box, as well as what had been found on the flash drives and memory cards. Brandon had taken a quick look at both. They were all password-protected, but he didn't think he'd have trouble getting around it. But before he tried anything, he wanted to make sure they wouldn't self-erase when he did. He'd have to go to police headquarters and use their equipment.

"Tell him I need them yesterday," Ed demanded.

Silence. A long silence. After a while, Bill asked how Justin was.

Ed shrugged. "We haven't talked since Saturday."

Seventeen

Bill sat at his desk and read his messages. The Tremways' lawyer had called about the boys. He'd return it later. He stared at the photos of Andrew that sat on his desk. One picture was of him sitting in front of his seventh birthday cake. There'd been a party planned, invitations went out, and no one responded with an acceptance. It was the year after Gavin moved in.

Bill remembered how his parents, Ed and Kristin saved the day by making the day one surprise after the other. IHOP for a pancake breakfast where everyone sang happy birthday. Disneyland for the rest of the day and pizza for dinner. Then home for a cake. Bill and Gavin decided against parties after that. Instead, they tried to make his birthday special by granting him a wish, which usually was a Lakers basketball game with Gavin, Ed, Kristen, and Justin.

For his fourteenth birthday, his freshman year in high school, Andrew asked if he could invite friends. Bill, fearing a repeat of what happened previously, nervously agreed. That year, three of Andrew's friends joined Bill, Gavin, Ed, Kristin and Justin to a game.

He smiled at Andrew's senior year picture, and his throat tightened as he thought about how much he'd miss having him at home. He picked up his office phone and dialed.

"Hey Dad. What's up?"

"Is there enough of Grandma's lasagna in the freezer for four people?"

"Let me check."

Bill stared out of his office window at the UCLA campus. He thought of the Tremway boys as he waited.

"Yeah, there's plenty."

"I'm thinking about inviting Ed and Justin over for dinner one night this week."

"Sounds good. When are you going to be home?"

"I have a report to write and a meeting downtown. I'll be home around 6:30."

"Chicken for dinner?"

"Sounds good." Bill's iPhone chimed. "Hold on. It's Ed...What's up?"

"Got another one. I'll text you the address. He was killed today. His wife found the body."

"Andrew. I'm going to be late. Make yourself dinner."

"I'll cook the chicken and put some aside for you."

"Thank you."

"Love you," Andrew said and hung up.

Bill pulled out of the parking structure onto Wilshire Boulevard. and headed east to the Fairfax District. His empty stomach growled. The street was blocked with police cars and an ambulance. He parked his car. After checking in with the policeman in charge of signing in people, he approached Ed.

He gestured towards a woman seated on the back end of an ambulance, wearing an oxygen mask. "She came home from work and found her husband..."

Mrs. Russell pulled off her mask and said through tears, "Why would anyone do that to him?"

A man in his twenties approached the house but was stopped by one of the officers. She looked his way.

"That's my son," she called out.

Ed waved him in.

"I'm Kevin Garland. My step-father..." He put his arms around his sobbing mother.

"We'll leave you, but I'll want to talk to you both before I leave."

"What happened?" he asked his mother as Bill and Ed walked away.

"Mr. Russell was out of work," Ed said to Bill. "He was a VP of some bank."

"This isn't very far from Xavier's. I wonder if they knew each other."

"I was thinking the same thing. Maybe one of the Thursday night crowd...I didn't think any of those bank execs got laid off."

They put on gloves and booties and stepped into the house.

Mrs. Russell had gone to work, came home for lunch at one, and then headed back. When she returned, she found Mr. Russell naked and tied to his desk chair, blood pooled at his feet.

"He's not castrated?" Bill said with surprise.

"No. Femoral artery cut like Adams. Bled out."

"What the fuck. Any message left?"

"Nothing."

"No smelling salts packs. No antemortem slashes. Other than the femoral artery cut, it doesn't look like there was any torture."

"Other than. But you're right. Notice the puncture wound. No forced entry. Guy must have knocked, shot him with the tranq gun, tied him up, cut him and let him bleed out."

"The house isn't tossed either."

"He's not on any of the safe deposit boxes, but whatever is going on, he's part of it."

Mark arrived.

"Sorry to drag you here," Ed said, "but I want consistency."

"No problem. I'm getting overtime." He checked out the body and the room. "This is obviously the same guy, but isn't he de-escalating? Isn't that odd?" He stepped closer to the body. "I wish you'd catch this guy. Since I've started working this case, I haven't been able to pull wood without thinking about it."

An officer entered the house, "Detective Coyne." Ed turned. "I think we may have caught him on tape."

Bill felt a rush of adrenaline. The officer signaled them to follow him. They left the Russell house, and the officer said as they walked, "I was talking to the neighbor two houses down. He's a gay guy, lives with his boyfriend. They're being harassed by someone in the neighborhood."

"Harassed?" Ed said.

"They put out their garbage and find it tossed all over their lawn the next morning. They've had shrubs torn up and..."

"You said there's a video."

"They installed a camera. It records the front of their property and the street—the one with the BMW parked in the driveway."

The art deco house was well maintained, painted a dark grey with black trim, and landscaped with white azaleas and red roses in full bloom. Bill noticed a camera at each corner of the house facing the street.

"He showed me what he has. We know the guy was alive when his wife came home for lunch at 2:15."

They approached a well-dressed young man standing in his doorway, whom the officer introduced as Aaron. He invited them in.

The interior of the house looked to be newly remodeled. The old wood floors were restored, and the furniture was also art deco. They walked through a hallway and entered a room with windows overlooking a large, beautifully landscaped backyard with a pool.

Aaron sat at his desk and typed on his computer. He turned the screen toward Bill and Ed. "I just got home from work. I saw all this going on. When I heard what happened, I checked what I might have caught." He started the video. "Okay, so this is at 2:15 p.m." They watched as a man wearing a helmet, blue jeans, and a black jacket drove past the house on a motorcycle. He fast-forwarded the video. "Here he is at 3:12 p.m. going the other way."

Ed studied the now-captured image of the man on the motorcycle. "This might be him. He brings everything he needs and takes it with him. Even the vics shoes. How many guys riding a Harley carry something like that on their bike?" Strapped to the back of the motorcycle was a large duffle bag. Ed sat down at the desk. "Can you run it in slow motion?" he asked Aaron. "No way to see the plate?"

"No, all I've got here is the side of the bike. He's wearing a helmet and the face guard is down."

Remembering the man in the elevator at Dr. Adams' office building, Bill said, "There is no way that guy is six-foot two and one-eighty. No way."

"I know," Ed said. "That's what I was thinking. Fuck. We get a break and all it does is add to the confusion."

"Can we have this?"

"I already cut you a copy." Aaron handed him a disc.

"Thanks. Can you make two?"

"Of course."

Bill stepped away. Ed followed. "Someone is killing pedophiles. If this Russell guy knows Xavier, he's probably one of them, otherwise how does our killer know who they are? They don't advertise."

"If he's one of them, would he all of a sudden turn on them?"

"I doubt it."

As they started for the door, Ed asked the young man about his troubles with the neighborhood.

"I thought it was kids on the block. But I'm pretty sure it's this older guy up the street. I caught him on a video dumping my garbage onto my lawn. He's not really identifiable—it's just his size. He's a big guy, overweight."

Ed stepped outside and called to another officer. "I want you to view the video that Aaron has of a neighbor dumping garbage then pay this guy a visit. Tell him that if anyone harasses these men, he'll have to deal with me." He handed Aaron his card. "If this happens again, call me."

"Thank you, Detective Coyne."

To the officer who brought them to the house, Ed said, "So the murderer was heading east. My guess is that he went up to the boulevard. He could have turned right or left, but the freeway is about two miles south. There are gas stations on every corner to the entrance of the freeway. I'm sure they have cameras. Start there and if you spot him work your way back here. Check any business along the way that might have cameras. I want the plate on that bike."

"Yes, sir."

Bill said, "I'll give this to one of the tech guys. They can pull his height and weight. Maybe we can even get enough on the bike to narrow that down."

Ed looked at his watch. "He could be anywhere by now." He stared at Bill. "You've got that look. What are you thinking?"

"Statistically, serial killers work alone. But we have our six plus foot guy at Dr. Adams' office and now we have someone who looks to be much shorter. If this guy killed Mr. Russell and our six-footer killed Adams, we have two possibilities. One, the two cases are not connected—I think they are. Two, we have these two guys working together or they are in communication, and one kills Adams, the other kills San Diego guy, and on and on."

"Like a competition?"

"Anything is possible. This might also explain the differences in the torture and mutilations."

"Fuck," Ed groaned, his arms crossed over his chest.

Bill noticed Ed staring at a couple of men chatting across the street. Ed went back into the young man's house and then headed across the street. Bill followed him.

"Did you men know the Russell's?" Ed asked.

"Yes," said an overweight middle-aged man. "I knew him and his family. Nice people." The other man agreed. Ed questioned them both about what they might have seen that day. "Just an ordinary day, I'd say." The other man agreed.

"Did either of you see someone on a motorcycle?"

Neither had.

Ed stepped closer to the overweight man. "You have a problem with the gay couple across the street."

The man looked surprised. "No, not really."

"He has you on video, dumping his garbage on his lawn and pulling up shrubs. I just saw it. I told him to press charges against you right now. I told him I'd be happy to take you in for harassment and destruction of property."

"Me? You're sure it was me?"

They glared at each other. "He said if it happens again he would. If it happens again, I'm personally coming out here and taking you away in handcuffs."

The man nodded.

Ed stepped closer, staring directly into the man's eyes, "We clear?"

He nodded again.

Bill and Ed walked across the street.

"Asshole."

"I want to ask Mrs. Russell something." Bill said.

She was seated in the passenger seat of her son's car with the door open. Kevin was squatting down and talking to her as Bill and Ed approached. He stood.

Bill said, "How's she doing?"

Kevin shook his head. "Is it okay if I take her to my apartment or does she have to stay here? I can leave her with my girlfriend if you need me here."

"Sure. But I'd like to ask her a few questions. Is she up to it?"

"I really don't think…"

"I'm good." Mrs. Russell's voice was heavy with pain.

"Did your husband have anything like a Thursday night card game or meeting with friends?"

"Not regular, but once in a while he'd get together after work."

"Was that on a Thursday night?"

She took a breath. "Wednesday or Thursday. I'm not sure. Usually, those are my days off and it was one of those."

"Did he ever travel with his friends?"

She shook her head. "No."

"Did he ever go to Thailand or Romania?"

"Thailand. But it was on business—bank business. He went a couple of times."

"It was more like four or five," Kevin said. "He said they had business there."

"And you never accompanied him?"

"No."

"Thank you. I'm sorry for your loss."

Mrs. Russell nodded as more tears fell.

Ed pulled Kevin away from his mother. "How old were you when they married?"

"Nine."

"Where's your dad?"

"He lives in Santa Barbara. He teaches Chemistry at UCSB."

"Is there anything about your step-father that we should know?"

He turned away from his mother and lowered his voice. "He's a real prick."

Bill asked, "Why do you say that?"

Kevin looked away and shook his head.

"Was he abusive?"

Kevin tensed. "It started soon after they married when I was nine. I was finally able to convince my mom and dad that I'd be better off going to high school in Santa Barbara."

"Was he sexually inappropriate with you?"

Kevin exhaled loudly and nodded. "I'm dealing with it in therapy. My mother and father don't know. And I didn't kill him—I was in class at UCLA when this happened—a chemistry lab. You can check."

"Thank you We've got your information if we need to follow up."

As Bill and Ed walked away from the car, Ed asked, "How did you know?"

"Gut feeling. This Russell guy knew Xavier."

"Card games on Thursday nights and Thailand," Ed added. A TV van was parking. "I'm surprised it took them this long."

"When is our meeting with Chief Henson?"

"I changed it to tomorrow afternoon."

"How about you and Justin come over for dinner later this week?"

"Okay. You said that my history was only a burden to me. You don't think hearing it will affect Justin?"

"Of course it will. He loves you."

"But it will change the way he looks at me."

"Yes, but you're assuming that it will affect him in a negative way. Right now, he sees you as a very good detective who is grieving his mother and who he is having a hard time opening up to. Your history could be a bridge for him to you and not an obstruction."

Eighteen

The next morning, Tuesday, Bill stopped at the FBI tech department on his way to his office and gave them the flash drive of the motorcycle rider. They had a complete database of all cars, tires, and motorcycles licensed in the United States. He gave the disc containing the video caught at the Russell crime scene to the techie and asked that it be analyzed as soon as possible. Then he went to his office and called the Tremways' lawyer.

"I called DeeDee's sister after hearing from her assistant Donna," the lawyer informed him. "They didn't know they were named as guardians. They asked where the boys were. I told them they were in a hospital. How are they?"

"At the UCLA Hospital on the child psych ward."

"Really? Why?"

"For observation. They'll be there for a while." Bill didn't want to give him any more information than necessary.

He called Dr. Bellows and explained all that he had seen and learned at the Xavier house and expressed his concerns. She'd been focusing on building a rapport with the boys and not looking to press them about what they might have experienced.

"I'm sure they've been abused," Bill said, "but I want to wait until we get the results of their physical from Dr. Cartwright. Then we'll have to change course. If Connor reacts badly, he's in the right place."

"You have something for me?" Bill asked the techie.

"It's a 2016 Harley Davidson Iron 883 Sportster. Nice bike worth about ten grand."

"The guy riding?"

"Once I had the bike, I fed the image capture into this program we have. He's 5 foot 8 or 9, weighs 140 to 145. Shoe size, nine or nine and a half."

"You got his eye color?"

He smiled. "Odds are they're brown."

"Thanks. I was hoping he was six foot two and two-hundred pounds."

"Not even close."

Bill and Ed headed to LAPD Headquarters to view the flash drives found in the Tremway's box. "Tech confirmed that the guy on the bike is 5'9," 145."

"So, we're thinking two guys. One over six plus the other five-eight?" Ed shook his head. "They did find footage of the suspect on the bike getting onto the freeway, heading east. Couldn't get anything on the plate."

They entered a room filled with electrical equipment and computers. Ed introduced Bill to Brandon, a flaxen-blond-haired young man sitting at one of the monitors. "He's our wunderkind when it comes to computer stuff."

He stood, distressed, and shook Bill's hand. "I've never seen anything like this." His voice sounded hollow.

He had uploaded everything they found in Romeo's safe deposit box. After he clicked on a file, the three of them stared at the monitor watching two naked boys sitting on a bed.

Bill immediately recognized Connor and Dylan. He watched as they began fondling each other. Bill's stomach churned.

"Okay." Brandon looked away. "We have memory cards and flash drives. They're coded..."

"God Damn it." Ed growled. "Kiddy porn. That motherfucker." He pulled up a chair and sat looking at the screen. "Their father couldn't have known."

"...Each memory card has a matching flash drive," Brandon continued. "The memory cards are from a camera and are the raw footage. The flash drives are the edited version of the memory card." He hit fast forward.

"Damn," Bill said, watching a naked adult wearing a black ski mask enter the scene. "We're watching the stuff from the memory card, the unedited stuff?"

Brandon nodded. "You never see his face." He returned the video to normal speed. He pointed to the monitor. "Did you see the angle change?

"Someone is filming this shit?" Ed asked Bill. "Doesn't that look like DeeDee's studio?"

"Maybe, yeah." Bill felt himself getting sick as he watched the boys perform fellatio on each other and then on the male. He sensed in Ed the rage and disgust that he too was feeling. A rage so deep, so pure, that it wouldn't let him breathe.

"I don't need to see any more of this," Bill barked. "How far does it go?"

"This one goes on for an hour, but it's edited down to thirty minutes. He penetrates Connor, and it ends with his orgasm. This video is one of the last ones made." Brandon clicked on another file. Up came a video of the same masked man with a very young boy. "That's the older boy..." Brandon looked at Bill. "...Connor, but at about four or five years old, is what I'm guessing." He fast-forwarded the video. "Fondling and oral sex."

"Is there penetration?" Bill asked.

"No." Brandon looked at him and not the screen. He sighed. "By the dates, there's no penetration until Connor is seven. These were made for an audience. The two videos before the penetration...when Connor was six..." Brandon shook his head as if denying the truth of what he had seen, "...at the end of the video, they announce the upcoming event. That being, this guy penetrating Connor for the first time."

"Doesn't that look like Romeo?" Bill asked Ed.

"Fuck. That fuck got off easy just having his junk cut off."

Brandon pulled up another file and opened it. He fast-forwarded and then let it play at regular speed. The video was horrendous. Connor fought and cried as the man in the mask raped him. Ed turned away from the screen, enraged. Both Brandon and Bill were staring at him. Finally, Ed said through his teeth, "I'd cut his cock off myself."

Bill looked toward Brandon. "Do any of these videos show Dylan being raped?"

"No, but..." he turned his chair and opened another file. "...the last video...it was made... the date is Monday, two weeks ago. They announced at the end that it would take place soon."

"Maybe we can get a voice comparison," Bill suggested.

"No voice. They scripted it and scrolled it at the end. No adult ever speaks."

Ed apologized to Brandon. "I'm sorry to ask you to do this, but I want you to view each of these, the raw footage. And I don't want anyone else handling them except you."

"There's something else you need to see." Brandon closed one video file and opened another. "This is the unedited stuff." The video was of Connor and Dylan.

"When was this taken?" Bill asked.

"Dated six weeks ago."

"Why are we watching this?" Then he saw Connor force Dylan onto his stomach and lay on top of him. Dylan begins to struggle, and the filming stops.

"I don't think that was planned."

The video begins again with Connor and Dylan beside each other when a masked man enters the scene.

"Damn." Bill groaned. "That's not good."

Ed said, "I need a report about what's on each of the memory cards. And if you ever catch the person holding the camera..."

"Can I fast-forward through them? I can catch..."

"Yeah."

As Ed opened the door, Brandon asked, "You're thinking the guy that killed Romeo knew this was going on?" Ed nodded. "When you catch him, I want to shake his hand. There must be some kind of medal the city can give him."

Bill started toward the door and then turned back. "The raw footage was edited."

"Yes. And from what I can tell it was done carefully. Almost professionally."

"So it's Romeo. They're filmed at the studio, and they're edited. Isn't that what they do there—make porn and have it professionally edited?"

"You're right," Ed said. "We'll talk to Tristan."

They left the room. Ed said, "Not sure I feel any differently than him."

Bill glanced at him questioningly.

"Giving this guy a medal."

"Yesterday, you wanted to nail his balls to the wall." Bill stopped and looked back at the door they just came through.

"What?"

"Blond boy. That woman, Victor's neighbor, Mrs. Silver. She said she saw a blond boy going into his house and staying the night with Connor." He opened the door and said to Brandon. "We have info about a blond boy who spent the night at the house. If you see him on there, let me know."

Bill joined Ed. "Do you know Stewart Dawson?"

"No, can't say that I do."

"He's our regional guy who works kiddy porn and child trafficking stuff for us. He's been working it for about ten or fifteen years. He knows everything that's out there. I should give him a call. He can work with Brandon, and he'll know if this stuff is on the Internet."

"Sounds good."

On their way to the precinct, Bill and Ed sat in traffic. Neither of them spoke for a while.

Then Ed said, "Little of what I see affects me anymore—hazard of the job. But this shit is different. That motherfucker raped his son!" Ed cried out. "That boy, his son, tried to get away from him. He held him down!"

"I know." Bill exhaled loudly. "There is nothing I abhor more than violence to a child."

"You've seen this before, haven't you."

"The rage you're feeling. Imagine sitting in a room with the abused child and their family, and knowing that one of them is the abuser, and feeling that anger, and having to control it."

"I can't."

"I had a patient, a twelve-year-old girl, Michele. She had a psychotic break. I couldn't be alone with her. When she became anxious, she'd either move toward me and try to put her hand on my genitals or she'd get on her hands and knees and thrust her buttocks into the air."

Bill had had a physical examination done. It was determined that she was vaginally and anally scarred. Michele had two older brothers, a younger brother, an alcoholic mother, and a born-again Christian father. Bill had to determine who abused her.

When Bill met with the family, Michele would be fine talking to her brothers, but when her father addressed her, she would get out of her chair, get on her hands and knees, and present her buttocks.

"I confronted him. He called her a slut. I threw him out of the room. Then the older brother told me that his father had been anally penetrating him until Michele turned eight. When the oldest boy moved out of the house, the father told him that if he told anyone about what was going on he would deny it and turn to his other sons for sex."

"Damn. What happened?"

"I testified at his trial. Then his daughter and sons testified. He was convicted."

"So you traded in your therapy hat for a Glock."

Nineteen

Bill sat in Ed's office, called Dr. Bellows and described what he had seen on video. "There are over thirty memory cards and flash drives. They go back five years." Silence. "Dr. Bellows, you there?" She was. She needed a moment to collect herself. "At least now we know what we are dealing with. You should start by telling the boys that I've seen the videos and that we know what happened to them, but don't tell them what I saw, only that I saw the videos."

"I worry about Connor. He's so fragile."

"I understand your concerns. But by letting him know that what they've suffered is no longer a secret, and that the devil hasn't appeared, you've given them permission to put words to their abuse. They survived the abuse and they can survive the telling of it. As they open up slowly, and with compassion, move them towards specifics."

"Okay."

"A supervisor once told me that specificity is the essence of reality. You know that being able to sit with that reality makes it safe for them to get to their emotions. It's therapeutic. You are the container, of the specifics, and then their emotions. That's the most difficult part. If you avoid it, they will pick up on that and then hold onto the fear that their experiences are too terrible to put into words."

"That's what Connor is doing," said Dr. Bellows.

Bill decided that, for now, he would wait for more information as to whether Connor was aggressively abusing Dylan.

◈ ◈ ◈

Before they left for the precinct, Ed had sent for Donna, the Tremway's business manager, their video editor, the two guards, and Tristan. The guards were the first to arrive. A policeman escorted them to an interrogation room. Bill poured himself a cup of coffee and entered the observation room.

Ed began. "We're going to talk about these nighttime shoots. I understand that a guard was always there."

"Yes, and Tristan was always present and made sure that all guests were signed in?"

"More often than not," one guard reported, "people hired one of the stars to join them. It was one of Romeo's selling points—to do a three way with your favorite."

Tristan took them into the studio, helped them set up, and then sat with the guards until the party was over—usually two to three hours. Sometimes Tristan was paid to film the scene. However, most of them were private parties and used their own cameras. After the clients were done, they signed out, Tristan closed down the studio, and the guards locked up. He left when they did, they reported.

"Had you ever seen the boys at the studio late at night?" Ed asked.

Yes, but not often, they said. When DeeDee was filming. Sometimes it went late into the night.

"Do you remember the boys being there when they were shooting private videos?"

They did not.

Ed then talked to Donna. "This editor, Ben, he's the only editor you used?"

"Romeo sometimes used someone else for the gay porn if Ben was swamped."

"Who was that?"

"I don't know. Romeo dealt with it. Romeo and Tristan. Tristan knows who he is. He wrote the checks and Romeo signed them. It was all kept separate."

Ed left the room and came into the observation room. Bill said, "I don't think she knows more than she's telling. She's nervous, but who wouldn't be."

"I want you in there with me when I question the editor. If he's editing these..."

They entered the room. Ed brought his laptop.

Bill had not seen Ben arrive and was surprised. He expected an older man. Instead, Ben looked to be in his late twenties. Blond, blue-eyed, and tanned, he wore a navy-blue tee shirt with flowers across the chest, shorts, and sandals.

"How long have you been working for DeeDee?"

"Nine years."

"You're a professional editor?"

He smiled. "I graduated from USC film school fourteen years ago. I get this all the time. I'm thirty-six."

"Tell me about working for DeeDee," Ed said.

"She was tough. I mean she wanted quality. Some studios play games with the footage. Run the same shot over and over, so that a thirty-second shot becomes a three-minute scene. She wouldn't do it. She shot with two handheld cameras and fixed cameras. At first, she was with me for every edit. The last year or so she let me work on my own, but she reviewed everything."

"You did mostly the straight porn?"

"All the straight porn. If I wasn't busy, I'd do stuff for Romeo."

"What about that side business he had?" Bill asked.

"Those people pretty much just took what they shot. It costs a lot to edit videos. It was just for their use. I think I might have done two over the last three years. Stuff that Tristan shot that involved our actors—you know, they hire a porn star to play with and they want it on video. Some people like to throw their money away."

Ed opened his laptop and clicked on a file. The video was forwarded to the point where Connor was being anally penetrated. "Did you edit this?" Ed turned his laptop toward Ben.

Ben looked at the computer. He blanched. His eyes widened and filled with tears. He looked up at Bill. "That's Connor. No, no, I've never seen that before." He glanced at the computer screen, shook his head, and then turned the computer away. "I swear, I've never seen that. Fuck, I've seen and edited almost everything you can imagine. But not stuff like this. I swear on my mother's grave." He lifted his tee shirt to wipe his eyes. "Those poor boys. Where are they? Are they okay?"

"You never suspected anything like this was going on?" Bill asked.

"No! Never. I mean I knew DeeDee was a lousy mother, but Romeo. Those boys hung on

him."

"Lousy, how?"

"Never had anything to do with them. Never talked about them. I'd be there during a shoot, you know, to see what she had in mind. We'd have meetings after a shoot. The boys would be there. Romeo and Tristan took care of them, lunch, naps, schooling. She never seemed to interact with them. She was all business."

"Who do you think the man is?"

"I don't know." Ben sighed. "It can't be Romeo. It just can't."

"Someone filmed this," Ed said.

Ben looked surprised. "If you watch it longer, you'll see the movement of the camera. Look, look at this. And that does look like the studio."

"I believe you."

"They say the boys were never not with one of their parents," Bill said.

Ben kept shaking his head. "I mean she was a bitch, but there is no way any mother would stand for this. She wasn't cruel. She just ignored them."

"Then Romeo did this without her knowing?"

"But he couldn't have. He..." He sat and shook his head. "I can't believe he'd... I know them, knew them...it can't be."

"I'm going to have more questions for you," Ed said, curtly. "Just wait here."

Ed and Bill agreed that Ben was most likely telling the truth. Bill called the hospital to talk to Dr. Bellows. She'd just gone into session with the boys. Bill said to Ed, "I think you'd better let me question Tristan. He's pretty fragile."

They returned to the interrogation room where Tristan was waiting, slouched over in a chair, pulling at the label on a water bottle. He immediately sat up straight.

Bill noted that when he met Tristan at the studio, he was clean-cut and well-dressed, but now he looked tired and hadn't shaved in a few days. He was wearing a wrinkled tee shirt, shorts, and tennis shoes.

"Did you find who did it?" he asked.

"We have additional questions for you," Ed said.

Tristan nodded, looking nervous.

Ed opened his laptop as Bill said, "You were in charge of the off-books shoots?"

"I got paid on the books, but..."

"These nights?" Bill interrupted. "You were always present?"

"Yes. A guard and me. He was there for security. I was there for...well, to get them set up, any questions..."

"Were there ever shoots when the guards were not present and you were?"

He shook his head. "No. DeeDee insisted. There's a lot of expensive equipment there and for insurance purposes a guard had to be present."

"Were there times when the boys were there during these off the books shoots?"

"Connor and Dylan? No, not that I can remember. No. I mean Romeo and DeeDee weren't there." He seemed to be thinking.

"What?" Bill said.

"Well, when this all first started, there were times when Romeo was there, but DeeDee and the boys weren't. Romeo was making sure I knew what to do."

Silence.

"What's this about?" he asked.

"You filmed scenes?"

"Some."

"My understanding is that not all the gay porn was edited by Ben. Is that true?"

"Romeo had this other guy who did editing. Out of his house."

Bill and Ed glanced at each other.

"You ever do editing?"

He shook his head. "Just the business end: casting, acting and lately some filming, but editing is another whole thing."

Ed sat staring at Tristan. Bill asked, "How old were the boys when you started working with Romeo."

"They weren't even born yet."

"You ever film the boys?" Ed turned on his laptop.

"Sometimes when there would be a long day, I'd hang out with them. You know, entertain them. I'd take a camera and we'd play like we were making a movie. You know, like sword fighting." He paused. "I don't understand what this is all about..." he said, as Ed turned the computer toward Tristan. The video was playing.

He stared, swallowed hard, and looked up at them. "Oh my God, that's them." His shock was palpable. He wiped tears from his eyes. He glanced back at the screen, shaking his head. "Oh my God, Romeo."

"You're sure that's Romeo," Ed asked.

Tristan looked around the room, stared at the trashcan, and then ran to it. An officer, who was standing at the door, quickly moved toward him, but Bill put up his hand. Tristan began to vomit.

Later, he sat, sipping bottled water.

"How can you be sure that's Romeo?" Bill asked.

Tristan's tears kept falling. He wiped his face. "I know his body better than my own." His voice cracked. "That's Romeo. If you zoom in on this part of his chest..." He pointed to the area that was mid-chest and to the right, "...You'll see a small mole. He always had it covered with makeup when he did scenes." He pushed the computer away and began to cry. "I knew something was going on with Connor. I knew it. I felt it," he pointed to his chest, "I just didn't want to believe it."

"There are more than thirty hours of this shit on memory cards. Starting from five years ago," Ed said.

"But Connor was only four."

"If you didn't film and edit and Ben didn't, then who did?"

"Not me. I swear. Please believe me. Probably Victor. Romeo has known him forever, since he was a kid."

"Victor Xavier," Bill said.

"Yeah, that's him. He came to the studio a couple of times—picked up work and a check. But mostly Romeo went to his house."

Tristan's tee shirt was wet with sweat. Bill understood his distress. He, too, felt like vomiting when he saw the video. But Tristan's anguish seemed beyond just his care and concern for the boys.

Bill's phone chimed. He pulled back, answered, and then stepped outside the room.

"Dylan told me what happened," Bellows said. "Connor just sat frozen in his seat. Dylan said that his father told him that he was going to 'make love' to him soon."

"So, it was Romeo. Did he say who was behind the camera?"

She sighed. "Their mother..."

Bill immediately thought of the message on the Tremway's mirror. MW 18: 9.

"...There's more that Dylan told me. Recently, Romeo was letting Connor have 'sleep overs' with other people at a man's house. When Dylan told me, Connor started crying. It was the first time I've seen tears from him." She paused. "Connor said..."

"Connor spoke?"

"Yes. He whispered but it was like he was trying to shout. He said his father left him at a house with strange men."

"Men not a man?"

"And another boy."

"Did he know who these men were?"

"No. Just their father's friends. Men who wore hoods. But the boy's name was Jamie. It was hard for me to not break down. He's so hurt and fragile. He said that he stayed with the man with a boy named Jamie a lot. I asked what a lot was. He looked at his hands and then put up eight fingers, but who really knows. Right?"

He could hear the pain in her voice. "I'll be in tomorrow. I know this is hard but you're exactly what they need. Connor speaking is a testament to how well you are doing with them."

Bill stepped into the room and asked Ed to join him in the hall. He told him what he had learned. Ed turned his head toward where Tristan waited. "He's five-nine and probably close to one hundred and forty pounds. However, his shoe size doesn't look to me like a size nine. More like an eleven."

"I can't see him killing anyone. Certainly not like what we've seen."

Bill went back to Tristan.

"I didn't know any of this. Please, you've got to believe me. I'd never..."

Bill nodded. "Are you in therapy?"

Tristan shook his head.

"Drug rehab, group therapy?"

"I was."

"Did you talk to them about being sexually abused?"

He shook his head. More tears

"How old were you?" Bill asked.

"I don't know. I mean..." he breathed in deeply. "It started before I remember. I know it was happening when I was in first grade...I remember that," he said, looking down at the table.

"By whom?"

He stared at his hands. "Ah..." he shook his head. "My father and...I ran away when I was thirteen and moved in with some old guy, but it got really bad. So I ran from him."

"That's when you started working for your pimp. What was his name?"

"Carl. He lived up in the Hollywood hills."

"This has opened a dark place for you, Tristan...Look at me." Bill waited until he was able to make eye contact. "You should talk this out with someone."

"I just lost my job."

Bill took out his card. "There's an outpatient psych clinic at the UCLA Psychiatric hospital. Their fees are on a sliding scale. Call them." He wrote down the number. "Tell them that I referred you for an intake. When you make an appointment, let me know. I'll do what I can for you."

"Thank you."

"You're at risk, very high risk of using."

"I know Mr...I mean Dr..." he looked at the card.

"Russo. William Russo."

"Sorry. My mind is kind of..."

"Make the call."

Ed and Bill watched him leave.

"By his father and before he can remember." Ed shook his head. "There's a lot of this shit going on."

"One in five boys, maybe."

"Shit. If someone touched Justin..."

"Tristan doesn't even remember when it started. I'm sure Connor has no memory of not being molested. He was four."

"That kid going to be okay?"

"Kid?"

"Tristan."

"Don't know. I hope so." Bill realized that he too, at some level, thought of Tristan, who was now a man in his late twenties, as a person emotionally stuck in pre-adolescence. "So, where do we go from here?"

"I have a warrant for Xavier's box." He looked at his watch. "Tomorrow. Hopefully, that will give us a lead."

Silence

Bill explained to Ed what Dr. Bellows said. "The blond boy, Jamie, was known to Romeo. Jamie and Connor were at Xavier's house at the same time. We've got to find Jamie."

"Tomorrow we'll get into Xavier's box." Ed glanced at his watch. "We've got the Chief in forty-five."

Twenty

Assistant Chief Henson's office, on the top floor of the LAPD Headquarters building in downtown Los Angeles, with its bookshelves, desk, conference table and chairs, faced south with a view of the Pacific Ocean and access to a rooftop garden. Henson was a tall, handsome, fit man, with an ebony complexion, dark eyes, and a baritone voice that added to his commanding demeanor.

Bill, Ed, Dr. Boudoir, Mark, and Brandon waited around the conference table. When the Chief arrived, they all stood.

"Gentlemen. Doctor. So, Ed, what do we have?"

"As of now we have eight victims."

"Eight? When I gave this to you there were four. What is going on?"

"Sir, we've linked two previous murders, one in Malibu, probably his first, and another in San Diego. Yesterday, we found yet another, killed prior to the Tremways. And yesterday he killed again. So, since we met, there has been one additional murder."

Bill chimed in, reading from his notes. "His first was Dr. Ralph Q. Adams, a plastic surgeon, who lived in Malibu, was killed on March 11th. We believe the killer took an address book from the doctor, perhaps containing the names of these other men. There isn't another murder until April 5th or 6th. We're not sure of the date Victor Xavier was killed. Mr. Xavier lived in West Los Angeles and was a film editor.

"The severity of the torture and mutilation is significant. Dr. Adams had his femoral artery cut. He bled out. Xavier was tortured—cuts all over his body, anally raped with a baton and his genitals were removed. Mr. Eric Rodgers, a wealthy San Diego businessman, who owned several car dealerships, was killed on April 2nd. He was cut and had his genitals removed. On April 7th, Brett R. Levin, a CPA who lived in Santa Monica was murdered in the same manner as Mr. Rogers. On April 9th, Leland Jay Rheingold, a lawyer, was killed in his office. He like Levin and Rogers was cut and had genital mutilation."

"There's a de-escalation," the Chief noted.

Bill nodded. "Then he takes time off. My guess is that he was doing surveillance of Xavier, Rodgers, Levin and Rheingold after he killed Adams. Then on April 15th, last Thursday, he killed the Tremways and his M.O. stayed the same, except where in the past he was able to separate these men from their families, this time he included DeeDee."

"She's part of his kill list."

Again, Bill nodded. "Yesterday, April 19th, Mr. Russell, an ex-VP of a bank, who lived in West Los Angeles, not far from Mr. Xavier, was killed. Again, he was able to isolate Mr. Russell away from his wife."

"This guy is doing his homework, isn't he?"

"What's odd here, is that all he did to Mr. Russell was cut his femoral and let him bleed out. A further de-escalation."

There was a long discussion about the pattern that was developing: the use of Ketamine, the torture and removal of the genitals, the removal of computer hard drives, the use of the victim's shoes, and the lack of fingerprints, hair, or fibers.

"At the Xavier crime scene," Mark said, "we found a sex dungeon – whips, dildos, ropes and a suspension device. There were cameras set up to record whatever went on in that room."

"Is this about sex then?" Henson said.

"We found safe deposit keys and got into the boxes of DeeDee and Romeo. I just got a warrant for the Xavier box. In the Tremway's box we found memory cards and flash drives," Ed said and then looked at Brandon.

"I was able to get by the passwords and download the content of them. On them we found hours of child pornography dating from four years ago to the present."

Ed said, "The videos were of Romeo molesting his sons."

Henson leaned back in his chair. "Child porn and his own kids."

"DeeDee filmed what Romeo was doing," Bill said.

Silence.

The Chief crossed his arms over his chest and stared into space. "So, what, this guy is killing pedophiles?" Everyone sat silently. "Profile?" Henson asked Bill.

"There are questions as to whether this is one guy or two." Bill explained that they had one image of a man over six feet tall, possibly one hundred and eighty pounds, and another much shorter and weighed less. "However, since we have no physical evidence left at the scenes, we're guessing. The guy on the bike might just be someone who was in the area at the time and had nothing to do with the murders.

"As far as a profile goes, I'd say we're looking for a white male between the ages of 25-40. He's highly intelligent and has medical knowledge. He could be a doctor, EMT or even a medic out of the military. He's a good planner, systematic in his actions, organized, focused to the point of being compulsive. He's driven and won't stop before he gets what he needs or is caught. And there's his MO."

"The escalation and then the de-escalation," Henson said.

"That leads me to believe," Bill said, "that our killer knows these people and his brutality is commensurate to his rage at each of them."

"Or," Ed said, "we have two killers."

"So, we have a group of pedophiles being killed by..." Henson said.

"Someone who is also in the group and killing off everyone who knows him, or one of their victims."

"Or," Bill said, "God forbid my son was sexually abused and filmed by these guys..."

"A vigilante who is working their way through the group," Henson said.

Brandon said, "After seeing those videos, maybe we shouldn't be so quick to catch this guy."

"As a father," Henson said, "I agree. But as a member of the LAPD I'm afraid that isn't an option."

Bill said, "I'd like to bring in our guy who heads up child pornography and trafficking. He might be able to tell us more about what we found."

"Who is that?"

"Special Agent Dawson."

"I don't know him, but I'm fine with that." Henson stood. In response, so did everyone else. "Lady and gentlemen, let's meet again next week. But Ed, call me with updates as you make progress."

"Yes, sir."

Standing in the parking structure, Bill said to Ed, "Thursday, dinner at my house."

"I know. Justin told me. Andrew is making dinner."

"He's learning how to cook before he heads to Stanford. But so far all he's doing is defrosting my mother's leftovers."

Ed laughed.

Twenty-One

They stepped out of Coyne's car in front of the USA Bank. The sky was clear. The trees stirred in a breeze just strong enough to take the searing edge off the hot sunlight. After they served the warrant, Victor Xavier's safe deposit box was drilled open. Craig pulled it from its vault and handed it to Ed. It was heavy.

He and Bill entered a private room as two uniformed policemen stood by. Ed set the box down. "If this is all gold and cash, there's a fortune here."

There were gold coins and cash amounting to what looked to be over three hundred thousand dollars. Also, twenty VHS tapes, an equal number of CDs, and over one hundred flash drives, each coded as before. "Videotapes. If this is more child porn, it can't be the boys. These have to be much older than them."

"Let's hope they're home movies," Bill said.

They tagged everything and took it into evidence. The tapes, CDs, and flash drives were sent to police headquarters downtown, and the cash and gold to the precinct. Bill called Agent Dawson and asked that he meet them downtown.

"I heard he's being transferred to D.C. to head up child porn on a national level," Bill said.

"Can't say I'd want that job."

"Agreed."

❖ ❖ ❖

Entering the lobby of the police headquarters, a tall man with graying hair, kept stylishly longer for an FBI agent, approached Bill and Ed. He wore a grey Italian silk suit with a black shirt and black tie, setting off his pale white skin. They followed Dawson into the elevator.

"I looked at the stuff you found—the adult and the two Tremway boys. I haven't seen them before. We've searched the web and the kiddy porn sites we monitor, but we'll do a deeper dig." They talked about how they might proceed as they approached a video-viewing room and waited for Brandon.

He arrived with a box. "Don't see VHS much anymore. I don't think we have to worry about passwords." He put a tape that was coded with a number and a date and hit play.

They watched a monitor. The image was of a bed in an artificially lit room. He then put the corresponding CD into the computer and pointed to another monitor where they saw the title *Cody*. There appeared the image of a towheaded, blue-eyed young boy lying on a bed in a tee shirt and jockey shorts.

"These are the Cody tapes," Dawson said. "They were some of the first child porn tapes to make it on the Internet in the 90s." Their attention went to the other monitor.

"It looks like the VHS is the raw pre-edited footage," Brandon pointed out. They watched Cody entering the picture in his tee shirt and underwear. He climbed on the bed. A voice gave him instructions.

"Damn, these really are the original tapes," Dawson said. "These videos went all over Europe, Canada, and the US. We could never find the..."

"Wait, did you see that?" Brandon said. An unmasked man walked in front of the camera and posed Cody on the bed. They tried, but they couldn't make out his face.

Dawson said, "This guy is in some of the videos. He wears a ski mask, but maybe we can get a look at him from the raw footage."

"The bastard does to this boy what Romeo did to his sons?" Ed asked.

"Yes."

Brandon said, "Okay, I've got earlier tapes, at least if I've got the code right. But they're not all Cody tapes. The name on these is Zachary."

"Put one in," Ed instructed. "I want these tapes viewed and I want the best images you can get of this guy. Hopefully, you can get a face shot."

"You think its Xavier?" Bill asked.

"I'm guessing." They watched the second tape. The same man wearing a mask was fondling a young dark-haired boy—Zachary.

"Okay, every face, body," Ed said, "anything we can use to identify this guy and the kids."

Brandon looked at Dawson. "I could use some help. There's about forty hours of just tape here. Then I've got..."

"I'll send you someone...Hundreds of people worked on this case. I was just starting out and stationed in Vegas, so this was probably fifteen, sixteen years ago. What's in here will be videos of a boy called Zachary which were first reported in Europe, then Canada and the United States. He looked to be ten or eleven. He was first shown alone and then with a masked adult. Then came the videos of Cody. He was much younger than Zachary, about six or seven. There were videos of Cody alone, then with Zachary who had reached puberty. Zachary was shown seducing Cody, then he disappeared or at least he's not shown on any of the videos that follow. What does follow is Cody with this masked man. Then Cody with another boy about the same age—Nicky. Then those two with Zackary. And he was by far the most aggressive of the boys. He sexually assaulted both Nicky and Cody. The investigation was being run out of the LA office," Dawson said. "We did everything we could to find this guy."

"The guy? What about the kids?" Bill said. "They were right here under your noses."

"We found nothing on any of them."

"My guess is that this is about child porn. I'm sure you're busy..."

"Actually, I'm not. I just received a promotion and I'm moving to D.C."

"I heard."

"I've been backing off cases. Other than packing up my office and home and running back and forth to D.C. to find a place to live, I'm free."

"Great. Your help is invaluable. We'll call you and keep you updated as to what else we find."

Dawson headed back to his office in the Federal Building. As Bill and Ed were about to leave, Brandon called to them. They followed him into the lab. "I might be crazy, but I think this boy called Zackary is actually Romeo. The age would be right." Brandon handed Ed printouts. "Okay, here are a dozen or so still shots of the Cody boy over a five-year period."

"Fuck," Ed said, "He looks like he was five or six." He snarled, "This is fucking sick shit."

Bill nodded. "That's when they started with Connor."

"Here's Nicky," Brandon said. "I'd say he's about the same age as Cody. And these are the dark-haired boy called Zackary." They stared at the pictures as he went through each image. "He's older than Cody. See here, he's gone into puberty, and see that," he said, pointing to the picture of Zackary, "that's a mole in the same spot as Romeo's."

Ed said, "Shit, that could be Romeo."

Bill said, "It looks like him."

"You get anything we can use on the adult?"

"A lot of his body," Brandon said. "Several times during the unedited tapes he steps into the frame, telling Cody how to sit or what to do." He showed them images of the adult from behind. He had straight brown hair combed back, perhaps covering a balding spot. Then Brandon showed them several stills of the man turning and walking toward the camera. There was a partial profile, then several of a fuller profile with his nose and mouth, then a partial view of his face but only showing his lips. "So far that's the best I have of him. I'll go through all the tapes. I did this fast-forwarding. I might have missed something."

"That could be Xavier," Ed said. His body had been too decomposed for a comparison, but they had pulled his driver's license photo.

"Tristan saw him," Bill reminded Ed. "And he seems to be good at making identifications."

"You have Zackary and Cody together?" Ed asked Brandon.

"Yeah, here," Brandon brought up a still shot.

"There's Romeo's mole. Good catch."

Bill peered at the pictures. "So Romeo is eleven or twelve here. He's thirty-five now. So this boy would be in his late twenties now...Let me see a later face shot of this boy."

Brandon handed him a photograph. "He's about nine or ten here."

"What are you seeing?" Ed asked.

"Damn! This kid fits the description, and the timeline would be right."

"For?"

"From County Hospital. Years ago."

He pulled out his phone and dialed. "Yes, this is Dr. Russo. Put me through to Dr. Gail Brennan."

One early morning in late August in 1994, a young boy, approximately age ten, was found roadside lying naked with a skull fracture in Griffith Park. He was unconscious, near death, clinging to a white sheet. He was rushed to USC/County Hospital.

He was running a fever of 104, had strep throat, cerebral edema, and pneumonia. He was given fluids, IV antibiotics and put in ICU. Thought to have little chance of regaining consciousness, he was put on critical care and monitored.

Police investigated. Johnny Doe had been washed down with bleach, wrapped in a bleached white sheet, placed in a shallow grave, struck with a large stone, and buried. He was able to crawl out and to the roadside, where he collapsed. The schools and surrounding neighborhood were scoured for information as to his identity. They found nothing.

He was given a complete medical exam. It was found that he had internal anal scarring. He eventually responded to medical treatment. However, he remained unresponsive to his surroundings. There were indications that he was not deaf, but although conscious, he remained mute.

Dr. Lisa Straus, who had been responsible for placing special needs children into foster care, was consulted. She worked for County Hospital but was on a health-related leave due to cancer. She had seen and written about children like Johnny—extreme emotional neglect, severe physical and/or sexual abuse. She reported that these children dissociate from their internal world and are unresponsive to the world around them. She referred to the abuse as 'Soul Murder.'

She visited Johnny Doe, sat bedside, and read while holding his hand. For days he just stared at her. One afternoon, after reading to him for over an hour, she stood to leave. Johnny tightened his grip on her hand—his first communication. She explained that she would return in a few minutes. He loosened his grip.

After consulting with the mental health staff, she decided to provide foster care for him. He was moved to the Straus home.

Bill had taken a seminar at LA County Hospital with Dr. Lisa Straus. Now he and Ed sat in Dr. Brennan's office, one of Bill's supervisors when he did his post-doctoral work at County. He showed her the picture.

She studied it. "Cody? We never had a name." She looked up. "That's him. Johnny Doe, as we called him."

"I'm sure Cody isn't his name—his real name."

She sighed. "We knew he was sexually abused."

"When I had the seminar," Bill told Ed, "I believe it had been eighteen months since Johnny had moved into the Straus home. He had made significant progress but had few memories of his life previous to his hospital stay. Then he started having flashbacks, which caused panic attacks and major depressive episodes. He remembered that the man he lived with was told by a doctor, that Johnny had a 'sex disease.' He asked Mrs. Straus numerous times what a sex disease was and how you get one and if he had one."

"Did he have AIDS?" Ed asked.

"No," Dr. Brennan said. "But he did have chlamydia and gonorrhea and his symptoms mirrored what they must have thought to be HIV exposure. They couldn't bring him to a hospital. How could they explain a ten-year-old being HIV positive or having any other sexually transmitted disease."

"Johnny told Dr. Straus that when he became sick, they gave him pills to swallow. I imagine they were antibiotics," Bill said. "Prior to that they gave him other pills and he'd go to sleep in one place and wake up in another with a strange man. He started palming the pills. He remembered that when he didn't get better from the sex disease, they forced pills into his mouth and then washed him with bleach."

"So he did have memories?" Ed asked.

"Yes," Dr. Brennan said, "his room, the pills, being taken to different places, but no memories of the men themselves or what happened with them. Dissociation is a very powerful defense against severe abuse."

"Where is Johnny now?"

"I don't know. I don't even know if he's alive. If he is, he'd be in his late twenties, early thirties. They were never sure of his age when they found him and that had to have been about fifteen or twenty years ago."

"Why wouldn't he be alive?"

Bill said, "Severe depressions like that due to that kind of abuse puts him at high risk for drug abuse and suicide. You know where Dr. Straus is now?"

"She passed away. But if memory serves me, she was married and had a child or children of her own. Maybe they know."

Bill and Ed walked to their cars. Ed said, "So, this might be our guy. He grows up, waits twenty years, and decides to torture and kill the men who molested him."

"If these men molested Johnny Doe and Romeo, I have no doubt that they continued their perversion after they buried him. So there are others— Romeo, and the boy Johnny Doe's age and I'm sure others who are now in their twenties and thirties."

"So much of what I see bothers me, but at some level I get jealousy, or rage, or gang shit... but sex with kids? I'm sorry," Ed said, shaking his head.

"Let me see if I can find out anything about the Straus family."

Ed's phone chimed. He listened and nodded. He said to Bill, "I'm heading back to the precinct. We just got all the information on the San Diego murder."

While Bill drove down I-10 to his office, Andrew called. On the phone speaker, his son asked if he was going to be home for dinner.

"I'm going to try to cook something special. Love you."

Bill half smiled. "Love you." He hung up. His jaw clenched as his thoughts went to Dylan, Connor, and Johnny Doe.

Andrew had the table set and dinner ready. As Bill sat, Andrew poured him a glass of his favorite Chianti.

"Can I have some?" Andrew asked.

"You going out tonight?"

"No."

"Half a glass."

Andrew poured a couple of ounces of wine and sat.

"Should I be worried? Spicy chicken corn tortilla soup."

Andrew laughed. "Because I got dinner for us? I've done this before...Actually, there is something I wanted to talk to you about."

"What did you do?"

"Nothing. It's about graduation. You know how after all the stuff we go to dinner with Grandma and Grandpa..."

"And Ed and Justin."

"Right. Well, there's this thing called grad night."

"I was in high school. I know what grad night is. Are you taking a date?"

"I want to go with the guys from the basketball team. No one is going to drive. And it's going to be at Disneyland."

"All night at Disneyland. And how are you getting there and back."

"Limo."

Bill took a mouthful of soup. "Damn, this is good."

"So...?"

Bill nodded.

"Yes," Andrew shouted.

Twenty-Two

Bill called *LA Magazine* the next morning from his office and asked to speak to Emma Straus, Dr. Straus' daughter. He was told she was due back late the next day from a two-week vacation on Kauai. He left word with her assistant to have her call him when she returned. Bill then called and asked Tristan to come back in.

While he and Ed waited in his office, Stewart Dawson knocked. "Got a minute?"

Dawson started to close the door. Bill said, "Leave the door open. I'm waiting for someone we're interviewing." From Bill's office door, he had a view across the seventh floor.

"I was wrong. The videos of Connor and Dylan have been found on the dark web. We're trying to trace it back to where and when they showed up. But I doubt we'll get much soon."

Bill noticed Tristan walk onto the floor with an attractive man. "Stewart, the young man we're interviewing just arrived." Dawson turned and watched Tristan talking to an agent who pointed toward Bill's office. "We're hoping to get an ID that will firm up the Xavier thing and maybe get an ID on the Cody boy."

"Great." Dawson stared at Tristan. "Do you mind if I watch."

"No. Why don't you head to the observation room now."

As Ed walked Tristan to the interrogation room, Bill introduced himself to Tristan's boyfriend, Christopher.

"How's he doing?" Bill asked as they shook hands. He felt Christopher's strength and the gentleness of his grip. He was tall, athletic, and attractive and looked to be in his mid-thirties—dark brown hair with a brush of grey at the temples.

"He told me you suggested he see someone." He shook his head. "He said no at first. I mean, he was adamant about it. But he started having night terrors and his panic attacks were getting worse by the day. Finally, I convinced him to call and set up an appointment. The whole thing has opened up a lot of painful memories."

"Has he done that yet?"

Christopher shook his head. "No, he hasn't. He's not still a suspect, is he?"

"He's pretty low on the radar. We called him in today to help us with an identification, not to interrogate him."

Ed stood in the hallway as Tristan took a seat. Ed said to Bill before they entered the room. "He's pretty nervous."

Bill explained to Tristan what they had found. "We're needing your help with identifications. I know you're going through a lot of emotional distress right now. If we could do this without your help, I wouldn't have called you."

"No, no, that's okay. But do I have to see videos?"

Bill thought he looked pallid. "No. We have still shots."

Tristan's lips pulled into a frown. "You don't still think that I..."

Ed opened his laptop. "No. You're not a suspect and we're not trying to extract a confession. We just need your help. It would mean a lot to us."

First, Tristan was shown pictures of Cody, whom they knew as Johnny Doe. He stared and looked to be on the verge of tears. "His eyes look sad."

Bill said. "He'd be about eighteen or twenty years older now. Maybe he's one of the guys who worked with Romeo at the studio?"

"Why would you think that?" Tristan pushed the computer aside.

Ed turned it back with a photo of Zackary. "Who does this look like?"

Tristan took a brief glance at the screen. "That's Romeo."

"That's what we thought."

Bill was surprised at how quickly Tristan was able to identify Romeo. "Are you sure?"

Tristan pointed to the screen. "Sure, I'm sure. That's him. Those are his eyes and that mouth. See the shape of his mouth. And see there, right under his right nipple there's a little mole or something. I told you about that. Romeo used to say that he had an extra nipple."

Tristan's hands shook as Ed showed him the images of the adult with Cody. "They're not very good." He wiped sweat from his upper lip. "This is that Victor guy." More images of Victor came up. "Yeah, the mouth is the same and the nose. Too bad you can't see his eyes." Tristan's tee shirt was wet with sweat in spots. He swallowed hard. "He always made me feel weird."

"Why is that?" Ed asked.

"I don't know. My skin would get all tingly and my stomach would feel like...you know, when you're on a boat. Like that."

They questioned Tristan at length about Victor. When they were done, Bill said, "Look, I know this is hard. I want to thank you for being so cooperative and helpful. I have a question about a more recent boy. A boy who would be around Connor and Dylan's age. He's also a blond and he's called Jamie. I'm wondering if you ever saw this boy or maybe heard one of the boys mention his name."

"Jamie?" Tristan searched his memory. "Wow, that kinda sounds familiar. Maybe Dylan said something. How are they doing?"

"There at UCLA psych hospital."

"Do you think I'll ever be able to see them?"

"Maybe, when things move along."

"You talked about a man," Ed said. "Carl somebody. You said he found you on the streets."

"Not him, but one of his escorts."

"This Carl fellow ran boys who were 16-18 and had a boyish look to them. Like you."

"Yeah, like me. But he also ran guys who were older. Ones that started when they were my age, but they were in good shape, attractive, clean. I was doing drugs and a mess, so he let me go."

"And one of those guys got you to Romeo."

"Yeah. This guy who Carl had driving me to and from the trick's place. He knew Romeo. Romeo was always looking for new guys, young but legal."

"How again does Carl find these kids?"

"He has guys who hang around the Greyhound bus stops and sweet talk kids that have runaway to Hollywood. You know, the kids that are gay and thrown away by their parents. They especially wait for the buses from Utah."

"Utah."

"Mormon gay kids that their parents kick out. They also hang around the streets where kids look for tricks."

"Did he ever handle young boys?"

Tristan looked distressed when he nodded. "I saw boys who were pretty young."

"I thought he looked for only boys over sixteen," Bill said.

"To pimp out," Tristan said. "But he always had young boys living at his house. He called them his houseboys. Sometimes I'd see them walking around naked and cleaning the place and they'd serve him food and stuff. Then he'd have these parties and then these kids would be gone." He sat back in his chair and shook his head. "I'm sure they pulled tricks, too. You know, for special clients."

Bill and Ed glanced at each other. "Do you remember his last name?" Ed asked. "And where his house is?"

Each time they pulled him into his past, life seemed to drain out of Tristan's body. He slouched in his chair. "He lived in the Hollywood hills. He had a pool and a view." He looked at Bill. "It was a weird name. I could take you there. I remember how to get there."

"You don't remember his last name?" Ed repeated.

"I try not to remember those days. A lot of drugs and..."

Bill noticed that Tristan had become ashen. "Okay. We might call on you to take a drive with us but that's enough for today."

As they approached the door of the interrogation room, Tristan hesitated. "That blond boy with Xavier..."

"Cody?" Ed said.

"Ah...Cody? Right his name was Cody?"

"What is it?" Bill asked, noticing that Tristan began to shake all over.

"I can't breathe," Tristan mumbled. "This room doesn't have enough air. I feel trapped." He fell to his knees and collapsed to the floor.

Bill knelt beside him. "Look at me Tristan."

Ed pulled out his cell phone. "Should I call the EMTs?"

Tristan's eyes darted back and forth. "I need air."

"I think he's having a panic attack," Bill said.

Tristan kept taking quick and deep breaths, gasping.

Bill placed his hand on Tristan's chest. "Tristan, look at me. Tristan." He made eye contact. "You're hyperventilating. You're having a panic attack. My hand is on your chest. Do you feel it? I want you to slow your breathing. Breathe as I move my hand pressing against your chest." Bill applied pressure and then eased up. "Breathe with my hand."

They stared into each other's eyes. "Good. You're doing good," Bill said.

He continued to slow Tristan's breathing for several minutes, then summoned Christopher. They stayed with him until he was able to calm himself.

"I'm sorry," he said to Bill.

"No. *I'm* sorry. We're putting a lot of pressure on you. But I promise you, you are being very helpful." Bill and Christopher sat with him until he looked well enough to leave. "This is bringing up a lot for you. Your own molestation and what followed."

"I know...I never think about it anymore. Actually, it's been kind of a blank. Like I was never a kid. Like my life started when I got clean and sober. But now it's all I think about." He looked at Bill questioningly. "Before...when we were talking...I kept thinking I knew someone by the name of Cody when I was a kid, but maybe not." He fell into thought. "No, I'm thinking of someone else. Anthony. Not Cody. He reminded me of Anthony."

"Where do you remember him from?"

"Who?"

"Cody or Anthony."

"When I was a kid and when I was being molested, he was there. He was a friend of mine." Tears fell. "I really don't want to talk about this anymore. Can I go, please. I feel really tired."

"Yes. Of course."

Christopher said to Tristan while looking at Bill, "Maybe Doctor Russo has a phone you can use here so that you can call and make an appointment. Just in case there's a problem." Tristan looked emotionally spent. "Tristan."

"Yeah, sure," Tristan said.

Bill sat with him as he called the clinic and made an appointment. Then Bill called in and asked that the man he had in mind be assigned to Tristan.

"Thank you," Tristan said.

"Could you do me a favor? If you remember anything else..." Bill wrote his government-issued cell phone number on the back of his card. "Or if you need my help with this appointment or anything else, please call me."

Tristan took and studied the card. "I try not to remember stuff. But if I do, I'll call."

Christopher said, "How about I hold onto that for you."

Bill watched Tristan leave, feeling a deep concern and curious about Tristan's emotional reaction. He reasoned that it was because his own molestation mirrored that of Connor and Dylan.

"I feel for him," Ed said.

Then their attention went to the opening door of the viewing room.

Dawson stepped out. "I thought I might get more information that would help with the tapes. What do you think that panic attack was about?"

"Memories. He suppressed them through a haze of drugs for years. Now with Connor and Dylan's abuse by Romeo, their father...well, I imagine memories, vivid memories of his abusers are breaking through."

"So who was this Anthony boy?"

"Probably a childhood friend."

Ed said, "I was hoping to get info on his pimp. Maybe we can take him for a ride along," he said to Bill. "Maybe he knows this Jamie boy."

"I want to give him time. His therapy appointment is Wednesday. Once he has someone to talk to, then we can interview him again."

"I think he knows stuff he's not revealing," Dawson said.

"Probably. But he will," Bill said

"I'll talk to you guys later. I'm going to head home and go for a long run and try to get this out of my head."

Ed said, "We have to find this Johnny Doe. Have you heard from Emma Straus?"

"She called from Hawaii. She's arriving tomorrow late evening. She said she'd be at my office Monday, between one and two."

Ed checked his phone appointment calendar. "Okay. I'll be there. So, dinner at your house tonight?"

"Nothing special. Andrew is defrosting and heating up my mother's homemade lasagna."

"I'll be there at seven. Justin said he's helping Andrew get dinner ready."

Twenty-Three

When Bill arrived home, the house had a wonderful aroma of Italian cuisine, lasagna in the oven. Andrew and Justin had prepared the table.

"Every time you guys do this, I start wondering what bad news I'm going to get," Bill teased.

"I'm just practicing for when I'm away and entertaining," Andrew said.

"You'll be living in the dorms."

"The first year. Can you teach me how to make lasagna from scratch?"

"Sure," Bill felt an ache. The thought of arriving home day after day to a house without Andrew saddened him. "I'm going to change. Ed will be here at seven."

Later, sitting at the table as Andrew dished up the lasagna, Bill asked Ed, "Have you looked into renting an RV?"

"I still have to do that."

"Where will you guys go?" Andrew asked.

"First San Diego," Ed said. "I know beaches where the waves are gentle enough for a beginner." He glanced at Justin. "It takes a while to get the hang of it. Then we'll head up the coast."

"I heard there's a nude beach in San Diego," Andrew said. "Did you surf in the nude?"

Ed chuckled. "Actually, I did. In high school, when I thought I was all that."

Everyone laughed.

"Wait, I thought you learned when you were in the Marines," Justin said.

Ed put down his fork and picked up his glass of wine. He took a sip and looked at Justin. "You know that I was an only child. I've told you that my mother passed away. Actually...she was a prostitute. One day, when I was in the first grade, she dropped me at school and never picked me up."

Justin and Andrew stared at Ed.

"...Years later, after I became a policeman, I tried to find her, but she'd passed away. So, anyway..."

"She just abandoned you?" Justin said.

"I was in foster care. It wasn't terrible. I mean, I was never abused." He took a deep breath. "But there was never love, not like in a family. Not the way your mother loved you, and I love you." To Andrew, he said, "Not the way you are loved."

Andrew glanced at his father.

Ed's last home was in San Diego. He barely made it through high school. "It was alcohol, sex, rock-n-roll and surfing. Sex with guys and sex with girls." He was almost whispering. He rubbed his face and looked at Justin. "Your mother knew everything that I'm telling you. I want you to know that I never kept anything from her."

Justin nodded.

"I joined the Marines and was stationed at Camp Pendleton. I met Joseph there. Our friendship turned into a sexual relationship. After we were discharged, we moved to LA, rented a one-bedroom apartment, and committed to each other. I had never allowed myself to depend on another person, but I had fallen deeply in love with Joseph. Then, one day, a few weeks before my first college finals, Joseph moved out. He left a note.

"Your mother was my teaching assistant for a psychology class I was taking. I went to her looking for a way to postpone my final. I couldn't focus. I was having anxiety attacks. I was depressed. I was a mess. I was alone again, and I didn't know what I had done wrong. I had no one. Your mother helped me get an incomplete and talked me into seeing a counselor. I took the next quarter off. When I was able to pull myself together, she arranged for me to take the final."

"So, you're saying you're gay?" Justin sounded doubtful.

Ed shook his head. "I know people always look at bisexual men and think they're gay and don't want to accept it. But I'd say that I'm bisexual. Your mother and I fell in love. Before we married, she made me promise that if I ever had an affair that it wouldn't be with a woman."

"Did you ever..."

"Never...Never with anyone. Justin, I loved your mother...but...this grieving...part of it is about losing your mother, but part of it is stuff...stuff about me...I guess..."

"I get it, Dad. Really, I do." Bill, Ed, and Andrew looked at Justin. "Everyone has left you. One day they're just gone."

He nodded.

"I love you, Dad." Justin stood up. Ed stood. They embraced and held each other.

Bill looked at Andrew, and Andrew looked at his father and half smiled.

While the four of them cleaned up the kitchen, Ed again congratulated Andrew on his acceptance to Stanford. Andrew said, "Thank you. I'm trying to convince Justin to apply."

"I don't know that I have good enough grades," Justin said.

"Except for your first semester your grades are about the same as mine, you've got swimming and your work with meals-on-wheels, and you're on student counsel. You just have to study for the SATs and ACTs and write a really good essay for your application. If you want, I'll help you study and help you with your essay. I've got all the stuff."

Standing at the door as Ed and Justin left, Bill asked. "What time tomorrow at the bank?"

"Ten. I'll see you there."

Twenty-Four

Ed waited with Bill in the bank lobby for Mrs. Adams. "I brought a warrant for both boxes in case they give her a hard time about getting into his."

And sure enough, they did. Mrs. Adams had brought identification and her husband's death certificate as Ed suggested, but the bank president wanted to see Dr. Adam's will, proving that she was the rightful beneficiary.

"No need for that." Ed handed him the warrant. "I didn't want to do it this way," Ed said to Mrs. Adams. "It means that whatever is inside will be police property until we are done with it."

"That's fine with me. I can't imagine there is anything in that box that is something that belongs to me. Do you mind if I accompany you?"

"Not at all."

Craig pulled the Box 182 and handed it to Ed. "Feels empty," he said as the three of them walked to a room. He gave Mrs. Adams the only chair.

Bill and Ed stood on opposite sides of her as she opened the box, and indeed it was empty. Bill apologized for bothering her.

"I'm glad it was empty. I was afraid of what might be in it."

They watched Mrs. Adams leave the bank, then Ed turned his attention to Craig. "We have a warrant for Box 131—Adam's other box, but first I have questions."

"I got into trouble last time I talked to you. You'll need to deal with my boss before I say anything else."

The bank manager joined them, accompanied by a locksmith.

"We want information about this box and the boxes we already served you warrants for. If you read..."

"What do you want to know?"

"Who last signed in on the Adam's box, Box 182?"

Craig pulled up the information. "Mr. Xavier was the last."

"When was that?"

"March 15th of this year," Craig said.

Bill noted that it was four days after Adams was killed. "Did Xavier open any other boxes that day?"

Craig studied the screen. "Yes. He signed into Box 182 at 10:06 a.m. and then signed into the large box—4209—at 10:14 a.m. The one he had with Romeo Tremway."

"Maybe he removed whatever was in 182 and put it in 4209," Bill suggested.

Ed handed the bankers the warrant for 131—Adams' box.

After the locksmith drilled it open, Craig gave it to Bill. In it was a small cardboard box, and in that box, Bill counted twenty numbered keys. "Safe deposit keys."

They laid them in front of Craig. "Might any of these fit boxes in this bank?"

"These could." Craig pointed to three. "The rest of those wouldn't."

"And there's no way to tell which bank they belong to, is there?"

"No."

"And you can't tell us who those three keys belong to."

"All I can tell you is that Adams is secondary on these other boxes. I can't tell you who the primaries are but it's not anyone you have a warrant for."

As they got to their cars, Bill said, "We're missing something. Mr. Six-Foot went back to Adams' house and then his office. We're assuming that he was looking for the key to Adams' Box 182. But Xavier had a key to that box and he emptied it. Maybe he was looking for and found the key to Box 131."

"So, if the killer found the key, he couldn't use it."

"Why does Mr. Six-Foot break into Adams' house and go to his office to get a key he couldn't use?"

"Mr. Six Foot knows about the keys. Knows that there are keys in Box 131. But he can't get in the box. Makes no sense."

Silence.

"They didn't want us to find the key to either box. Maybe it leads us to this bank. From Box 131, we get to 182 and then that gives us Xavier's name," Bill said. "We get Xavier's name and then Romeo's name and reach out to them and start asking questions."

"Bingo. If they can keep us out of this bank, we're in the dark as to what is going on. That keeps us away from these pervs. But, fuck, is the killer trying to protect these guys from being found out or kill them?"

"Or protect himself by killing them. Killing them before they can identify him for some reason."

"Maybe Johnny Doe, after being molested by these guys joins the group like Romeo did. Maybe he's afraid someone is going to talk and turns on them. Kills them."

"We have to find Johnny."

"But if Johnny is Mr. Six-Foot, who is Mr. Five-Foot-Eight? And don't say it's part of the puzzle."

Bill smiled.

Twenty-Five

John drove and parked his motorcycle a block from the house. A short, overweight man in his forties, wearing dark blue pants and a white short-sleeved shirt, entered a small ranch-style house off Santa Monica Boulevard. Having tracked him for the last week, he knew that Glenn Paulsen, a real estate broker, lived alone and seldom had visitors. It was now late on a Friday afternoon.

Carrying what looked to be a computerized clipboard and an official-looking nine-by-twelve manila envelope addressed to Mr. Paulsen, he approached the house. Under the clipboard, he held his tranquilizer gun. He rang the bell, knocked, and readied himself.

"Yeah," a voice called out.

"Messenger service. I have something for a Mr. G. Paulsen at this address."

"Just leave it."

"Has to be signed for."

"Who's it from?"

"Sorry. I wouldn't know."

The door opened.

"Mr. Paulsen?"

They made eye contact. There was a pop, like the sound of a small firecracker, as John fired the dart. He pushed his way in and closed the door behind him. Glenn tried to fight back but would have been no match even if he were not drugged. John watched him slip into unconsciousness.

He checked outside. It looked to be clear, so he nonchalantly strolled back to his motorcycle for his duffle.

Then, by the numbers, he began his much-practiced routine: *One.* He removed his shoes, put them in the duffle, and put on hospital scrubs over his clothing. *Two.* He put on two pairs of gloves, one over the other, tucking in the shirt scrubs. *Three.* He taped the gloves to the sleeves of the scrubs. *Four.* He put on booties and taped them to the legs of his scrubs. *Five.* He removed Glenn's shoes and put them on. *Six.* He pulled a black ski mask over his head for effect.

Same size feet. He checked Glenn. *Still out.* He undressed him, pulled him into a windowless bathroom, tied him to a dining room chair, put a ball gag in his mouth, and secured it behind his head.

He looked himself over, making sure he'd done everything as practiced. Satisfied, he made his way through the house, going through drawers, closets, shelves, and anything else he could find that might hide flash drives or DVDs containing child porn.

He sat at the computer and wondered if he could be as lucky as he'd been at Victor's house when he caught Victor in the process of editing the raw footage of Romeo and his two sons. Victor wouldn't give up the name of the man who had kidnapped him, and when he asked who the female voice was giving Romeo and his sons direction, Victor smiled. "Their mother. It's a family affair." It was at that point that he decided to make Victor's death especially gruesome.

He checked his watch. Glenn should be coming out of it soon. With his toilet kit in hand, he returned to the bathroom, where Glenn sat naked, legs tied to an armless chair. A rope crossed his chest, securing him to the back, and his arms were tied behind him. His pale white skin hung on his body. His belly sagged and covered his genitals.

He passed smelling salts under Glenn's nose. "Hello Glenn."

Glenn shook his head as he regained consciousness. His eyes opened wide and darted around the room until they became fixed on the stranger standing in front of him. They made eye contact.

"That expression on your face. I know and remember it well. It's fear. It's how I felt when I woke in a strange room one night when I was six years old and realized I was naked. And then in came a naked man who stood over me, smiled and then raped me. Don't worry. I know that wasn't you."

Glenn made muzzled sounds.

"Let's see...you're wondering who I am and what I want...and probably what's going to happen to you, right? Actually, we've met."

Glenn shook his head violently.

"Yes we have, but a while ago. A long while ago."

Glenn made sounds.

"When? You want to know when. Let's see...about twenty years ago." Glenn furrowed his eyebrows. "That would put you in your twenties and me... about eight."

Glenn shook his head.

"Yes, think back. An eight-year-old skinny blond boy." He lifted his mask.

Glenn's eyes widened.

"See, you do remember...Oh, I know you're sorry...So, what do I want?"

John removed a scalpel from his bag. Glenn focused on it.

"First, I want the truth." He put the scalpel to Glenn's thigh. "Your femoral artery is here, and one quick cut and you'll bleed out in minutes. It won't be terribly painful. You'll feel the cut and then your life drifting away. Not a bad way to die."

Tears.

"You lie, I cut," John pulled the scalpel over Glenn's skin, making a shallow cut. Glenn tensed and tried to shout. "It's just a nick, and no one is going to hear you." John moved inches from Glenn's face. "The truth."

Glenn nodded.

John put the scalpel on Glenn's thigh. "You remember me? I was called Cody." John pressed the scalpel to Glenn's thigh.

Glenn nodded.

"Good because I remember you..." They stared at each other.

"I have Adams' diary. This guy was one paranoid piece of work. He coded that fucking thing and used initials and partial addresses. I'm still trying to figure it all out, but with your help...Well, let me tell you what I know. You were part of a group of around twenty men on and off."

Glenn tried to speak.

"Just listen now. I'll let you speak. Boys were kept—me, a boy you would know as Nicky, and another known as Zackary. Videos were made. Recently, this cabal took trips to Thailand and Romania where they found other boys and made more videos." John unfolded a piece of paper he pulled from his bag. "Okay, Glenn. This is a list of men currently in your little group—it is coded, but it didn't take long to figure out parts of it. But Mr. Adams wasn't all that dumb. He listed the street but no address and a phony name. And these numbers."

He showed him the list. Eight of the twenty names were crossed out, and two, coded, had no information at all. What John feared was that the man he was most interested in finding was the one with the least information: Jack411—no street name.

"My problem is that you guys used different names with each other and no last names. See, your code name was Harry. The names are followed by three or four numbers. I've learned these are safe deposit boxes, and the word that follows those is the street where they live."

Glenn stared at the list.

"You're looking at Brett, your ex-lover's name. Yes, it has been crossed out. Xavier, the man who kept me at his house all those years, told me where he lived."

Glenn groaned.

"You know he's been killed?"

Glenn looked at John and nodded. He moaned.

"Yes, I talked to him a couple of weeks ago. He gave me your name and address."

Glenn closed his eyes and hung his head.

"Okay, now I need information from you. I'm going to remove the gag. Your impulse will be to scream. But first, no one will hear you. Second," John moved the scalpel to Glenn's throat, "I'll cut your throat and you'll hardly make a sound.

"Got it?"

Glenn nodded.

John removed the gag.

"Please, please, don't kill me. Please."

Most of what Glenn told John, he already knew. His old lover, Brett, ushered him into the group when he was in his twenties. To protect the group from possible law enforcement infiltration, the initiate was put in a room with a boy—John or Nicky. The boy was fully dressed, and the initiate was unmasked. What happened next was videotaped. In Glenn's case, the boy was John. Adams kept member information and the unmasked videos secure as insurance. Victor Xavier and Ralph Adams were the only people who knew everyone's true identity and where those videos were stored.

"Brett was the only person I really knew. He gave you my name and you killed him anyway. You're going to kill me."

"You don't know that."

"I never brought anyone in. That would be the only way I'd know someone."

John said, "There were three men who ran this group: Adams, Victor, and another man who I haven't identified yet. And there's the man I'm especially looking for—my kidnapper. The rest of you..."

"I only knew the guy who you've called Adams. Oh, and I knew the guy who kept you, and I knew Brett."

"Who else?"

"Please, I don't want to die."

"Who else? You went to Thailand. I have the diary that Adams kept. Three years ago you went to Thailand and made videos with boys. Who else?"

"The guy you lived with went. He always went, and Brett and two guys you've crossed off your list and..."

"And."

Glenn pleaded again, bargaining for his life. There was another man. Glenn gave John his code name and then his actual name. "He screwed up. He told me his first name. He's a married guy and he liked for the boys to call him Daddy. He lives here in Los Angeles."

John felt sick. He remembered the man who insisted on being called Daddy. He felt his teeth clenching. *Focus.* John pointed to the list of names.

"There, that one, the fifth one down. Highland Park. His name is Richard Henning. That's all I know, I swear."

"When I talked to Adams, he said that only Victor knew the one man I'm looking for—the man who took me from my mother. But I'm sure he was lying. Others must know. Victor refused to give me his name. He said, 'Do what you want to me, but I'll go to my death knowing that I fucked you one last time.'"

John held up the list in front of Glenn.

"Please, I don't know anyone else..."

"The man I'm looking for is tall, although I was a kid, and everyone seemed tall. But compared to my mother, he'd be over six foot, I would guess."

Glenn shook his head.

"His hair was reddish brown, not red and not brown, kind of a dark rust color."

Glenn looked to be thinking.

"He had ears that stuck out, really stuck out."

"I don't know him, but I met him by mistake. No, I didn't meet him, I just saw him."

"Tell me."

"His box is at the same bank as mine. They told us to stay off child porn sites because the FBI was monitoring. They worried about the mail, so we used the boxes."

"Tell me."

"I went to the bank. I saw a tall guy with sticking-out ears going into the safe deposit box area."

"You remember him because of his ears." John didn't believe him.

"No. The DVDs and flash drives. They were in plastic containers and wrapped in brown paper and taped over. Only one person at a time can go into the box area. I noticed him take a wrapped DVD out of his box and then put flash drives in the box. Most of the videos we got were from places around the world—men with boys, boys with boys. But some were private stuff.

"There were two boys. Sometimes they were alone, most of the time with a man."

Romeo and his sons, John thought.

"Then, one boy showed up in videos that were made in Victor's house. He was with a blond boy who at first was always with the tall man, but lately with different men. I'm sure these were never on the Internet."

"Maybe I can help you figure out which one the guy is."

"So he wasn't just picking up DVDs. He was putting stuff in his box."

"He's not the guy in Highland Park. You've got eleven left on your list."

John stared at him and nodded.

"I've seen the videos from Romania. Victor went several years ago. Mr. Ears was on one of those trips."

"They're hooded, aren't they?"

"Yeah, but... I recognized him. He was on the old tapes with you and other boys, and recently that blond boy. After a while, you get to know them by their body." Glenn never saw Mr. Ears after that Romania trip until he showed up in recent videos with the blond boy. "He's tall and lean and in good shape. You said that you knew when I went...We were supposed to destroy the videos, you know...just in case. So we couldn't..."

"You've got them?"

"Please, don't kill me. I'll tell you everything I know. I'll help you any way I can. I know what I did was fucked up. Please."

"Where are they?"

"In my bedroom. Move the nightstand on the left side of my bed. You'll see a floorboard that is loose. Under that is a safe." Glenn gave him the combination. "Get them. I'll tell you which ones he's on. I know which they are. Then you'll know when he went to Romania. Maybe it's in the diary."

John hesitated but agreed. He secured the ball gag in Glenn's mouth and returned to Glenn's bedroom, moved the nightstand, and lifted the cut piece of wood flooring. He found the safe and opened it, then returned to the bathroom with three plastic storage canisters. He stood before Glenn as he opened each of them.

Glenn made sounds. John took off his gag. "I won't scream."

"There are hundreds of DVDs and flash drives here. These are all of you guys with boys?" John's voice filled with anger.

"No. I told you, someone in the group collected stuff off the Internet and he'd leave those for us too. Most of that stuff is from the Internet."

"Then which one is it?

"I dated them." John went through the stack of DVDs. "That's it. That's the one with Mr. Ears in Romania. Keep going. That's the one with him and the blond boy, Jamie."

John stood. "I'm going to take a look at this...if you're bullshitting me, you'll be more than sorry." He started for the ball gag.

"Wait. I know you think that if you leave me alive, I'll go to the police, but I won't. I've got a copy of the video they made of me with you...without the mask. You can take it. I won't be able to go to the police. If I do..."

The thought of Glenn watching his rape filled him with rage. At that moment, he wanted to kill him. "They didn't have DVDs then."

"No, it was on VHS, but I transferred everything to DVD and flash drives."

John's teeth clenched. "And which one is that?"

He gagged Glenn, went to the den, and watched the Mr. Ears videos. He remembered his cheap cologne and that his mouth smelled of tobacco. He remembered the weight of his body on top of him and the grunting sounds he made. John's body tensed to the point that he began to shake. He forced himself to continue watching. The man in the hood was the man who kidnapped him. He checked on Glenn, who remained as he left him. Then John watched the latest video of Mr. Ears with a young blond-haired boy—Jamie.

Then, he watched the video of Glenn the night he was initiated. All those memories had returned, but seeing and remembering were two entirely different things. He had to pull himself together, or he would make a mistake. He thumbed through the rest of the DVDs and noticed one that was dated just days before he killed Dr. Adams. *This can't be from Thailand.* He slipped it into the player. He watched as Connor, who he immediately recognized, and the boy with blond hair undressed each other while kissing. When Connor turned to give the other boy fellatio, John ejected the DVD.

He removed Glenn's gag again. "What can you tell me about Jamie?"

"He's in that video of Mr. Ears in Romania. I think he got him there and brought him back here." Glenn pleaded, "You can keep the video of me without a mask. There's no way I can ever go to the police. Maybe I can help you find this guy. I know what he looks like. What are you going to do if he's the guy with no address? He lives here in LA. He uses my bank. You'll need me to point him out."

John took a syringe from his bag.

"What's that?"

"What I shot you up with."

"But why? I have more information I can give you."

John had decided to end it quickly but then hesitated. "What information?"

"Jamie. They are auctioning him off. I'll show you which one, a flash drive. It made me think that Mr. Ears is the guy who has the boy. I can help you find him."

"And how would you do that?"

"That day at the bank. I saw his box. Mr. Ears' box number is 411. He must be Jack:411."

John gritted his teeth. He was tiring of Glenn. "There's no information on him. How can you help?"

"I don't know, but we can figure that out."

"I do have one question. When you entered that room, undressed me, and raped me, what were you thinking?" Glenn's eyes filled with tears. "I was eight years old. You must have seen the fear and pain in my eyes."

"I was shown a video of you before I entered that room. You were with a boy your age. And you seemed so comfortable with each other and wanted to be with each other."

"Nicky." John felt an ache in his chest.

"When I entered that room, I guess I convinced myself that you wanted to be with me."

"*I* wanted to be with *you*."

"I'm sorry."

John injected Glenn and watched him fade.

"Really, I am…"

"Sorry for what you did to me." John put the scalpel to Glenn's scrotum and cut it open. He removed one testicle, cut again, and removed the other. Then he pushed Glenn's girth upward, grabbed the penis, and cut it off at the base. Blood spurted onto the floor. John put his fingers to Glenn's neck and felt his pulse slow and then disappear.

He gathered what he used and put everything in his bag. He sat down at the computer and inserted the flash drive.

As Glenn said, they were auctioning off Jamie. John looked at the timeline set for bidding. *He's been sold by now.* John read on. One of the conditions of the sale was that the boy would not be available until the last week of May. What followed next were scenes of Jamie with Connor and scenes with Jamie and a hooded, tall, pale-skinned man who John was now convinced was his kidnapper. He sat back and stared out the curtained window into the backyard.

He gathered all the flash drives and put them back into the safe. He closed it and replaced the flooring, leaving it a bit off-kilter, and the nightstand at an angle, to be sure the police would notice. His hope was that they'd see the video of Jamie and get to him.

He removed the computer hard drive, gathered all the DVDs and wiped down anything he might have touched with a rag wet with bleach. He spread a plastic sheet on the floor, stood on it, and took off the gloves, scrubs, shoes, booties, and hair cover. He rolled it all up and put it in his duffle. He glanced outside. It was now dark, and the street was quiet.

Leave nothing behind.

Driving away, he calculated how long it would take him to get back to Sequoia National Park.

Twenty-Six

Emma Straus arrived at FBI headquarters for her interview at exactly one o'clock. Bill met her at the reception desk and introduced himself. A young woman, tall, fit, and brunette with bright blue eyes, her tan spoke to her recent vacation.

"How was Hawaii?" Bill asked as they walked to his office.

"Beautiful. I go there with college friends each year."

They entered Bill's office. "This is Detective Coyne."

Ed stood. "Miss Straus."

Bill offered her coffee or water. When she declined, Bill sat behind his desk.

"I understand that Kauai is beautiful," Ed said.

"Why am I here? Surely, not to talk about my vacation."

"I didn't know your mother personally," Bill said, "but I did take a seminar from her at County Hospital. She mentioned the boy she fostered."

"John," Emma offered.

"We've recently obtained videos made of him being sexually abused. Detective Coyne and I are interested in knowing as much about him as possible. The last that we know is that your mother took him in after he was released from the hospital. Whatever else you can tell us would be appreciated."

She stared at Bill and then began to speak—guardedly, Bill thought, seemingly wanting to maintain control of the conversation and the information to protect John.

When Dr. Straus brought John home, he was unresponsive, refusing food in the presence of anyone. She sat by his bed and read to him as she had in the hospital. Her choice of books, *The Three Musketeers,* was deliberate—good versus evil, no family ties, and adventure based in historical fiction. John listened intently, never saying a word until she came to the last page. He touched her hand and said, "More, please."

Lisa taught him to read and was amazed at how quickly he learned. She began homeschooling him. She tested him and soon became convinced that he had eidetic memory.

"Is that like a photographic memory?" Ed asked.

"A person with a photographic memory can recall something that she read ten or fifteen years after reading it. It's visual. A person with an eidetic memory can recall auditory, olfactory, tactile, gustatory, and visual stimuli. John was eidetic."

Bill's stomach churned as he recalled that John was buried alive, wrapped in a sheet in a shallow grave. *How does he live with those memories?* "Your mother said that he was having flashbacks. Memories of the abuse?"

She looked away and shook her head. These memories were clearly difficult for her. "Names could set him off. We first realized this when my mother read one of her books to him."

"Do you remember the names?"

"Richard. Jack... Daddy. Oddly, the name Romeo. I remember that because she was sure that reading him Shakespeare would be free of modern names and when she read him Romeo and Juliet he reacted badly."

Ed and Bill glanced at each other. "How so?" Bill asked.

"He'd curl up into a ball and moan. He never cried. My mother would ask him what he was remembering. But he couldn't or wouldn't say. He couldn't watch TV because sometimes that set him off. Sometimes it was so bad, he'd remain in bed for days."

Socially, John remained excessively shy and skittish. Each day, when Mr. Straus came home, John retreated to his room. When Emma's older brother Ryan returned from Berkeley for Thanksgiving and shared the bedroom with him, John slept fully dressed, sitting up in bed and completely shut down for days.

He had no memory of his family or if and how he was related to the man with whom he lived. He did not know the date of his birthday or his age. When he reached puberty, Dr. Straus assigned him the age of twelve and a birth date of June 21st, the summer solstice. It was his favorite day because it had the least amount of nighttime, which he feared.

His education progressed rapidly. He loved geography, math, and science—maps covered his walls. He remained leery of Mr. Straus but very slowly formed a tenuous relationship with Ryan, who was majoring in biology.

"My brother was small for his age. Picked on a lot. You know, the nerdy kid with glasses, cute but not one of the guys. His best friend was Shadow, our black lab. He was the kind of kid that was always taking everything apart and wanting to know how they worked and how to fix them. One day, my parents took us to church. Ryan had been playing with Shadow in the backyard. Anytime they left, Shadow had to be put in the house or he'd jump the fence. Ryan left Shadow out. While they were gone, Shadow went over the fence and was hit by a car. Neighbors took him to a vet but it was bad. They kept Shadow alive long enough for Ryan to say goodbye. He was twelve years old. He took it badly. He insisted that a good vet could have fixed Shadow. So, he became one."

Bill glanced at Ed.

"John got his GED at sixteen and there was talk of him going to college, but he rarely ventured from the house, except with my mother. And he refused to learn to drive. Two years later, when Ryan was in his first year of veterinary school at UC Davis and I was a sophomore UCSB, Mom's lung cancer reoccurred. During chemo and radiation therapy, John attended to her the way she had attended to him. I don't think there was anything he wouldn't have done for her. He did everything, everything except dress and bathe her. All that she had given to him he gave back to her in those two years. He even learned to drive."

"Where was your father?" Bill asked.

"My father was a recovering alcoholic who relapsed. The more my mother needed him, the more he drank."

"John has a driver's license?" Ed asked.

"I assume so."

"He would have had to have some type of legal identification."

"All I know is that my parents went to court and filled some kind of papers."

"What name did he use?"

"John Adear."

"Adeer?"

Bill smiled. "John Doe. Doe a deer..."

"No, it was spelled ADEAR. My mother used to say to him, "You are such a dear.""

Bill asked, "Did he give her trouble, act out, fits of anger?"

"Never. Actually, I remember that she expected it and was concerned that it never happened. His affect was always the same – pleasant but kind of flat. Ryan had graduated when her cancer started progressing. On his days off, he'd come to LA and help take care of her. It was during that time that John and Ryan finally let down their guards and became close."

"What was the problem?"

"John never really trusted a male person and kept his distance. And in Ryan's eyes John not only took over his room but the affection of his mother. He felt he was replaced and he resented John. But I think they bonded over this love they had for my mother in her final days."

She turned her gaze to the floor and fell into thought. "When we knew the end was near for my mother, Ryan and I came home. We were sitting in the living room. My dad was in the kitchen drinking a beer. John was sitting beside my mother's bed, reading to her from her favorite book of poems. I can still hear the soothing tone of his voice. Then there was this wail. That sound lives within me. We knew immediately what happened. Ryan sat in the living room crying. My dad and I ran into the bedroom. John was on his knees beside her bed, holding her hand and sobbing.

"He retreated to his room and didn't go to the funeral. He was almost catatonic." She sat silently, staring into the air.

"What happened to him?"

She sighed and glanced at Bill. "Ryan went back to school as did I. One day, my dad called and said that John had left."

"Left?"

"All his stuff was gone, as was the car."

"The car?"

"My mother signed it over to him."

"You've never heard from him?" Ed asked.

"You said you found the original tapes and they show John being abused by this man? But it's my understanding that the statute of limitations is up on this. Right?"

"We found the original videos in a dead man's safe deposit box."

Bill watched as her composure changed. Her back stiffened. She shook her head and said angrily, "Dead. You found the guy who made them and...? Was it his father or a relative?"

"We don't know. We think not."

"It only took you how many years to find him? And you didn't *find* him, did you?"

"Yes, that's true."

"So why bother him or me with this. It will destroy him. He functions but any reminder of what happened to him has always..."

"So, you've seen him recently," Ed said.

"I didn't say that," she snapped.

"You said Ryan and John had a strong bond. Do you think Ryan might know how we could get in touch with John?"

'I haven't spoken to Ryan in over a year."

"Really," Ed said in a tone of disbelief. "And why is that?"

"How's that any of your business?" she shot back.

"I think it's best if you let me decide what's my business."

"When John was found we asked the police over and over what they had found out, what had happened to him and what we received as an answer was 'you know what we know.' Well, Detective, you know what I know, and I'll get back to you if I learn anything else. Like we learned from the LAPD, don't expect to hear from me."

She stood to leave. "I hope you don't find him. You'll use him for your own gain and toss him aside again. People, victims, are nothing more to you than a means to an end."

"Ms. Straus, I understand your concerns and so does Detective Coyne. If we get a chance to question John, we'll do our best to take into account the trauma he's experienced."

Ed added, "We are going to find and question your John. If we have any further questions for you..."

"Come with a subpoena," she said and started to leave. She turned back. "Detective Coyne is it? Do you have a family?"

"Yes."

"This man, the one who's dead...he was murdered, right?" Ed did not respond. "I looked both of you up. You're a Behavioral Scientist, Dr. Russo. And you're a homicide detective, Major Crimes. You're looking for a killer.

You're profiling. You think I don't know. Your single mindedness may work for you as a cop, but your lack of regard for anything or anyone else while solving murders, leaves people in misery, I have no doubt, and I'd say that includes your family." She looked at Bill, "And your slick 'take it easy on her' way of handling me to get what you want, I'm sure plays well for you too. At least he's straightforward with being an asshole. So, how's that for a profile."

She turned and left.

Bill said, "So where do we go from here?"

"We try to find John. John Adear."

"If the brother is a veterinarian he has to be licensed. I'll run a search for a Ryan Straus."

"John Adear. He has a driver's license."

"I'm not sure she said he legally changed his name. What she said was that was the name they gave him, like the date of his birthday."

"Well, I'll check. Maybe we can get a picture and description. If it comes back that he's six foot ten and three hundred pounds...Damn, I was going to ask her for a description."

They stood at the elevator. Ed said, "You should think about hiring her. She nailed me."

"She could say that about ninety percent of the men walking the earth."

"Maybe you can call her and ask her for a description of him."

Bill smiled. "You heard what she said. My slick ways won't work on her."

The elevator doors opened. "She looked us up?"

"She works for *LA Magazine.* Their search engines are probably more up to date and better than ours."

Twenty-Seven

Bill stopped at the UCLA Psychiatric Hospital to speak to Dr. Bellows in person. She was with Connor.

"Where is Dylan?" Bill asked the charge nurse.

"He's in the dayroom. They're doing math."

Bill entered the dayroom, where nine children sat at a table writing in workbooks. Dylan looked up and smiled. Bill smiled and called him over. He jumped up and quick-stepped it to Bill.

"Hi Doctor."

"How are you doing?" Bill asked as they walked to a treatment room.

"Okay. Can we go home?" Dylan asked as he entered the room.

"Hopefully, you can live with you aunt and uncle soon." Bill left the door open. "Did you see Dr. Bellows today?"

"Yeah, she's nice. She makes Connor cry though."

He sat down. "Makes him cry?"

"He told her that men hurt him, that my daddy hurt him. He's crying a lot."

"Well, sometimes crying is good. It's good that he's talking to her, don't you think?"

"Yeah. The devil can't get in here. The doctor showed us that the door is locked and only doctors and nurses can get in."

Bill noticed Connor standing in the doorway. He and Dr. Bellows entered the room. Connor looked at Bill and said, "I can talk now." His eyes were red. He looked exhausted.

Dr. Bellows and Bill went to an empty office on the ward. "You're doing well with them. He trusts you."

"I'm not sure how he has the strength to trust anyone. They were given a physical examination under mild sedation. Connor was anally scared. The examining doctor told me that she thought that Dylan might have also been anally penetrated. I asked Dylan about it. He said, 'My daddy just put his fingers in and Connor put his penis in and did stuff like Daddy did to him.'"

Bill slumped in his chair, remembering the short, interrupted scene he'd seen where Connor aggressed toward Dylan. "I was concerned about that. Do you know if Connor was coerced into it or did he do it because it was done to him?"

"I don't know. Your thought is what?"

Bill sat silently for a moment, thinking. "It will determine how we will approach him in long-term therapy."

"It makes a difference, doesn't it? I mean if he initiated things with Dylan."

Bill could hear the apprehension in her voice. "You're doing great with him. How are you doing?"

"This is not my first sexual abuse case. But when Connor described the rape by his father and then several other men." She shook her head. "He was terrified. Terrified of the pain and of being left with these men he didn't know. He threw himself into my arms and..." Her voice broke. She took a deep breath.

"This is tough work. Maybe the toughest."

They talked at length. Bill agreed they should remain on the ward as long as they could justify it. "Best they go from here to their relatives. I don't want them having to transition too much."

"Any word from their relatives?"

"They've been communicating with a lawyer, but nothing yet."

*   *   *

Bill left feeling encouraged, hearing Connor was talking and opening up emotionally. But the fact that Connor might have been molesting his brother of his own volition concerned him. *Conner's young. We can help him,* Bill assured himself.

As he left the hospital parking structure, Bill received a call from Ed. "We caught another one in West Hollywood. He's been dead for a few days. I'm on my way there now."

"I'll meet you there."

"I found information on our John Adear."

"Yeah, I just got a call about Ryan, he's up north..."

Bill had put out a query regarding Ryan Straus' veterinarian license. He was currently practicing in San Luis Obispo. He was able to find the phone number and address of the clinic and his home address and cell phone number. Ryan also had a landline to his house.

Driving to meet Ed, Bill also received a call from Stewart Dawson. He and his staff had gone through all the Zachary and Cody tapes. There was nothing new on the unknown adult, but they were able to confirm that it was Xavier.

"I wish we had caught the bastard before he was killed," Dawson said.

"Statute was up on him."

"They've got to change that. These guys get away with so much of this shit because of that and they don't stop. Maybe we could have gotten him on something recent."

"I wish we could figure out where he got John from. Romeo might have known but he's gone too."

"I understand this Xavier guy's house was ransacked and the safe emptied. You got nothing?"

"Nothing. My guess is that there's more than what was on memory cards. He had the room wired for videos."

"Do you think this John guy is the one doing the killings?"

"That's the guess right now."

"You have someone else in mind?"

Bill explained that there had to be other boys who this man abused and that it could have been any of them who matured to adulthood. "We're not even sure that he's working alone."

"Really?"

"I'm just arriving at another murder site. I've got to go."

"Another? You think it's this John guy again."

"Don't know. I'll get back to you if we find anything you need to look at," he said and hung up.

Mark was soon on the scene. They all knew the drill. The coroner found the injection site. "Looks like the others," she said.

Mark called out from the bedroom, "We've got something here."

Bill and Ed stood in the bedroom and watched as Mark moved the nightstand and pried open a loose floorboard, which exposed a safe. As soon as an officer entered with the requested search warrant, they broke it open. It contained dozens of flash drives.

"Give them to Brandon. I want to know what's on them ASAP," Ed demanded.

Twenty-Eight

Ed's alarm went off at 5:00 a.m. Running with Kristin had been one of his favorite things, early mornings or evenings when they could be alone doing something they both enjoyed. As he dressed now, there was a knock at his bedroom door.

Justin looked in. "Heard your alarm."

Ed bent down to tie his running shoes.

"Can I come with you?"

"Really? Yeah, sure. That would be great."

They headed down their street into the darkness of the morning. "It's been a while since I've done this," Ed said.

"I'll go easy on you."

Ed chuckled. "I'm really looking forward to surfing with you."

"I've been telling everyone that you're going to teach me. Did you really surf in the nude when you were in high school?"

Ed smiled. "Yes. It's hard to believe now."

"I think that's so cool. I want to do that someday."

"Just remember to load up on sunscreen or you won't be able to sit for days."

They jogged at a fairly good pace. Ed was feeling the effects of not running regularly for the past two years. He started to slow down. Justin slowed too.

"I really want this trip to be for you and me," Justin said. "But can we go again in August with Andrew?"

"Sure. He wants to learn?"

"Very much."

Silence.

"Dad, I want us to do more stuff together, stuff like this. We can run at night, like you and Mom did. Before bedtime. I'd love that."

"So would I." Ed checked his watch as they ran. "You're not even winded." Two miles in seventeen minutes. He was feeling it. "How far do you want to run?"

"We can head back."

"No, but let's slow down." They did. "You run with Andrew?"

"Yeah, and Brian and Evan."

"You're going to miss Andrew," Ed said. "You two have gotten very close."

"Yeah. We talk and kid around, tease each other. It's easy with him. He said that if I get accepted to Stanford, we could be roommates. He said we're going to be friends forever, like you and his dad."

Forever, Ed thought and then thought of Kristin. "I hope that's true."

"It will be. He loves me and I love him."

"I heard you tell Andrew that."

"And he tells me."

Silence.

"Not like sexual attraction love," Justin said. "Like friendship love. Like you love Uncle Bill and he loves you."

"I guess my generation doesn't express emotions like that freely, even though we may feel that way."

"That's kind of sad. Don't you think?"

When they arrived home, Ed paced around the driveway breathing hard and fast.

"You did good, Dad." Justin put his hand on his father's shoulder. "If we do this often enough, you'll be able to keep up soon."

They both laughed.

Entering the house, Ed said, "Get ready and I'll drop you at the pool."

"I kind of want to talk to you about something."

"How about we talk while I shave? You can shower in my bathroom if you want."

Justin turned on the shower. "Ah...well..."

"Is something wrong?"

"No…nothing. Andrew said this guy was interested in me. And…"

"Interested, like in dating?" Ed lathered his face and watched Justin in the mirror, noticing his broad shoulders, muscular back, and small waist. *Swimming has been good for him.*

"His name is Luke." He stood outside the shower, waiting for the water to warm.

"How old is he?"

"Seventeen. I mean he just turned seventeen. He's in my class. He's on the basketball team and he's friends with Andrew." Justin explained that Luke was not out to anyone at school except Andrew. He stepped into the shower. "He told his older brother first, then his sister. They convinced him to tell his parents, so he did."

"How did that go?"

"Good, I guess. Like with you and Mom."

Ed nodded.

"He called last night and said that he'd like to get together this weekend. He told me that he really doesn't want to be out at school. He's going to come out when he goes to college, but not in high school… He's nervous… being on the team and all."

"So how does that work? He and you going on a date?"

"Well, the three of us, Andrew, Luke and I, are going to go out Saturday… tomorrow night if that's okay with you. We'll go to a movie or something, go to Antonio's for pizza…"

"What if you run into people you know?"

"That's why Andrew is coming. It'll be the three of us, you know, just hanging out."

"Okay…" Ed sounded unsure.

"What? Just say it."

"I appreciate you telling me."

"I'm asking you if it's okay."

Ed nodded. "Okay. I appreciate that even more."

"You're concerned about something?"

"I remember being younger than you." Justin opened the shower door to better hear his father. "Fifteen, if memory serves me right."

"Were you with a guy first or a girl?"

"I was with this guy. He was in the foster care home I was in."

"And..." Justin said, moving soap around on his chest.

"We knew about safe sex, but we weren't. I guess we were too stupid to care."

"Two things, Dad. First, we are both completely virgins. I've never even touched a guy other than myself. Neither has he. Second, we'll be with Andrew, so it's not like..." Ed gave him a questioning look. "Okay, so maybe we'll find time to be alone. But it's not like we're going to fuck on the first date." Another look from Ed. "And I'll have condoms with me. Dad I promise you. No exchange of fluids as they say. One more thing. Luke said his father would like to call you."

"Why? I mean it's fine, but why?"

"Luke told him that you're a police officer and that you know I'm gay, but his dad said he wanted to make sure that this was okay with you. I mean you are a COP."

"Give him my cell number."

Justin saw that his father was finished shaving. He stepped out of the shower and grabbed a towel. Ed stepped in and pulled the door closed. "I have to tell you that if you told me two weeks ago that I'd be having these conversations with you, I would have said you were nuts." He looked toward Justin, who was still drying himself off. "Justin, the idea of talking to you about what I did when I was your age or what you might do with a guy..."

"It's a good thing, Dad." He started to leave the bathroom but stepped back in. "Can I ask you something?" Justin called out. "You don't have to answer."

"What?"

"Do you think you'd ever date someone again?"

"I guess I haven't really thought about it, but maybe sometime, if I found someone interesting. But your mother will be a hard act to follow."

"Do you think you're still bi-sexual or would you say you're straight now?"

"Do you think you'd ever be straight?"

Justin chuckled. "Okay, so then that person could be either a woman or a man."

"That's what bi-sexual means."

"Cool."

"Cool? Why cool?"

Justin shrugged and smiled. "Andrew and I were saying that we thought it would be funny if we wound up as step-brothers."

Ed shook his head. "We're friends. Very good friends."

"Yeah, I know. He's your best friend," he said and smiled. "Just something to think about."

"Like I said...if anyone had asked if I'd be having these conversations..."

"Does it bother you?"

"No. Not at all. I'm happy we can talk. This is what I want, but I just didn't think it could happen."

"Thank you, Dad, for being cool."

"I'm not good at this, Justin. Your mother understood, but...I want you to know...No," he said, shaking his head. "It's not enough for you to know. I want to say that I love you and that I admire the person you are. I want you to hear it from me. I think about you during the day, or when Bill and I talk about you and Andrew, and my chest swells with pride. Then I think that I don't tell you that enough."

"I feel the same about you, Dad."

Twenty-Nine

Ed found that John was John Adear, his legal name since he was sixteen; he had a driver's license and registered a car. "He last renewed his license with an address in San Luis Obispo. He's five feet nine and weighs 140 pounds."

"That sounds like the guy on the motorcycle."

When Bill ran John and Ryan's names, he discovered Ryan owned a veterinary clinic in SLO, and twelve acres of land approximately ten miles outside the city limits. He traced John to working at the clinic Ryan owned. John's bank account showed the same amount being deposited each month. He had one credit card with little activity, except for the purchase of gasoline.

The car that had been registered to John, a Toyota Civic, was now registered to Ryan, who also owned a motorcycle, a camper, and a BMW.

"What type of camper?" Ed asked.

"A Cambria. It looks like the front end of a pickup but the back is a camper. The Harley Davidson motorcycle is the same as the one on our video."

"That can't be a coincidence. That had to be John on that bike."

"Or Ryan. He also owns a 2002 five series BMW which I wouldn't mind owning."

Up until a year ago, John had over twenty thousand dollars in his bank account. Then there were monthly withdrawals, and then six months ago, he emptied his account except for one hundred dollars.

They arrived in SLO early and drove out to Ryan's house. They walked the roadway, seeing what they could see.

"Twelve acres," Ed said. "One house."

It was a large adobe-style house with tan stucco walls with rounded edges and exposed timber beams, hewn by hand. They stopped at the gate and looked around.

"Doesn't look like anyone's at home." Bill opened the four-foot black wrought iron gate. They nodded at each other and walked down a wide flagstone path lined with flowering bushes toward the house. On the covered porch, which ran along the front of the house, several redwood flower boxes filled with dry soil sat unattended. They knocked on the door. No answer. Bill glanced through a window into a large entryway, with a dark heavy wooden table and a Mexican style hand painted vase.

A fat orange Tabby surprised Bill as it jumped onto the window sill. "Seems empty."

They walked around to the side of the house.

Ed said, "I don't see a motorcycle, but it could be in the garage."

"No camper, no Toyota, or BMW either. That's a small garage for all of that."

Ed walked toward the back of the house. It was U-shaped and had a patio with a flagstone floor. There was a large lawn and a fenced-in pool. Beyond the pool, there were fruit trees. Two horses roamed the back acres.

"There's the Toyota," Bill called out. It sat parked by a shed.

They drove into town and pulled into the parking lot of an outdoor mall where the clinic was located.

"There's the BMW." Bill checked the license against what he had written in his notebook.

Ed looked at his watch as they stepped out of the car. "It's early. Let's hang here a bit." Ed's phone chimed. "Brandon, you're on speaker phone. Dr. Russo is here."

"I've got a lot of kiddy porn. It's not great quality. I mean it looks like stuff that's old and transferred from 8-millimeter and was black and white but has been colorized."

"Give it to Dawson. No, wait. Just hold on to it. Thank you."

"Wait. There's more. That blond boy we saw with Connor."

"What about him?"

"God, I can't believe I'm becoming familiar with these kids. One of the flash drives. It's some kind of auction to sell him to the highest bidder. The bidding has been closed, but the boy won't be available until the end of May. That's like in a month. Fuck, it's like they're selling a car. This is so sick."

"Shit. Okay. Look, I'll be in tomorrow."

"You think we can find this kid?" Brandon said.

"John is at the top of Ed's list. This boy is moving to the top of mine," Bill said.

Ed put his phone in his pocket. "Damn. Auctioning off a boy..."

Bill looked at Ed. "I wonder if our guy knows about the auction?"

They sat silently.

"I would live here," Bill said. "It's beautiful."

"What, and give up one-hundred-degree weather, air you can see, and parking lots called the freeways." They found a bench and sat. "Do they have an FBI office here? You'd be a lot closer to Stanford."

"Just up the highway."

"They probably don't need a homicide detective. Probably not a lot of murders."

Bill caught Ed's inference about needing both. "Probably a good place to retire," he responded.

What would it be like to settle here with Ed? To be more intimately involved? It was not the first time he'd fantasized about that. Had Ed ever considered it? He dismissed what he said as just an acknowledgment of their friendship.

"The boys spent eight hours last weekend studying. Andrew said that Justin helped him with his senior paper, and he went over the math for the SAT with Justin."

"That kid has his mother's verbal abilities and her trouble with math."

"How's he doing?"

Ed spoke of their morning run and their summer plans.

"Maybe it's time to ask Ryan how he likes his camper?"

Ed checked his watch. "Let's head in."

The receptionist greeted them. They took out their identification and asked for Dr. Straus.

"He's finishing up. Have a seat." She picked up the telephone.

Ryan entered the lobby in scrubs, looking younger than his thirty-five years. Bill estimated him to be about five-foot-ten, one hundred fifty pounds. Shoe size nine to ten.

He had straight brown hair and blue eyes. His sister was right. Ryan was attractive, almost pretty. Bill thought he looked like a man who, as a boy, would have been bullied.

Introductions were made, and Ed asked if he had time for questions.

"I'm working until six and without a break, but I do have to have lunch."

"We can eat," Bill said. "I saw a coffee shop a few storefronts down."

"What's this about?" Ryan asked, leaving the clinic.

"We can talk over lunch," Ed said. "What's it like living in San Luis Obispo? It's beautiful here."

"It is beautiful. People are friendly. It's a great college town but we are running out of water."

"So is everyone else in California."

After being seated, Ed said, "We're here to talk to you about John."

"John? Is he okay? I thought this was about my sister."

"Your sister?" Bill said.

"Yeah. She was raped last year—a date rape, by a guy that I knew."

"No. We didn't know about that. We've found tapes of John that go back to when he was very young," Ed said. He explained the tapes and DVDs but did not mention the murders. "We talked to your sister about John's time with your family. Hasn't she talked to you?"

"We haven't talked for over a year. John...John came here after my mother passed."

Ryan, unlike his sister, was shy and awkward when talking about John. "When we moved to SLO, John studied all my medical books then started working as an assistant at the clinic."

"Where is he?" Ed asked.

"Camping. He's at Sequoia right now."

"How long has he been there?"

"He moves around. One of my colleagues just asked when he might be coming back. I told her that I didn't know. Everyone misses him. John was never affable, but since his move to SLO, he's been as happy as I've ever seen him. He likes being needed. We asked him to assist with surgeries. He could recite the textbook as we operate. Though we had to put animals down without him knowing. It upsets him. Most people wouldn't know, but I do. I see it at home for days. He's withdrawn, sleeps curled up, sometimes he has bad dreams."

Bill noticed that Ryan was talking about John in the past tense. "You say he was helpful at the clinic. Is he not still helpful?"

The waitress brought their lunch.

"He had a breakdown about a year ago."

"Breakdown?"

"He could spend hours reading books or on the computer. He never watched TV. I think he was working his way through the library, book by book. One night I woke up a little after three. He wasn't in bed. I looked for him and found him pacing around the backyard. He looked crazed. Nothing I'd ever seen before. His eyes were darting back and forth. He kept putting his fingers through his hair and then pulling on it. It scared me. I tried to talk him down. When I reached out to him, he shoved me then he hit me. I called for an ambulance. He kept pacing and mumbling."

"What was he saying?"

"Names, people's names, first names."

"Do you think it was the names of people who..."

"Why are we talking about this?" Ryan reacted angrily. "I'm not ignorant of the law and neither is he. There's a thing called a statute of limitations."

"He remembered his abusers?" Ed asked.

"I don't know what he remembered. I had to have him hospitalized."

"How long?"

"Almost four months. He became catatonic at one point. It was terrible. But the doctors wouldn't give up on him. When he came out of it..."

"Did he regain his memories," Bill pressed.

"I don't know! He never talked to me about it."

"Did you ever find out what caused the break?"

A couple of days after John's hospitalization, Ryan went onto John's computer. "Along with his concern for animals, John donated much of his paycheck to children's charities."

Bill thought of the Tremway boys and how care was taken to minimize their trauma.

"One of those charities dealt with children from third world countries who were born with facial disfigurements. You know, doctors in this country raise money to go there and do hundreds of surgeries."

"Plastic surgeons."

"Right. The last site John visited was a video of a surgeon talking about the work being done."

Ed looked at Bill. "Adams?"

"Adams?" Ryan repeated.

"A plastic surgeon we know. Probably one of John's abusers."

"That makes sense. I never heard that name, but if it was one of them..." He sighed.

"Clearly, you love him," Bill said.

Tears came to Ryan's eyes.

"He's not with you anymore?"

"Five months ago, he said he had to spend time alone. That's when he left and went camping. He calls me every Sunday...tells me where he is, where he thinks he's going."

"But you haven't seen him?"

He shook his head.

"He's got your camper?" Ed said.

Ryan nodded and then looked at Edward. "You know I have an RV?"

"And he has your motorcycle?"

"Yeah, he has that too. What's going on?"

"Some of the men that had control of John, those who molested him and made videos have been found murdered."

"Murdered? And you're thinking...No way. He's not capable of murder."

"Torture and murder."

"No way. No way."

"Well, we hope you're right, but until we can talk to him and eliminate him, he's a suspect," Bill said. "Whoever it is has to be stopped. Nine people have been killed. That we know of."

"Do you use tranquilizer guns?" Ed said.

Ryan didn't respond.

"It wouldn't be in your interest to lie or obstruct a criminal investigation."

"We have two...had."

"Had?"

"We had a break in and stuff was stolen."

"Drugs?"

"Ketamine. It's a street drug. Since then, we've installed a safe. It's all locked up."

"What about Versed?" Bill asked.

"No. We have no use for that." Ryan shook his head. "Oh God...It wasn't, couldn't have been John." He stared into space.

"When did you put in the safe?" Ed asked.

"Four months ago."

"After he took off?"

Ryan nodded. He was clearly distressed, drifting off into thought. His pain was palpable. He'd lost someone he loved.

"You remembered something," Bill said.

Ryan shook his head and stared.

"Look, Ryan, anything you can tell us can help us understand John and that can only help when we talk to him."

"It's just stupid stuff. You know, the little things you remember. The things you don't notice or the things that you take for granted, but then when they're gone..."

"Like what?"

"You've got to understand that he was broken. He never expressed feelings. I never even heard him say that he'd rather have chocolate ice cream than vanilla. The only reason I knew that, was that if I bought both, he never touched the vanilla." He moved in his seat. "When we slept together, he always had a hand on me someplace, on my back, on my chest, on my arm."

"You were lovers," Bill said.

Ryan's face tensed.

"No judgment. I promise you."

"I have a gay son," Ed added, "and his son is my son's best friend. So, no judgment here either."

Ryan nodded. "Lovers, yes...but not like you think. I don't know how he did it. I never woke during the night that he didn't have a hand on me, and he always woke before me but never got up before I did. He never said good morning, he never said I love you or asked, 'How did you sleep,' nothing. But he'd always smile at me, scoot down and lay in my arms."

Ryan's chest quivered as he breathed in. "That was all before the hospital. After that if I reached out to touch him, he'd recoil, he'd look like I sickened him and then his eyes would tear up. He'd say he was sorry and then he'd go and close himself in what had become his bedroom for the rest of the night. Soon after that is when he said he had to go away, be alone. He said he hoped to come back and feel differently. I told him I'd wait."

They walked Ryan back to the clinic.

"Do you have John's phone number?" Ed asked.

"Yes, but he won't answer. His phone is off. When he first left, I tried to call him. I'd leave messages, but he said he'd call me on Sundays and he only calls on Sundays. He's like that. Once he decides something..."

"He sets firm and rigid boundaries," Bill said.

"Very."

"Can we have his number?"

Ryan took out his iPhone, went through his address book, and turned his phone toward Ed. He copied the number.

"Can you give him a try?"

Ryan tapped the screen and then turned the phone toward them. They listened. Immediately the phone went to voicemail. "You've reached me. I'm busy. Leave a message."

Ryan put his phone away. "That's him."

He promised he'd try to convince John to come in for questioning when John called on Sunday. He said he'd never owned a firearm and was confident that John wouldn't own one either.

Driving back, Ed said, "He's our guy—though Ryan fits the body type for the guy on the bike too. I've got a statewide alert on the camper and the bike. I'll run the phone when we get back. What do you make of the breakdown?"

"Makes sense. Adams and Xavier were probably the last people he saw as a boy before he was found near death in the road. He's sitting at his computer, in his safe home and he comes face to face with Adams—a video, so he heard his voice too. All those memories came crashing through."

Silence. A long silence.

"Justin joined me on a run this morning. We talked."

"How was it?"

"I think it was the perfect time. He told me that a guy who is Andrew's friend on the basketball team is interested in him."

"What did you say?"

"I didn't know what to say. This is something Kristen would have handled. But I asked him if he was interested, and he said he was."

"You sound concerned."

"I worry that he'll get involved and get hurt."

"You can't protect him from a broken heart." Silence. "What did you tell him?"

"That I was happy we were talking about this and that he could date but had a curfew. I have to admit that I felt nervous but later felt happy about the talk."

"This is what you wanted—him opening up to you...I saw Luke. At the basketball game. Very handsome. Seemed shy."

Entering the San Fernando Valley on Highway 101, Ed said, "I wonder what happened to John's parents. Maybe that Xavier guy was a foster parent and John was turned over to him by the state?"

"No. He was never in the system prior to being turned over to the Straus family. Maybe he can tell us."

"I hope he stops what he's doing and runs," Ed said. "Actually, if he has Adams' address book ..."

"Maybe we won't find him for a few weeks."

Ed smiled and shook his head as they slowed to stop. "Fucking traffic."

"We hit it at the worst time."

"San Luis looks damn good." Silence. "Why do men do this shit to kids?"

"Most men who were sexually abused never abuse. But every pedophile I worked with was molested. Romeo was sexually abused by Xavier. He maintained a positive relationship with him. He must have reasoned that since he turned out okay, so would his sons."

Thirty

As the sun rose over the Santa Monica Mountains, the tall man parked his dark grey Range Rover on Sherwood Drive in West Hollywood. He checked his phone for the address he found for Tristan McGuire. He was dressed in a pair of black joggers, a lightweight black hooded sweatshirt, and Nike running shoes. He put on his sunglasses and EarPods and stepped out of the car.

Jogging up and down the street, he found both Tristan and Christopher Adams' cars. As he passed Tristan's building, he slowed and considered its layout. The neighborhood was still quiet. He circled back and entered the courtyard looking for Apartment 6. It was on the first floor, and its windows were still dark. He walked to the back of the building and found what he was sure were Tristan's bedroom and bathroom windows. They too, were dark.

He moved his car to a better view of Christopher's car and their apartment. At 8:17 a.m., Christopher exited. The tall man watched him drive down the street and turn onto Santa Monica Boulevard. His heartbeat quickened with anticipation. He decided to wait to make sure Christopher did not return. At 8:45, he put on a pair of latex gloves, loaded a syringe with Ketamine, and put it in the pocket of his sweatshirt along with a surgical scalpel.

Making sure he was not seen and noticing a light on in the apartment, he took a deep breath and knocked. He heard someone approach the door and the chain being secured.

The door opened. Tristan was wearing just a pair of sweatpants.

"Yes," Tristan said.

"Tristan McGuire?"

"Yes."

"I was wondering if..." He saw the expression on Tristan's face change. He'd been recognized. He threw his shoulder and the weight of his one-hundred-and-eighty-pound body into the door before Tristan could close it. The door flew open and hit Tristan in the head, causing him to fall to the floor dazed.

He pushed his way into the apartment, closing the door behind him. He then quickly straddled Tristan's torso and put his left hand around Tristan's throat, almost choking him.

Tristan tried to scream but couldn't. He gasped for air.

"You know me. Can't have loose ends," the tall man said. "And you are a loose end."

He took the syringe from his pocket, injected Tristan, and watched him fade. He sat on his chest staring down at him, and gently stroked his face. *You were my favorite. John always resented me, but you...you would curl up into my arms and surrender yourself to me.* Then he pulled off Tristan's sweatpants, cut his scrotum, and removed his testicles. He cut off his penis and watched the flow of blood. When he peeked out the curtained window, the courtyard was empty.

He put his fingers to Tristan's neck, then his ear to Tristan's chest, and heard nothing. Satisfied, he moved to the door, opened it a crack, and listened. Nothing. He pulled the hood of his sweatshirt up over his head, put on his sunglasses, and then exited the apartment, closing the door behind him.

Thirty-One

The Tremways' lawyer told Bill that DeeDee's sister decided she didn't want custody of them after she was told that the boys were in a psychiatric hospital and why. Donna, the manager, was also named as a guardian. She agreed to foster them when they were released.

"They know her. That might not be so bad."

He called Dr. Bellows to ask how she and the boys were doing. "When I told you that Connor anally penetrated Dylan, you asked if it was coerced by their father, or if Connor initiated it. Dylan told me that their father didn't know about it. Connor was the aggressor and used objects like a pen and the handle of a hairbrush."

"I was afraid of that."

"Another boy on the ward reported to his therapist that Connor tried to touch him."

"Okay. I'll be in on Friday. We'll set up a treatment plan."

Bill's cell phone rang a moment later. He checked the caller ID. *Christopher Adams? Who the...? Oh, Tristan's Christopher.*

When he answered the phone, Christopher said, "He's dead. There's blood everywhere."

"Who's dead?"

"Tristan is dead. What do I do?" Christopher sobbed.

"Are you in the apartment?"

"Yes. What do I do?"

"Step outside and don't touch anything. We're on our way. I'll stay on the line with you until you get outside, but I'm going to be on with Coyne too."

By the time he arrived, Christopher was leaning against a car, talking to Ed. He looked at Bill. "I took time off from work. It was his first time going to therapy and I was going to go with him. He cried all last night. He said there was so much no one knew and that he couldn't tell me. He was afraid he was going to go nuts."

Bill noticed blood on Christopher's right hand and shirt. "I touched him," he explained, starting to cry again. "I thought he might be alive. I thought I could..."

"It's okay," Ed said. "Stay here with the officer."

"Suicide?" Bill asked as they walked the pathway to the apartment.

"Assault. Mark is inside."

Bill exhaled loudly. They ducked the yellow tape and stepped into the apartment. He noticed that the door jamb was damaged.

"He must have opened the door with the chain on," an officer said. "The guy must have thrown his shoulder into it."

Bill looked around the room. Mark was kneeling over the body. He looked up. "Looks like when our guy pushed open the door, this kid..."

"Tristan."

"Tristan got hit with it." He pointed to a broken tooth in Tristan's mouth. "His boyfriend said his tooth wasn't like that this morning. He must have stumbled across the room to here," Mark pointed to an area beside the sofa, "That's where our guy must have shot him up." He pointed to a puncture wound on his chest. Tristan's pants and underwear were pulled off. "He stripped him, then did his thing, cuts his junk. What's different is that this seems quick and unplanned. The others were so orderly. This isn't."

Bill said to Ed, "Maybe Tristan recognized him." Nothing else was disturbed. No messages on the bathroom mirror. "Something is not right."

"Their laptops are in their bedroom and it doesn't look like the hard drives have been taken," a policeman said.

Bill stared at Tristan's body lying on the floor in blood. Sadness washed over him. It was one thing to come to a scene like this where he didn't know the victim, another when he did.

They stepped outside.

"Something changed," Bill said. "Almost every other scene we've been at has had locks and chains. Tristan doesn't fit the profile either. Tristan is young, not wealthy...certainly not one of John's molesters."

"These fuckers are getting nervous. They know their friends are being killed."

"But how the fuck would anyone know that Tristan was involved in the case? And we don't need him to identify John. We have Emma, Ryan, and everyone at that clinic."

Ed nodded.

Bill exhaled loudly. "I don't think John did this. We have someone else."

Ed stared at the damaged doorway. "Tristan opened the door. He sees who it is...he recognizes the guy...he knows he's in trouble...tried to close the door...this guy forces his way in...he's got to be big."

"Our Mr. Six-foot-two..."

"Does Christopher know anything?"

"I don't know. I don't think so."

Then Bill stared at Ed, lost in thought. "The blond boy. Jamie."

"What about him?"

"We asked Tristan about him and who might have him or be selling him. He said he'd help us with finding his old pimp."

"The guy in the Hollywood Hills."

"Fuck, how would anyone know that?"

Sunday afternoon, John set up in a Sequoia National Park campsite. He talked to the managers about trails in the area, made himself dinner, and climbed into bed, where he studied a map of Highland Park. Then he did a search on his computer for information on Richard Henning. *Fuck!! Henning is a superior court judge.*

Monday morning, he packed his backpack with enough food for two days and headed off for where he would take time to consider his plan of attack. Henning was going to be tough. Since he was a superior court judge, cameras and guards would be everywhere in the courthouse and the parking structure.

He set up his tent alongside a stream. After beans and rice for dinner, he lay in his tent, trying to sleep. Memories. Daddy used to bathe him, fondling him as he washed his privates. Part of the game was for John to ask for more.

When Daddy refused, John had to beg. If John didn't play his part, he was punished severely. Daddy finally gave in to his son's demands and raped him.

This wasn't the man who kidnapped him. But he hoped that someone in such an important position would have the information on his kidnapper that he so desperately wanted.

Wednesday afternoon, after his hike back to the campsite, John turned on his phone. A text from Ryan read, *You have to call me now. It's an emergency.* John called.

"What are you doing?" was the first thing Ryan asked.

"Hi to you too."

"Sorry, how are you?"

"Good. I'm at Sequoia again. It's so beautiful here. The trees..."

"Sounds wonderful. I miss you and I'm worried."

"Don't worry. I'm fine."

"John, the LAPD and the FBI were here yesterday. They had all kinds of questions about you. They think you're killing the people who molested you. Are you? John, please tell me you're not. Please."

"What did you tell them?"

Ryan repeated their conversation the best he could remember. "I told them that I didn't know if you remembered who these men were. They mentioned a plastic surgeon. I told them you saw him on your computer. John, you're not doing this are you?"

Silence.

"I care about you. If it's you, they'll find out. You'll go to jail."

"I'm not going to jail. Don't worry about it. Who were these guys?"

Ryan gave him Ed and Bill's information. "If it's not you, call them. Go in and talk to them."

Silence.

"John, I can't go a full week without talking to you with all this going on. I'll be sitting here thinking you're in jail or worse, dead and I won't know otherwise until Sunday."

"I'll call you during the week. Stop worrying. I'll be okay."

"They know you have my camper and motorcycle. John, they're looking for you."

John changed the subject and asked about the people who worked at the clinic. As usual, they talked at length, Ryan working to keep John on the line. John asked questions. Ryan spoke at length.

"I promise I'll call you during the week," John repeated.

Silence.

"Will I ever see you again? Will we ever be happy again?"

Silence.

"John?"

"The only time I've ever been happy has been with you."

"If you're doing this, come home, we'll pack up and take off. I've always wanted to live in Costa Rica. I've got money put away. I can practice there. If you're not doing this, then call them. Talk to them and then come home."

"I'll call you."

"Okay. Be careful. John... I love you."

"Ryan, I've never said that to you..."

"It's okay."

"Let me finish. I've never been sure what feeling goes with the words I love you. But I've been thinking about this. I didn't say it because the feeling that I felt toward your mother was what I thought I had to feel toward you. Like that was love. Well, it was love, but not the kind I feel toward you. The kind of love I felt toward your mother was like a child loves his parents. I understand now that I love you like a man loves another man, his best friend, his lover, someone with whom he wants to share his body, his entire body and in the most intimate way."

"That's the way I love you."

"I know."

"Then please come home."

"I'll call you," John hung up.

He lay awake most of Wednesday night. He was not afraid of being caught, but afraid he would be caught before he found his kidnapper. Now it was too dangerous for him to drive around LA with his kill gear, the drugs, tranquilizer gun, and scalpels. *They know my camper and motorcycle and license numbers. But I'm not going to pack up and go home. Not until I find him.*

He tossed and turned.

Costa Rica. I can't let this affect Ryan's life. I've burdened him and his family enough. If I get stopped, it's all over. There's no if, I'm going to get pulled over. I have to plan on it. So, I either give up and run, or...What if I'm stopped and the camper is clean? Do they possibly have something on me? If they did, wouldn't they have been more aggressive about looking for me? I've been careful. They told Ryan that they found the videos. So, they've guessed why I'm killing these guys, but do they have proof? I can't drive around waiting to get pulled in. Either run and hope I don't get caught or...take control of this.

He had a plan.

Thursday morning, he went through his camper three times. He was careful to gather everything that could link him to the murders into a large plastic garbage bag, including a new pair of scrubs he'd bought in Bakersfield on his last trip from LA. He had also bought another duffle at an army-navy surplus store but decided to keep it.

He sat and glanced around the camper. Usually, he was obsessively neat, but he thought it would look better if the camper didn't look like it had been cleaned. *Make it look lived in.* He gathered some of his dirty clothes and stuffed them in the duffle. He left some thrown on top of an unmade bed.

He looked at the names and numbers that Ryan had given to him. *An FBI agent William Russo, Ph.D. He's an Italian-American, just like my mother. Just like me.* He dialed.

"This is John Adear. I understand you're wanting to talk to me."

Bill sat up straight in his chair. "Uh, yes we do. We'd like to talk to you about a case we are working on."

"I know. Ryan told me all about it."

"Where are you?"

"Sequoia National Park. A campsite. It will take me maybe five or six hours to get there. You have an alert out for me, right?"

"For your camper and motorcycle."

"And what do I do if when I'm heading there..."

"Have them call this number."

Bill gave John the address of the Federal building and directions. He would be expecting John in the late afternoon. He hung up and stared at the phone, surprised by the call. He shook his head and called Ed.

"You really think he's coming in?"

"If he isn't, why would he call? He can't be thinking that he'd be buying himself six hours. He could have taken off days ago."

"Okay, I've got shit to do here. Let's have a late lunch and plan how we're going to do this. I'm going to ask a few of the CSIs to meet us there. Maybe we can look over his camper."

John took down his tent, packed the camper, and attached the motorcycle to the towing hitch. To bury his gear, he decided on the long way to LA, through Bakersfield, east to Mojave, south to Lancaster, through the Angeles forest, and into LA. He pulled off Highway 14 onto Agua Dulce Canyon Road and followed it until he found a grove of white alder trees. Carrying the garbage bag and a shovel, he walked into the groove of trees and marked one. Using his compass, he took one-hundred paces directly north. In an area covered with California buckwheat, he dug a hole and buried the bag. After walking back to his camper, he brushed off as much dust as he could and wiped his hiking boots with a wet cloth.

I should call Ryan. If I blow this, they'll take my phone. If he doesn't hear from me...

He called Ryan before getting back on the highway and tried to convince him that everything would be okay.

"They interviewed Emma," Ryan said. "She told me the FBI guy plays good cop and the detective plays bad cop. Please be careful."

"Can you give me Emma's cell phone number?"

John called Emma, who repeated what she had told Ryan and what she could remember of her conversation with Bill and Ed. "I'm not going to ask you if you're doing this. I don't want to know. But please be careful."

"I will. But I do have a favor to ask of you and please don't ask me any questions."

"Okay."

"I've been writing. It's sort of a memoir. I've put it on the cloud. I want to give you the address and the passcode, but don't open it until I tell you or..."

"Or?"

"Well, you'll know. I want you to read it over and publish what you think is important and appropriate. I trust you Emma. You'll know what to do."

"John..."

"I love you and I love Ryan, but I don't know how to live with all that's in my head. Will you do a I ask?"

"Yes. Of course. But John please..."

"You should write this down." After giving her the information, he asked her to repeat it, and then he hung up.

Thirty-Two

Bill took the elevator and met John in the lobby. He was dressed in a tee shirt, cargo shorts, and hiking boots with long leather laces. He took off his sunglasses and put them on his head. He was as Bill imagined: average height, lean but looked to be in good shape. The cut of his straight blond hair brought attention to his boyish blue eyes.

"I'm sorry about not being cleaned up," John said. "I was out hiking and the showers at the campsite..."

"No problem." Bill was not surprised by the warmth of John's smile and voice. His experience with serial killers informed his expectations, but he was surprised that John seemed nervous.

John took the glasses from his head and put them in a pocket in his shorts. "Usually, I check into a motel once a week or so and soak in the tub," he said as they stepped into the elevator. "It helps."

When he lifted his arm, Bill noticed a scripted tattoo on the inside of his left arm.

"Your tat. What does it say?"

John glanced at his arm and pulled up the sleeve of his tee shirt. "I am alone, as I have always been; abandoned not by men...but by the happy Spirit of Joy..."

"I've read that someplace."

"It's from *A Fragment of Life*."

Bill said, as the doors to the elevator opened, "Kierkegaard."

They walked along the hall and entered a large office space where Bill introduced Ed, then all moved into a mirrored interrogation room. Bill motioned John to a chair facing the mirror. A video camera pointed in his direction. Bill closed the door.

"We'll be recording this," Bill said as he and Ed sat. He announced himself and Ed and gave the date and location. "We are with John Adear..." he said, then proceeded to read John his rights. "Do you wave your right to council?"

"Am I under arrest?" His voice sounded hollow.

"No. This is standard procedure. You know, us covering our asses."

John nodded.

Ed pushed a piece of paper in front of him. "You'll have to sign this then."

John looked at it. "Well, since we're being so formal, perhaps I should tell you that my birth name is Anthony Rizzoli."

"Really," said Bill. "You remember your given name?"

"Of late, yes. So you want me to sign this as John Adear or ..."

Ed said, "Your ID says John Adear. So use that, but note that you were born Anthony Rizzoli."

John studied the paper, then took the pen and signed it first as John Adear and then as Anthony Rizzoli. "It's odd to see my name. I mean the Anthony Rizzoli. I never use it."

"Do you remember your parents?" Bill asked.

"Only my mother—vaguely."

"Do you remember her name?"

"Gina Rizzoli. I don't believe my father was ever in the picture."

"What happened to her? How did you wind up with Victor Xavier?"

"Was that his name? I only knew him as Leo." John explained being awakened in a motel room in Las Vegas by a very tall man with reddish brown hair and big ears. "He gave me chocolate milk to drink and said that we were going to get my mother out of jail. The next thing I remember is waking up in a strange room. I was six years old."

"You don't know what happened to her?"

John shook his head.

Ed said, "We've seen the videos of you being molested..."

"Molested? I wasn't molested." John growled. "I was raped. I was kidnapped, locked in a room with my kidnapper and raped over and over. I screamed and fought and no one came. Then Leo took his turn with me. For weeks, I cried and screamed and no one came. Then I stopped screaming."

Silence. A silence so heavy it sounded like those screams.

Ed exhaled loudly. "You're right. We've seen videos of you being raped. They were on VHS tapes that had been stored in a safe deposit box that we found. So, we know what happened to you."

"I promise you, it would take many very large safe deposit boxes to store all the videos he took. He filmed everything. So," John muttered, "I can assure you that you don't know all that happened."

John and Ed continued to stare at each other. Ed nodded.

Bill said, "You're right. We can only guess. The videos we saw were of you with Xavier, and later with another much older boy called Zachary."

"Romeo was probably about twelve or thirteen," John said.

"You knew his name?" Ed asked.

"Yes. The guy you are calling Xavier, he never talked to me other than to tell me what to do. All of the men I was with weren't there to talk either. So, when I was with Romeo or any other boy..."

"We have tapes of you with a boy your age or maybe younger..."

"Probably Tristan. He was another boy that they brought in sometimes."

Bill felt his stomach sink. "Uh..." He and Ed looked at each other. He recalled his first conversations with Tristan. *I've bottomed with Romeo many times, more than I can remember. He's always been good to me, got me off drugs, gave me a job, been more than generous.*

Bill took a breath and tried to pull his thoughts together. "...How about we step outside for a moment." They left John with an officer.

Closing the door behind them, Ed said, "Fuck...He's right. He was a child being raped."

"And he remembers it all; the men, their sounds, their smell, the pain, everything, every day. And those memories were exploding into Tristan's consciousness."

"So, you think it was Tristan McGuire?"

"Yes. Remember what his boyfriend said. Tristan had secrets he couldn't tell him. I thought it was about the abuse by his father, but..." Bill took his phone out of his pocket.

"Who are you calling?"

"Dawson. I'm going to see if I can get pictures of Tristan as a boy from the videos we found. We have pictures of him as an adult...Shit, I can't believe we missed this."

"There was no reason to think..."

"Yeah," Bill said into the phone. "Where is he? Okay, patch me through to his cell." Bill waited. He heard a phone ring in the room adjacent to the interrogation room.

"Dawson," Stewart answered.

"Where are you?"

Stewart stepped into the hall. "I thought I'd watch this. Maybe learn something about other videos and guys. Maybe we can nab someone."

"We need pictures of Tristan as a boy."

Stewart walked away, speaking into his phone.

Bill turned to an agent sitting at a desk. He wrote on a pad of paper. "Gina Rizzoli. Call Vegas PD and find out if they have any information about her being jailed some twenty years ago." He estimated the dates. "Give me the info as soon as you get it."

They returned to the room and Ed asked John if they could look through his camper.

"It's kind of a mess. But it is my mess and I know where everything is. If you're..."

"We'll leave it as we find it."

John tossed him the keys and told them where he parked. "You can't miss it, it's the one with the motorcycle hitched behind it."

Ed handed the keys to the officer in the room, who then nodded and left.

"We want you to look at some pictures," Ed said, putting a picture in front of him.

John picked it up. "That's Dr. Adams. The plastic surgeon."

"You remember him?"

"Ryan told you I saw him online. I'm sure you know that I wound up being hospitalized. That's when it all started coming together."

"Coming together?"

"Before that, I remembered voices, sounds, tastes, sensations, and names. Any names I remembered weren't real. Dr. Adams was called Ron and there was Leo. I knew another man only as Daddy. The faces were very vague, fleeting. But when I saw the video..."

Ed pushed the photo closer to John. "This man is dead."

"Yes, Ryan told me the men who raped me have been found dead...And that you think I had something to do with it. But like I said, I never knew their real names and there were other boys."

"Romeo and Tristan."

"And others—four that I knew of."

"Were Romeo and Tristan ever in the same video?" Bill asked.

"There were several videos of the three of us together."

The door opened, and an officer handed Bill a folder containing pictures. He opened it and then stared at one in particular—the boy called Nicky. He could see the resemblance to Tristan, the adult.

"I'd like for you to look at a couple of photos. They're driver's license photos. See if you recognize them." Bill put Romeo and Tristan's photos in front of John.

He picked them up and shook his head. "Who are they?"

"The dark-haired man is Romeo. The other is Tristan."

John studied them. "Yeah, I can see that."

Ed put the crime scene photos on the table.

John pushed them around. "Geez, that's pretty gruesome." He looked at another. "God damn. You said murdered, but..." He looked closer. "Is it all cut off?"

"Yeah, all cut off." Ed laid the first piece of his trap. "They say you have a good memory. Maybe you can tell me where you were when this happened."

"I'll try, but it doesn't work that way. Something has to trigger my memory. Seeing a picture that I have no association with isn't going to do it. But I'll try."

Ed put each crime scene photo before John and gave him the dates and times. "Can you remember all that?"

John looked over the pictures. "I think I was at the Salton Sea for that one."

Ed presented each picture in the order of the murders.

When he came to the realtor, Glenn Paulsen, John repeated the date and time. "I was camping in Sequoia."

"You weren't here in LA?"

John sat back.

Ed put the picture of him on his motorcycle in front of him, knowing that this was not from the scene of the Paulsen murder but rather the murder prior to it.

John looked at it. "Yeah, that's me. Seeing that does jog my memory."

"You were in the area that day?" Ed pointed to the pictures of Glenn Paulsen.

"That day? The day this guy got killed. I don't think so. I'm pretty sure I stayed in Ventura and then, that weekend, I headed up to Sequoia." He looked through the pictures again. "The reason I'm saying that is that I had come into LA, rode my bike around on this day and didn't come in again for a while." He hoped that was all the pictures they had. "Yeah, that's the day I went to a bookstore on Santa Monica Boulevard after I dropped my laundry off at a place on Fairfax."

"You remember where the laundry was?"

"Well, yeah. I went to a deli on Fairfax—they have the best pastrami on rye. I put my laundry in the washer, got a sandwich, went back, put my stuff in a drier and then headed up Fairfax to the bookstore. I came back, got my laundry, and headed back up to Ventura."

Bill said, "Do you remember what you bought? At the bookstore."

"Yes, of course. A book called *Essays* by Michel De Montaigne."

"You read French?"

John smiled. "I'm learning, but no. It's a translation by J.M. Cohen. It's in my camper."

"The duffle?" Ed said, pointing at the picture, sounding frustrated.

"I keep my laundry in the duffle. I mean it's a camper. Where else would you keep dirty laundry? And this is LA," he said, pointing to the picture, "I usually come into town on my bike. Not too many places to park a camper."

Bill put the picture of the boy called Nicky before John. "Is that Tristan?"

John picked up the picture and stared at it. He nodded. "Yes, that's him."

"And he knew Romeo?"

"There were videos made of Romeo, Tristan and me. And some with the three of us with Romeo's father."

"Romeo's father...?"

John sighed impatiently. "You say you found videos and you know what happened. Clearly, you know little. My kidnapper was the first to rape me. Then Leo, then Romeo's father showed up."

"Do you know Romeo's father's name?"

"Not his real name. But he was some English professor in some college."

Ed put a picture of Romeo tied to a chair before John.

"Geez. Is that Romeo?" John looked at Bill. "But why him? He didn't molest anyone."

Ed put a picture of Tristan in front of John. He looked at it. Bill watched his reaction. To the previous images, John seemed almost unaffected. However, when John saw the crime scene photo of Tristan, he blanched.

"This is Tristan, isn't it?"

"Yes."

He pushed the picture away. "Again, why kill him? He didn't molest anyone."

"Exactly." Again their eyes locked onto each other.

John finally looked away and glanced back at the picture of Tristan on the desk. "I liked him." He sat back in his chair. "Okay, so Romeo is killed. Tristan is killed and other guys who molested them and me. I get that you think I'd kill these guys." He pushed the pictures toward Ed. "But why the fuck would I kill Tristan...or Romeo," he added. "They were just as much victims as I was. You have to understand that I was a child without friends. No one. When Tristan and I first were put together I could see in his eyes the pain and loneliness I was feeling." John's voice strained with sadness. "When they brought Tristan to the house, it was the only time I felt happy. I didn't care what they asked us to do on film. I had a friend."

John picked up the picture of Tristan's crime scene. "I wish I had known he was living here in LA" Tears fell. He wiped them away using the sleeve of his tee shirt. "Maybe I'm next on this guy's kill list."

Bill was convinced that everything John said about Tristan was true. He sat back in his chair and crossed his arms over his chest.

"You suggested that it might be someone else who was molested," Ed said. "Clearly, it's not Romeo or Tristan."

"Okay. Look, I didn't tell you this, and maybe I should have, but you guys are scaring the shit out of me. I get that I look good for this. If I were you, I'd think it was me too."

"And what is it that you should have told us?"

"I talked to Adams."

"Talked?"

"I confronted him. I told him I remembered him. I threatened him. He said the statute of limitations ran out. He also said that I had no proof. I told him that I know a reporter at the *LA Magazine* who would love to write an article about a cabal of men molesting boys under the noses of the LAPD and FBI for years. I told him that I'd make it bad for him. He'd never be able to work again, and his family would know. I told him that I wouldn't say anything about him if he told me how I could find the guy whose house I stayed at and the guy who kidnapped me. He was scared. He said he didn't know who kidnapped me, but that he could find out. I gave him two days. He said I had to give him a week. That's when he'd be seeing Leo—the guy you are calling Xavier. That's where we left it. A week later, I waited for him where he worked. He didn't show. Then I heard that he was killed."

"You're right, you should have told us."

"The guy who kidnapped me is killing all his friends so that I won't find him."

"The problem with that is, why not just come after you? And who is to say that you're not going after each of these guys. I mean, like you said, the statute of limitations has run out. So, this is you taking your revenge."

"Revenge," John said brusquely. "No. The act of revenge is passionate, uncalculated..." he hesitated. "You know, messy and personal."

"So, if not revenge, then what?"

"If this were me, and again I say it is not, I'd think of it as retribution."

Bill asked, "A distinction with what difference?"

"Retribution," John turned his attention to Bill, "is an act that is... what? Morally justified. You know, like capital punishment—fully deserved."

"And it's not you, taking," Ed paused, "retribution?"

"It's not me. You said Leo, this Xavier guy, is dead, right? Adams thought Leo knew who my kidnapper was. I knew that Leo knew him."

"And why is that?" Ed asked.

"He was in the room filming this guy with no hood on. I was six years old and this adult man shoved his adult penis into my ass over and over, for days, as I screamed and cried."

Bill and Ed slouched as they sat back in their chairs.

"Then he was gone and Leo, Xavier, raped me. When he was done," John exhaled loudly, "like I said, when he was done, Romeo and his father showed up. Romeo stayed with me, slept with me, talked to me, and told me that he had been with Leo for years. He told me he'd teach me what to do so it wouldn't hurt. So the videos you saw of me with Zachary were soon after I was taken. The videos of Tristan and me were much later."

Bill and Ed remained silent.

"The man who kidnapped me returned many times. So, obviously, Leo, Xavier, had to know who he was. Maybe when Adams came to him and asked about him, Xavier figured that something was up and told this guy and then this guy decided to take care of business."

"Okay, but you, too, know who he is," Ed said. "You might not know his name, but you know him."

John shook his head. "So, you envision me walking around LA checking out every tall, red headed guy with big ears to see if it's him?"

Silence.

"What were you going to do if you found this guy? Kill him?"

"Depends on the day."

"You can't tell me you hadn't thought about it."

"Of course, I have. If I've dreamed of..." John leaned forward and pointed to a picture of Glenn, showing his castration, "...cut the Johnson off the guy who kidnapped, raped and left me to be raped by others or five years, I think that's not crazy."

Bill and Ed stood and left John in the room with an officer. Ed told Bill, "It's him. We've got nothing, unless we get something from the camper, but I know it's him."

Bill nodded. "He talked like he was shocked by the photos, but when he saw Tristan, he blanched. He didn't kill Tristan, just as we thought, and that photo surprised him. Maybe even scared him. Or it scared him because the boys in these videos—Romeo and Tristan—are being killed. He's right to be scared. He might be next on this guy's kill list."

"We can't hold him."

An agent supplied Bill and Ed with new information on Gina Rizzoli.

"We have bad news for you," Bill told John as they sat back down. "You said you were taken in Las Vegas and that your mother had been arrested.

Gina Rizzoli." Bill looked up from the document he was reading. "Actually, her name was Georgina."

"Okay."

"Your mother was never arrested in Vegas...she was found dead there. A couple of days before, her car was towed from a motel outside of Vegas. So..."

John breathed in deeply. "I guess I knew she was dead. I mean I guess I hoped she wasn't. Fuck..." He groaned.

"It was a cold case—unsolved."

They sat silently for a moment while John tried to compose himself. "I'm sorry. So, the guy that kidnapped me is a kidnapper, child-rapist, and a murderer."

"You say he was the first to molest you," Ed said.

"No. What I said was that he *raped* me."

"Yes, sorry. And he wasn't wearing a mask. Right?"

"Right." John confirmed that Xavier filmed him, and he wasn't wearing a mask.

"We've found tapes. We've found DVDs, CDs, flash drives and memory cards, but in all of what we've seen, the adults are wearing hoods, or if they're not, their face is not shown."

John sat silently for a moment. "There are maybe thirty videos of men without hoods." He explained that the first time he was with any given man, they were filmed not wearing a hood. "Either they're hidden someplace or destroyed."

An officer entered the room and whispered into Bill's ear.

Bill said, "They went through your camper and found nothing that interests us. We'd like to find this guy, the guy who kidnapped you. Vegas is sending us what they have from your mother's murder. With DNA testing, we might be able to pull something. You're the only one who knows what he looks like," Bill said. "If you come back tomorrow, I'll have a sketch artist here. She can work with you. We'll put you up for the night. It'll be on us. Dinner, breakfast, the whole nine yards. Also, we're looking for a boy named Jamie and it's highly likely that your kidnapper has him."

"I don't know if I can help. I know what he looked like twenty years ago."

"Work with us," Ed said. "We have software that can age a picture and adults don't change that much. Not like a child does over twenty years. Give us tomorrow and it might go a long way to catching this guy."

"Okay, but I'm not staying in a hotel. I'll stay in my camper."

"You can't park here and spend the night."

"It's only an hour to Point Mugu National Park. I'll camp there and be back tomorrow."

They stared at him.

"I came in today, didn't I? I'll be in tomorrow at ten. I want to find this guy as much if not more than you do. There's no statute of limitations on murder. Right?"

Bill tested John. "Avec votre aide, nous pourrions l'obtenir."

"En esperant que. Je serai demain a dix."

"Okay, then, tomorrow at ten."

Thirty-Three

Steward Dawson drove down each level of the Federal Building parking structure in his Range Rover Sport, looking for a camper with an attached motorcycle. He found it on the third level. Two men wearing blue shirts with the letters CSI were stepping out of it. He looked forward as he drove past it, not wanting to be noticed. He drove down to the second level and waited for John.

He and Victor Xavier were college roommate's freshman year. Their resident assistant, Liam Conway, was a 22 year old English literature graduate student. During their year of dormitory life, they shared their most private sexual secrets and desires.

Liam talked about masturbating while being allowed to watch his older sister and her boyfriend have intercourse. Victor admitted that when he was eight, he was tricked into giving his much older brother a blowjob. And when Dawson was prepubescent, a neighbor paid him one dollar each time he put the man's penis in his mouth and then allowed the man to 'kiss' Dawson's penis while masturbating to orgasm. They formed a confederacy of sexual perversion. The following year, they moved off campus, living in a two-bedroom apartment with the intent of furtively filming sexual acts with unwilling partners.

Heterosexuals in desire, they agreed to submit to each other homosexually while the third person filmed the encounter. The videos they each held would serve as surety for their commitment to silence. Their first attempts were puerile as they fumbled, gagged, and grimaced. Victor declared that if they were to be serious in their purpose, they would have to put aside their concern for their own and each other's sexual sensibilities and take each other by force—practice makes perfect. He volunteered to be the first to be tied up and raped orally and anally on video by his confederates.

They worked their way through a list of men and women. The last intentions involved adolescent girls and then prepubescent boys. They seduced, coerced, and drugged fellow college students. Their effort to seduce an adolescent girl almost brought in the authorities. They explained it away as an innocent misunderstanding. Panic led them to destroy the tapes and eventually end their partnership.

He transferred to a university in Arizona, where he studied computer science and criminal justice. Liam, having earned his master's degree, moved to Northern California, where he hoped to teach. Victor enrolled in a film school in Los Angeles.

Wishing to escape the lure of his past and being influenced by a woman he was dating and later married, Stewart Dawson became a born-again Christian. He applied and was accepted into the FBI and was stationed in Las Vegas, where he was assigned to a unit that specialized in stopping sex trafficking. However, the years he spent with Victor and Liam played heavily on his mind, but not with guilt or shame. Rather, it was with a longing for the excitement that he missed and for which he lusted. Finding Victor was not hard to do using his FBI resources. But summoning the grit to meet his partner in crime and acknowledge aloud to himself and another his desires, took years.

When he did make the call, Victor refused to speak on the phone, so he drove to Los Angeles, and they met at a coffee shop. Victor wanted to know everything about him and became extremely guarded when he heard that he worked for the FBI. He admitted that he had been obsessing about their exploits. Victor acknowledged nothing, but he did say that he had been in contact with Liam, who had a son, Romeo.

Driving back to Las Vegas, his imagination ran wild, thinking of the last item —sex with prepubescent boys? Did Victor mention Liam's son, letting him know that he had a boy available? His body roiled with anxiety and desire. Months passed before he called Victor. He asked if he and Liam might be willing to work with him again. He said he would do anything to prove he could be trusted and was willing to do it on film.

Victor and Liam agreed but under one condition. The kidnapping and raping of John while being filmed and then leaving John with Victor was the price he had to pay for an introduction to boys with whom Victor had access.

Shackled by his marriage and job location, Dawson worked to free himself of both. Pornography on the Internet was growing one hundred-fold each year, and child pornography was becoming prolific but hidden on what was becoming known as the dark web. Innocuous web pages, a site that advertised running shoes or used furniture, would be hijacked. The hijacker would come behind the page and put hidden hyperlinks, doors, and commands, or what were called 'hot buttons,' onto the page and, when located and clicked on, would take the user to another website on the dark web. He put his mind to developing a program that could scan for hijacked sites, then tweaked it so he could list sites as innocuous that were not.

Having given the FBI such a powerful tool, he was given a promotion and a transfer to any location he desired. Since the Los Angeles FBI offices had one of the largest departments working with child trafficking and pornography, it made sense to everyone when he requested LA. His transfer was approved at the same time his divorce was granted.

Stewart, Victor, and Liam freely indulged themselves in videos with the intention to make money. The first released were those of John and Romeo, to whom they gave aliases. The videos were for sale on the dark web through a backdoor hyperlink safe from Dawson's program. However, a few years later, the material surfaced after making its way through Canada, Europe, and Asia. Stewart watched as the FBI and Interpol tried to find the boys and who made the videos. Finally, they closed down their dark website and ended all online releases.

Now, he watched as John slowly drove through the parking structure and pulled out into traffic on Wilshire Boulevard. He followed at a distance, teeth clenched.

He followed John onto Pacific Coast Highway. He thought about Russo and Coyne standing over John's mutilated body, their imagined conversation. "What the fuck is going on here?" he said aloud.

He engaged his address book on the Rover's dashboard and put the call through to Liam.

Thirty-Four

John figured they would have never let him leave if they had anything other than suspicions. He drove north on Pacific Coast Highway through Malibu. Passing Zuma Beach, he thought of Ralph Adams and then the man who kidnapped him, and then Tristan's murder.

John had decided he could no longer live with the burden of his ever-present childhood memories. They had become a constant torturous companion. If caught by the police, he would commit suicide while in their custody. If he found and killed his kidnapper, he would leave the scene and later commit suicide. Yosemite, maybe, finish his memoir, and then head up to Half Dome. Jump from one of the steep trails.

I wonder if they will be able to find him from the sketch artist? Did he kill Tristan? Is he after me? Can I get to him first?

Ryan, he thought, glancing at his watch. *As soon as I get settled, I'll call him.*

He entered Ventura County and drove north a few miles to Point Mugu State Park. Being early spring, the park was nearly empty.

"Mr. Adear. You're back," Ranger Caputo said.

"For a couple of nights, maybe longer. How's Mrs. Caputo?"

"Good. She's making lentil soup. Why don't you join us?"

"Ah..."

Mr. and Mrs. Caputo had a son around John's age who was killed in Iraq. They'd taken a shine to him the last few times he stayed at the park, and he responded to their warmth and friendship.

Now, Mr. Caputo picked up his cell phone. "John Adear just checked in." He looked at John. "She wants you to come."

John smiled and nodded.

"He said yes. Okay, I'll tell him," he said to his wife. To John, he said, "I'll give you a call when it's ready. Probably in about an hour. I've got your number."

"Sounds great. Thank you. I have to set up and make a call."

He paid for a two-night stay and found a parking space in the most isolated area that he could find. He backed in, unhitched his motorcycle, settled into the camper, and called Ryan.

"It went okay?" Ryan asked.

He described his time with them, not mentioning the picture they had of him on his motorcycle. "They showed me a lot of pictures of the dead people."

"Must have upset you. How are you doing with all this?"

Silence.

"John."

"Confused. I guess nervous. Scared," John paused. "Anyway, I told them about being kidnapped and my mother's name. They found out..."

He heard something outside the camper. "Hold on."

"What's wrong?"

"Hold on." He leaned into the front cab and looked out. He saw nothing. He stepped to the door. "I thought I heard something. Probably just an animal." He opened the door and listened. Nothing. He closed and locked the door and sat down. "What was I saying?"

"You were saying they found something about your mother."

John took a deep breath. "They found out that she was murdered, probably the night I was taken and by the guy who took me."

"Oh wow... John I'm so sorry."

"Yeah. It's kind of bittersweet news."

"How do you mean?" Ryan asked.

"Well, I think...I've never said this..." He felt his throat tightening. "I've always wondered..." He fought not to cry but buried childhood anguish whelmed him.

"Ah, John."

John struggled against his tears.

"It's okay, John."

He wiped his eyes with the tee shirt he was wearing and drank from the bottle of water. "I think I've been scared that my mother gave me to this guy...you know, for drugs or money." The sound of his sobbing filled the camper. He took several deep breaths and wiped his eyes. "So, at least I know that didn't happen."

"I'm sure she loved you...she would have never given you away."

"I guess." He exhaled loudly. "I feel so stupid."

"Why?"

"I don't know. Anyway, they want me to come back tomorrow."

"Why? Are you going?"

"They want to find this guy. They want me to sit with a sketch artist. But I'm sure they also want more time with me."

"Fuck...I'm so worried. Why don't you just come home and forget this."

John's chest quivered. "I want to get this guy."

"Will you then head home...after you talk to them tomorrow?"

"Ryan...I don't think I can ever be with you the way you want, the way I want. I'm too damaged. I'll always be damaged. You deserve more from a lover."

"Okay, listen to me asshole. You don't get to decide what I deserve or what's good for me. Like I don't decide for you." Silence. "Have I ever asked you to do anything that..."

"Never. But..."

"I was...we were happy before. We can be happy again. This, my work, being here, all this seems worthless without you here."

"You love doing what you do."

"Yes, I do. And I can do it anywhere. But I love you more than my job. Come home. If you want to leave, we'll leave. I'll sell the clinic. We can go anyplace. Start new."

"I love San Louis Obispo. Why do you think I'd want to leave?"

Silence. "I thought maybe part of the reason you left was that you didn't want to be here anymore. You know, after the hospital."

"I didn't leave because of you. I left because I had to be alone." John longed to be close to Ryan, safe in his bed. But he knew he would never feel safe again.

"Can you at least think about it? Tell me you'll think about it, really consider it."

"Okay. I'll call you..." John glanced toward the door of the camper. "Hold on, there's that sound again." He stood and moved toward the door.

"John," a voice called out from outside the camper.

"Hold on, Ryan. Someone is calling me."

"Really, who would know...?"

"Who's there?"

"It's about where you're parked," the voice said.

"Okay, just a second."

"I'll call you tomorrow night. I love you." Hearing himself say those words with ease surprised him.

"I love you, too."

John hung up, put his phone down, and stepped toward the door. When he opened it, he saw nothing but darkness. Then before he could react, he saw something moving quickly toward his head. He was struck hard with a metal rod against the left side of his face. He fell back, unconscious.

Stewart grabbed his briefcase, left just outside. He closed the door, pulled out a syringe and vial, and injected John in the chest with a small dose of Ketamine.

The camper's two swivel armchairs were attached to the floor. Stewart pulled John onto one by lifting him from under his arms. He put on black leather gloves and shoved a ball gag into John's mouth and tightly behind his head. He wrapped a rope around John's right ankle, pulled his foot far to the right, wrapped the rope around the base of the chair, and then attached it to his left leg pulling it back. He had John sitting spread eagle. He tied John's arms to the arms of the chair, took scissors from his case, and cut John's tee shirt off him. Then snapped a pack of smelling salts under John's nose.

John was finally able to focus. He tried to fight his restraints, but they held fast.

"You remember me, don't you?"

John glared at Stewart.

"You just couldn't leave it alone. Could you? Let me introduce myself. Agent Stewart Dawson." He snorted. "Yes, FBI very Special Agent Stewart Dawson."

John's eyes widened with surprise.

"That's right. FBI. And I work with your friend Dr. Bill, a cocksucker like yourself. And I do mean that literally. I saw your interview this afternoon." He shook his head. "There's no way you're going to sit with a sketch artist. Oh, and by the way, even though they have no evidence, they know you killed my friends, all except Tristan that is. I killed him. He should have kept his mouth shut."

He ran his hand over John's chest. "God, I remember you when you were ripe for the picking." He cut through his shorts and underwear. He gently stroked John's penis. "I'll never understand what you homos see in these when they're big and hairy...And this is one mother-fucking big cock." He pulled on it hard. "You were big when you were a kid, but this...You know, I always hated the fact that you were uncut. I wanted Adams to circumcise you. But Victor said it would take you out of commission for too long. I think he always had a secret thing for an uncut cock."

The ring of John's cell phone caught their attention. Stewart smiled. "Ryan calling back?"

John began to struggle against the ropes. Dawson held John's testicles and slowly squeezed. "Quite a handful you've got here." John fought not to groan from the pain, but Dawson didn't stop.

"I told Victor to kill you that night and that if he couldn't I would. When I heard you were alive, I wanted to kill him and then come after you. I should have. Then I heard you could remember nothing. Amnesia, they said." He tightened his grip on John's testicles, pulled and squeezed until John's body shook with pain. "You should have stayed stupid. Now you're going to die."

John growled, trying to express his rage.

"Yes, I killed your mother. She was a greedy bitch. She wanted twice what we had agreed upon."

"No," John screamed, but all that could be heard was a muffled groan. He fought his restraints, shaking his head violently, in spite of the pain radiating from his jaw.

Stewart pulled a scalpel from his briefcase. "Yes, that's right. She was selling your sweet little ass. Why do you think she came to Vegas?"

John screamed again, "*No*," but it didn't sound any different than his growl. "*No*."

Stewart swiveled the chair so that John faced the front of the camper and was able to look out the windows into the darkness of the night. From behind, Dawson reached over John and placed the blade against his chest.

"Let's see. How did you do this?" He lightly pulled the knife over John's chest, cutting him enough to make him bleed.

John struggled and grunted.

Again with the blade, over and over, until John was close to passing out. He knelt before him and smiled. "Still with me?" He pulled at John's foreskin. "They say this is extremely painful." John glanced down and watched as Stewart placed the scalpel against his foreskin and began slowly slicing it off, exposing the head of his penis.

John's body shook violently, and then he passed out.

Stewart brought him back to consciousness using smelling salts and knelt before him again.

"Smelling salts. What a great idea. Thank you for that. I want you awake for all of this."

John managed to raise his head. He looked into Dawson's eyes, readying himself for what was to come. He closed his eyes. But instead of more pain, he felt something gently touching his face. He opened his eyes.

"You were so beautiful. I thought about keeping you for myself, but I couldn't figure out how to do that." He kept stroking John's cheek with the back of his gloved hand. "I hated sharing you. We made love."

John's eyes narrowed into a glare of hatred.

Dawson gripped John's bleeding penis and squeezed. A bolt of pain exploded throughout his body. He shook uncontrollably and gasped for air. Then he passed out.

Dawson popped another smelling salt packet. He waited until John became fully conscious.

"Well, enough play. I'd love to drag this out, but I do have to get home. I have a cute little boy—blond and blue-eyed, just like you—waiting for me."

Stewart stood, leaned over John, and ran the blade over the back of John's neck where he injected him. "That's what you did, isn't it? First the penis, and please don't pass out. Then the balls, right? Or is it the other way around? No, first we extract the balls, one at a time." Stewart took hold of John's scrotum with his left hand and sliced it open. He saw John's body shake and then go limp.

He stood and backhanded John across the face. John's head bobbled on his shoulders, his eyes fluttered open. As Stewart was about to cut, he heard a sound at the door. He hesitated. Then the door flew open.

"Don't move," a voice called out.

Stewart quickly slashed at John's throat.

The air was filled with the report of the gun and the smell of gunpowder. Stewart's body slammed against the wall of the camper. Mr. Caputo fired again and watched as Dawson's body fell to the floor.

John's head fell forward as blood ran down his chest.

Thirty-Five

Bill and Ed sat in Bill's office waiting for John to arrive. Bill looked at his watch. It was 10:05 a.m. "Probably traffic. He'll be here."

Ed leaned back in his chair. "You know I get it."

"Get it?"

"Him killing these guys. If one of these guys took Justin and raped him, he wouldn't have to hunt them down. I would…"

"I know." Bill moved his chair so he could see if anyone was approaching his office. "How these guys get away with a statute of limitations and avoid jail… and then their victims grow up locked away in their own prisons for life."

"Did Vegas know there was a kid missing, back when?"

"I talked to them this morning. Yes, they did. The motel called when John's mother didn't check out, and her car was left in the parking lot. The manager told police that she had a five or six-year-old blond boy with her. They assumed he was either taken or killed."

"And that was it?"

"They investigated. They contacted the Vegas FBI in case it was a kidnapping and then the case went cold."

"So we, law enforcement, failed him in Vegas," Ed said. "He's here for five years being raped and then left for dead. That goes nowhere. And now we're going to put him in jail for life or stick a needle in his arm. Doesn't all that seem wrong?"

A young woman entered the office.

"You the sketch artist?" Bill asked, standing.

"Yes. Is your guy here?"

The three of them sat and waited.

Thirty minutes passed.

"He's made a run for it," Ed said.

"You've got his number. Call him."

Ed dialed. John's phone rang four times. "It's gone to voicemail...Hey, John, this is Detective Coyne. We're waiting for you. Give me a call and let me know if you're coming in." He hung up.

"How many rings?"

"Four."

"His phone is on. It would go straight to voicemail if it was turned off." He picked up his phone. "Run a number for me. Exact location." He handed the phone to Ed.

Ed gave him the number. He waited. "What's there?" he asked. "Point Mugu State Park. Okay, thank you."

"His phone is where he said he'd be." Bill called Ryan's clinic and told his assistant he needed to talk immediately.

"Agent Russo." Bill could hear the nervousness in Ryan's voice.

"We saw John yesterday. Have you spoken to him?"

"He called last night. He said he was coming in so that he could help you get the guy who kidnapped him."

"He's not here and we called him and pinged his phone for a location, and we got Point Mugu."

"That's where he spent the night. When he hung up, he said someone was outside his camper. He said he had to go."

"We'll check it out. Maybe he overslept."

"John never oversleeps."

"We'll check it out and get back to you."

Bill hung up. "You've got the license plate of the camper?" he asked Ed.

Ed stepped away as he made a call.

The sketch artist asked Bill, "Do you want me to hang around?"

Bill leaned back in his chair and stared at her, thinking. "Just until we figure out what's going on here." He called and asked for the telephone number of the State Park. They transferred him to the campsite. "This is FBI Agent Russo."

"Yes, sir," a woman answered. "How can I help you?"

Ed handed him a piece of paper. "I'm calling because a witness to a crime is staying at your campsite. His name is John..."

"Adear, John Adear." Her voice was sad. "He was attacked last night. It was terrible, terrible. The police took my husband...they're going over what happened."

"Attacked? Is he dead?"

"I don't know. He was taken to the Ventura County Hospital in Oxnard. I just don't know."

"Okay. We'll be there," Bill looked at his watch. "In about forty minutes."

"Call the hospital," Ed suggested.

When Bill finally reached a floor nurse in the ICU, she refused to give him any information, but suggested that he was transferred there for a reason.

"Thank you. We need to talk to him about the attack. We should be there in about forty-five minutes."

She told him that talking to him wasn't possible now.

"He's in ICU." Bill grabbed his jacket and told the sketch artist she could leave. "My guess is that he's not conscious. We should go to the campsite and see what's going on there and then head to the hospital."

On the way to Ed's car, Bill called Ryan and told him everything he had found out.

"I just can't help but think about John being raped by these men," Ed said, his hand on the car's steering wheel. "Now this."

Silence.

"How is Justin? How did his date go?"

Ed sighed. "Good. He seemed happy. He thanked me. He said he likes that we're talking."

"You do get that it means a lot to him?"

Ed nodded.

There were two police cars parked at the ranger's office. Mrs. Caputo greeted Bill and Ed, wearing jeans, a sweatshirt, and sandals. Bill thought she looked to be in her fifties. The police had questioned Mr. Caputo at their office and returned him to the campsite just moments before they arrived.

"He's with them now... where it happened," she told them. She instructed them how to find where John had parked.

"Do you know how he's doing?" she asked.

"As far as we know," Bill answered, "he's still alive."

As they were ready to leave the office, Mr. Caputo returned. He looked haggard and much older than his wife.

"Mr. Caputo," Bill showed him his credentials, "I really hate asking you to talk us through this again, but..."

Mr. Caputo explained that he had called to let John know dinner was ready. He didn't answer, so he thought he might be having trouble setting up, and walked out to where John had parked, noticed the lights on, and glanced in the front window of the camper. "I... at first... we, the Mrs. and I figured that John was gay. Just things he said. You know how they talk."

"Ah..." Ed interrupted him.

"You know when they say they live with a friend and they never say it's a girl or a guy. My son always did that until he came out. Anyway, when I glanced in I saw this man kneeling in front of John and John was sitting and didn't have a shirt on. I stepped back right away because I thought... but then, like for a second I saw it in my head. There was something in his mouth and stuff all over his chest. It didn't make sense. I looked back. John was tied up and that stuff was blood."

"You saw the guy?" Ed said.

"Yes. I killed him."

"Where's the body?"

"They took it... the medical examiner took it."

"Do they know who he is?"

Mr. Caputo shook his head. "No, he had no ID. They're still looking for his car. It's not here, but maybe someone drove him. We're aways from anything close by."

"How bad was John?" Bill asked.

"I was too slow. I should have just shot the guy. He had time to slash John's throat. There was so much blood. I called the missus. She told me to press on his throat. She called 911 and ran here. She knew what to do. It was coming from his throat. Running down... I never saw anything like it before. but he was breathing and had a faint heartbeat. They rushed him off pretty quick. How the hell could he survive that?"

Bill and Ed walked out to the camper. It was staked out with yellow tape and had a police officer standing guard. CSI was still going over it. They looked inside.

"Wow, there is a lot of blood," Bill said.

The officer said, "Some of it is the perps'. I heard them say John Adear must have lost half his volume."

Back at the office, Mr. Caputo pulled the Ventura County map from his desk and gave them directions to the medical examiner's office.

Bill noticed that Mr. Caputo's hand was shaking. "You did what you could."

Tears filled Mr. Caputo's eyes. "It's just... I just wish..."

"I understand."

The ranger circled the map where they were and then where the Ventura County Hospital was located and explained it was about a twenty-minute drive.

"That's the same hospital where John is," Ed said as they walked to the car.

"This fucking case is an emotional rollercoaster."

They drove the eighteen miles with anticipation.

At the hospital, after showing their credentials, they were taken to view the body by Dr. Vaston. In his fifties, he was tall and lean, had hollow cheeks, thin lips, and a bulbous nose that didn't fit his face. His hands were small.

"We haven't yet identified him. They're running fingerprints now," Dr. Vaston said. He pulled the sheet from the body.

"Holy shit," Ed said.

"Damn," Bill stepped back. "No way. No fucking way."

"You know him?"

"Know him..." Ed said. "He's FBI."

"Agent Stewart Dawson," Bill said.

"FBI!" the doctor said. "My understanding is that this guy was chopping up some young fellow in his camper. You're sure?"

"I work with him. Damn..." Bill left the room.

The medical examiner took information on Dawson from Ed.

"The man he cut up. I understand he's in ICU?"

The doctor explained how best to get there. When Ed joined Bill, he was on the phone with his section chief, explaining what he just learned. "Shit is hitting the fan," Bill said as they walked down a long hallway toward the ICU.

"He does have the ears. Fuck, he's the right height. The guy at Adams' office... with the gear to distort the camera images... he killed Adams?"

They stopped at the nurses' station and showed their identification. They were told that John had indeed lost half his blood volume and had a brain swelling and a broken jaw from a blow he had received to his head. He was in critical condition and was now in a drug-induced coma. "What are his chances?"

"Not good. We've done all we can for him. The cuts to his torso and genitals were severe but not life threatening. It was the cut to his jugular and the blow to the head."

Bill text messaged Ryan that he and Ed were getting lunch at the hospital and would wait for him to arrive.

Bill said, "Since Dawson attacked John, he must be the one who killed Tristan."

"If Dawson is the man in charge of breaking child porn and pedophiles rings, why would he kill Tristan and go after John?"

"He's part of the group?"

"Shit, didn't Dawson watch the interview with Tristan?"

Bill nodded. "He watched John's interview too. He knew about the sketch artist."

"What in the Tristan interview would set Dawson after him?"

"...Jamie. We were asking about Jamie and Tristan's pimp."

"Jamie. You think Dawson... Fuck, he has Jamie?"

"We have no evidence. And Tristan's dead."

"John sets the killing spree in motion when he contacts Dr. Adams. Dawson panics when he hears John is looking for him. He kills Adams, takes the journal but needs the safe deposit box key not to be found. He goes to Adam's office. The FBI has the type of equipment that would block out his image on the video. And he's the right height."

"True," Ed said. "He knows John is looking for him and figures someone in the group is bound to give him up. So, he decides to get rid of everyone and frame John. But this all assumes that he's part of this group of pervs. I mean I don't know why he'd kill Tristan and try to kill John unless he was. We need proof one way or the other. And John is the only one who could tell us if Dawson is the guy who kidnapped him and he has a vested interest in us thinking so."

An idea occurred to Bill. "The boys. Connor. The boys' therapist said that Connor had been left with several men."

"If he could identify Dawson as one of them then, at least, we'd know that Dawson was part of the group... But they were hooded. Dawson wouldn't be with the kid unmasked."

"They were masked when they made videos. But John recognized Adams."

Bill called FBI headquarters and asked that a twelve-man photo array be made up with Dawson's picture included.

They met Ryan at the ICU, where the charge nurse refused them entry. "I'm sorry. Only family is allowed," until Bill showed his badge.

Ryan presented the doctor in charge papers showing his power of attorney and the right to make all medical decisions for John. The doctor said, "Clearly, he went through hell and lost a lot of blood, but he's lucky."

"Lucky?" Ryan repeated.

"What I think happened is that before his throat was cut, he went into shock and passed out. The loss of blood might have been worse. Also, those people at the campsite knew what to do to keep him alive. We have him intubated. His brain was starved of blood which caused the swelling of brain cells. His neck injury, we're afraid if we bring him to and remove the tubes and then his throat swells, we'll never get him intubated again. And he has a broken jaw. We're going to have to wire that."

"How long will he be intubated?" Bill said.

"My guess. Two or three days if he stabilizes."

Ryan said, "What are his chances?"

"It's hard to say."

"Please, I need to know."

The doctor stared at Ryan for a moment. "I'm concerned about the brain swelling - the cellular edema. His intercranial pressure is high. We are treating it with hypertonic saline and Mannitol to bring the pressure down."

"Can I stay here with him?"

"We can have a recliner sent in so you can get some shut eye."

"Thank you."

"Would you call me when he wakes?" Bill asked Ryan.

"Yes."

Thirty-Six

As they walked to the nurse's station, Dr. Bellows greeted them. "Dr. Russo," she called out.

She told them that the boys were in group therapy, but she could pull them out. "I told them that you wanted them to look at some pictures, but I never said why."

"Thank you."

Bill and Ed waited in a therapy room. "How do you think he'll react if he sees a picture of Stewart and he knows him?" Ed asked.

"Not well, would be my guess. He's pretty fragile. I hate doing this."

"Do you know what's going to happen to them?"

"They'll be on the ward for at least six months. The aunt doesn't want them. She has two daughters and doesn't want the boys anywhere near them."

"Damn, these kids can't catch a break."

They sat and waited.

Ed said, "Wait. If Dawson killed the Tremways because they could ID him, why wouldn't he kill the boys who could surely ID him? I mean, if he was molesting Conner."

"Good question. Maybe..." The door opened. "Hi Connor. Hi Dylan," Bill said.

"Hello." Dylan was smiling. Connor looked at both men and then looked away.

"This is Detective Coyne."

"He was at our house," Dylan said.

"You remember me," Ed said as they sat.

"You came with all those people and you helped me get dressed."

"That's right." He glanced at Bill in amazement.

"Hyper-vigilance." Bill asked Conner to look at some pictures. "I'd like you to tell me if you recognize any of these men." Bill put one of the twelve photos of various FBI agents on the table in front of Connor.

"I don't want to."

"You're safe here," Bill said.

"No."

"Okay. It's okay. You don't have to..."

"Can I look?" Dylan asked.

"I don't think you would know this man. He spent time with Connor."

"I know some of them."

Connor stood at a distance staring at Bill as he began showing the pictures to Dylan. He took one step and then another closer.

"Take your time," Bill said.

Dylan leaned in and scanned the picture. Then he looked at Connor. Connor stared back at him. Dylan studied each of the first five photos and shook his head. The sixth photo was of Dawson. Dylan focused on the picture. He looked up at Bill.

"I know him," Dylan offered.

"You do?" Bill said. "From where?"

"He came to our house. Daddy put Connor in our bedroom before he came. Mommy put me in their bedroom. They made me sleep there sometimes. Then that man came to our house with Jamie. When I heard Jamie, I snuck out of the bedroom and watched. The man put on a black hood that went over his face and head like Daddy always did when we made movies. Then he went into our bedroom where Connor was, and Daddy took Jamie into the den. Mommy put me to bed and then she went in the room with Daddy and Jamie with her camera." Dylan glanced at Connor. "Do you remember the man with the black hat thing that was at our house?"

Connor nodded.

"That's him."

Connor pulled back, wrapped his arms around his chest, and groaned.

On the way to Director Coulter's office, Bill made a call, requesting information on Agent Stewart Dawson—marital status and his address. He put his hand over the phone receiver and said to Ed, "If I remember, he was married at some time in his life."

"Yes," he said into the receiver, "When was he divorced?" He nodded and then repeated, "Children? Address?" He scribbled onto a pad of paper. He looked at Ed. "A condo on Wilshire Boulevard. No children."

They arrived at the sixteen-story building with a warrant in hand. The manager took them up to the fourteenth floor in the elevator. "You ever see Mr. Dawson with a boy," Bill asked.

"No. Don't see much of him, really. Never with a boy."

The manager opened the door. Bill and Ed quickly checked the one-bedroom apartment.

"It hardly looks lived in," Ed said, opening the refrigerator.

Bill looked through the bedroom closet and the dresser of drawers. "He kept clothes here. Toiletries in the bathroom. Nothing that would belong to a kid."

"He was moving to D.C."

"But the video said Jamie wouldn't be available until the end of May. That's in four weeks."

They went through the kitchen cabinets. Bill opened the dishwasher. It was empty. He stared out the living room window. He could see the Federal Building where he and Dawson worked. They exited the apartment and stepped into the hallway where the manager had been waiting.

"You said you didn't see Mr. Dawson much," Bill said to the manager.

"Maybe once a week, he'd pick up his mail, spend a night. He said he was FBI and in the field all the time."

"We're missing something. He's got the boy somewhere else."

As they stepped out of the condominium lobby, Bill's phone chimed. "Hello Mrs. Adams. I'm with Detective Coyne. You're on speakerphone."

Mrs. Adams told them, "My son-in-law was walking through the hallway from the bedrooms, past my husband's office...He realized the hallway was longer than it should have been."

"What do you mean?"

"Behind the piece of artwork in his safe, he found a button that released a latch. Behind a bookcase there was a room. The journal was on a shelf.

Names, dates, addresses, then three and four digit numbers and more addresses. Then there are dates going back twenty years. And locked drawers. I have no idea where the keys are, so we'll have to break into them. But I thought I'd call you first and see if…"

"We'll be there as soon as we can. Please don't do anything more. I'd like to be there when the drawers are opened. Chain of evidence and everything."

In the safe room, Ed and Bill found equipment for making and copying DVDs. A laptop, an old one. The journal had names with addresses, each having its own page. He and Ed glanced at each other when they came across names they recognized.

"Shit," Ed said, "this is what Dawson was looking for and what we thought John had."

The first drawer they broke into was empty. The next drawer held what looked like cases of unrecorded DVDs. Then they found rows of DVDs in their cases with numbers that corresponded to the numbers in the journal. The last two drawers held coded discs from video cameras and flash drives.

Bill thumbed through the journal and found the first entry for one of the 'No Name" people. The date corresponded to the period when John was kidnapped. They looked at the code and then went through the drawer. He and Ed nodded at each other when they found the corresponding DVD and flash drive.

"When we give these to Brandon, this will be the first one he views. It has to be Dawson and John," Ed said.

He called for a team to collect and log everything in the room and deliver it to headquarters. "Tell Brandon I want him working on this tonight, and I don't care that it's Friday. I want to be able to see what's on them by tomorrow, even if he has to stay all night. And tell him he can call in help."

Saturday afternoon Bill and Ed joined Brandon at the LAPD Headquarters. When they entered the room, Brandon looked at them, sighed, and shook his head.

The DVDs were more of the same—masked men raping preadolescent boys. The flash drives were protected with a very sophisticated system which had taken Brandon some time to figure out how to bypass. Each man's name in Dr. Adam's journal was a member of the ring and had a video of him with a young boy, many with John.

"The video that goes with the No Name guy, Jack 411," Brandon said, "is that FBI guy who was helping me."

"Dawson," Bill confirmed.

"The video is four hours of Dawson raping John. The last two-hours of the video, he's clearly drugged."

Then there were recent videos of several men with a blond-haired boy—Jamie. Ed and Bill sat watching as Brandon, using the material from Dr. Adam's safe room, identified each subject by name, opened the file, and fast-forwarded through the video as Ed and Bill watched.

"These are all actionable," Bill said.

"Yes," Ed said. "This has never been seen or reported to us. The clock starts running now."

"Warrants are being drawn up?"

"As we speak."

Brandon slid in another flash drive. He looked at Ed and Bill as he turned up the volume. They heard a man say to John, "Call me Daddy. I like to be called Daddy." Brandon asked, "Do you recognize him?"

"No," Ed said.

"He works down the street. He's a superior court judge."

"Fuck."

"We have a minister, too."

Thirty-Seven

It was mid-morning when Bill and Ed entered the LA County Jail. After they put their guns into locked cubbies, they met District Attorney Allen Foster, the head D.A. for Los Angeles County. He was tall and lean, had salt and pepper hair, and wore what looked to Bill to be a very expensive suit. They were bringing in the big guns to take down Superior Court Judge Henning.

"He wants to deal, but he's going to have to give up something big," Foster said as they walked down the hall.

"As far as we know," Ed said, "we have all but one locked up. Not sure what Henning could have."

Bill asked, "What does he want?"

Foster said, "Not to be sent to state prison."

"Where the fuck does he want to go?"

"Some Club Fed., I'm guessing."

A guard led them into a room where Judge Henning and his lawyer, Henry Collins, were waiting.

"Gentlemen." Collins stood and put out his hand. The three men ignored it and sat. The judge looked tired, nervous, and old.

Foster said, "I understand that you think you have information that would interest us."

"I'm a judge and I've sentenced many of the men in state prison..."

"I guess you should have thought about that before you started raping children," Ed said, never taking his eyes off Henning.

"My client is also aware that thirty percent of all those murdered in prison are pedophiles."

"Again, he should have thought about that..."

"We get your point, Detective. But like I said, we're here to give you information that I'm sure you want. We want something in return."

"What do you have?" Foster asked.

"Before that, let's talk about what we want."

Silence.

"The judge will do his time at the Federal Corrections Institution at Dublin. It's just outside of San Francisco and..."

"I know where it is," Foster said.

"...and he wants consideration at sentencing."

"That's not going to happen," Foster said. "He's doing the max."

"This is bullshit," Ed said. "We have you raping not one, not two, not three but four different boys. And I do mean tender age boys."

The two men glared at each other.

Collins said, "Actually, from what I understand you only have his face on one tape and that happened..."

"That's why I'm here," Bill said to Collins. "We are able to identify your client not only with the boys called Cody, Zackary and Nicky, but most recently with a boy called Jamie, who we are looking for. When your client was taken into custody he was photographed. I, for one, would be fine getting on a stand in front of a jury and presenting the video and comparing who we see sitting before us to naked photos of your client." He turned his attention to Henning. "You ready for that?"

Henning seethed. "You know there was a time when they treated people like you..."

"Cut the crap...," Foster moved his chair back from the desk.

"Okay. We'll..." Collins interjected.

"...no deal for any info unless there's an allocution and he takes whatever the judge gives him."

"What about Dublin?" Collins asked.

"That I'll deal on, but the info better be good."

Henning and Collins whispered to each other. Henning said, "I know of another sex trafficking ring here in LA Mostly pubescent boys, twelve, thirteen, up to sixteen years old. Some prepubescent."

Bill felt his teeth clenching. He wasn't naïve. He knew this was going on. But this man was a superior court judge. He glanced at Ed, who was giving Henning a death stare.

"You know this how?" Foster said.

"Is this necessary?" Collins said. "You want information, not more..."

"I also know who has Jamie," Henning said. "He's been sold. The man knows Dawson was killed. He's coming into town to pick him up."

"You bastard," Ed said. "And you have a son, don't you?"

"None of this comes out in court," Collins said. "His allocution is only to what is on video."

"Let's step outside," Foster said to Bill and Ed.

When they left the room, Foster said, "You searched Dawson's condo for this kid?"

"He's not there."

Bill added, "We did a property search, hoping to find where else he might have him. Nothing."

"I hate dealing with this bastard, but the boy."

"You think anyone else arrested might know where he is?"

"I've talked to them all," Forest said, "Some don't even know this Jamie kid. Never met him."

Ed said. "The videos only show Xavier, Dawson, Romeo and Connor and this asshole...and some guy we don't have yet, who we believe is Romeo's father. We've searched for a professor with that name in every California college. Nothing."

"Out of state?" Foster said.

"Yes. Nothing. We searched death records, too."

"I'd make the deal just to get the kid. Throw in another sex ring and info on this guy..."

"You can make it contingent..." Ed said.

"Definitely. We find the kid alive and we make arrests with the info or the deal is off."

"And he gives a statement in court and gets the max..." Ed said.

"How can you be sure?" Bill asked.

"Any judge that gave him less would be hung by his balls. Can't show favoritism. I want him to give an allocution to all charges. It will be on the record."

The deal was made. Papers were signed. Judge Henning gave them the name Carl Ronshow, Tristan's pimp, who pimped out the boys and lived in the Hollywood Hills.

"And Jamie?" Bill asked.

"Dawson sold Jamie...because he was being promoted. I don't know the guy's name. We didn't exchange names. But he doesn't live in LA He's from Northern California someplace."

Foster said, "That's not enough. The deal is that we find the boy."

"You've got the FBI here. He and Dawson were pals from years ago. They all went to college together."

Foster said, "Jamie. How did Dawson get him?"

"Romania. About four years ago. The boy was five. He went there and adopted him from an orphanage."

Bill stood. "A name, or I guess you're going to general population at a state prison. You should last all of about a week."

The judge sighed. "Conway, Liam Conway. He owns a house here in Culver City. That's where Dawson kept Jamie."

"Bastard." Ed growled as he stepped toward the judge.

Bill grabbed Ed's arm and held him back.

As they retrieved their guns, D.A. Foster said, "We have to talk about this John Adear. Do we have a case against him?"

"We'll give you a call," Ed replied.

As they headed to Culver City, Ed called for backup. They drove onto the street where Liam Conway owned a home and pulled up alongside a black Chevy Tahoe. The window rolled down.

"We saw movement in the house. An adult male," the plainclothes officer said.

"We have a no knock warrant," Ed said.

Four men from the LAPD, two from the FBI, and Bill and Ed approached the house, guns drawn. Two officers quietly moved along the side of the house and entered the backyard. Two stood at the front door, one holding a battering ram. When Bill nodded, one officer spoke into his radio, "Breech."

Simultaneously, the front and back doors were bashed open, and eight men rushed in. "Police," several of them called out. Liam was in the kitchen. He grabbed his gun and raised it, pointing it at an officer and was immediately shot and killed.

As the rest of the house was cleared, Bill came to a locked door. He stepped back and then threw his body weight against it. It flew open with a thud. He noticed a small naked boy race off the bed and scoot under it.

"Jamie."

The room was dark. The windows blacked out. Bill found the light switch and turned the lights on.

"Jamie." Bill got on his knees. He glanced under the bed and saw a naked boy staring back at him. "You're safe. I'm the police. I won't hurt you."

Jamie hesitantly moved toward him. Bill took his hand, grabbed a sheet off the bed, wrapped him, and carried him out of the room.

Thirty-Eight

"Superior Court Judge Henning. Fuck," Assistant Chief Henson read the list of men who were arrested. "My wife and I have had dinner with him and his wife. Fucking asshole." He glanced up at Ed and said, "You actually have him on film raping this John guy?"

"Yes, sir."

"Do we think John Adear is the serial killer?"

"I do," Bill answered. "I think he was set off by seeing Dr. Adams. He was able to identify various men in the group, but I do believe that he was looking for Stewart Dawson."

"The shit is going to hit the fan over there."

"Already has."

"Do we have a case against Adear?

"Not really," Ed said. "Circumstantial. The evidence would be slim."

"It might not matter," Bill said. "I talked to Ryan this morning. John's condition has gotten worse. He was put on a phenobarbital drip. He's in a medically induced coma and on life support."

Emma and Ryan were standing outside John's room talking to the doctor when Bill and Ed arrived. The doctor nodded at Ryan and then walked away. Ryan turned and walked into John's room. Emma waited as Bill and Ed approached.

"How's he doing?" Bill asked Emma.

"They're going to take him off life support. Ryan signed the papers. I think he's holding out hope, but…" she crossed her arms over her chest. "I'm really worried about him."

Ed said, "When we talked to your brother, it was obvious that he loves him deeply."

The doctor returned with a nurse. He made eye contact with Emma and nodded. Emma, the doctor, and nurse entered John's room, where Ryan sat, holding John's hand. Bill and Ed stood outside.

The doctor shined a light into John's eyes. "Pupils are fixed and dilated." Then he turned John's head from side to side, watching his eyes for movement. "No corneal or ocular cyclonic reflexes."

He stood back and looked at Ryan.

"We are going to disconnect the ventilator for eight minutes to see if he breathes on his own. If he doesn't, we'll pronounce him brain dead and reconnect the ventilator to keep viable organs functioning for transplant."

Ryan nodded.

The doctor removed and disconnected the tube. Everyone remained focused on John for the eight minutes. John was not breathing.

"Time of death," the doctor said, "2:44 P.M.," as the nurse reconnected John's breathing tube.

Ryan buried his face in John's chest and wept as the doctor and nurse left the room.

Emma sat on the bed and put her hand on Ryan's shoulder. Tears fell from her eyes.

Later, Emma called out to them as they walked down the hall to leave. They turned and waited for her.

"I just wanted to tell you that I'm going to write his story. Our editor has already agreed and it's going to be on the cover."

"I think it should be told," Bill said.

"He had been writing a memoir and storing it on the cloud. I downloaded everything yesterday. His last entry was the morning he left to be interviewed by both of you. I know I was defensive when we last talked. I'm sorry about that."

"No need to apologize."

"I was wondering if I could talk to you about that interview sometime soon."

"Actually, yes. There is information you wouldn't have about his mother and Tristan and Romeo and about a boy named Jamie."

"I read about you finding him. I'll go gently on the both of you, but not on the LAPD and the FBI." She glanced at Bill, "Especially the FBI."

"Good. I'll look forward to reading it."

Ed said, "About Ryan..."

"I'm taking a month off to write this story and stay with him in San Luis Obispo. A few of his friends are on their way here now. We'll get him through this."

Ed nodded.

"And thank you for your concern."

As they stepped out of the elevator, Ed said, "John's body died today, but his soul died the day Dawson kidnapped him and turned him over to Xavier."

"Did you notice his tattoo?" Bill asked. "A quote from Kierkegaard. *I am alone, as I have always been; abandoned not by men...but by the happy Spirit of Joy.*"

Ed sighed.

Silence.

"What's going to happen to Jamie?" Ed asked.

"Nothing good. It will be almost impossible to find a placement for him. He's a boy, near puberty. He's been sexually abused, and his English is poor at best. Right now, he's withdrawn. Much like John was."

"He'd never survive a group home. At least none that I was in," Ed said.

"Chances are he'll wind up on the streets."

"Fuck."

Ed parked by the Federal Building. "It's been good working with you again," Bill said.

"Yes. Very good."

They glanced at each other, smiled, and nodded. Bill opened the car door to get out.

Ed said, "I'd like to take you to dinner. Just you and me."

Bill turned. "Sure. Anytime."

Awkwardly, Ed said, "I'd like to spend time with you. Have a nice dinner and wine. Lucy's El Adobe Café on Melrose?"

"Spending time with you is always a good thing."

"Good, then how about Friday night?"

"I'm free."

"Then it's a date."

Bill smiled. "A date?"

"You said I should start dating. So, if you're okay with that...."

"Then it's a date."

Acknowledgments

I would like to thank: Mathew Fagan, Nancy Faranda, and Dennis Morrison for their advice on how best to tell this story, and Judith Stahl for her many years of friendship and support.

I am particularly indebted to Diana M. Gordon for her encouragement and assistance.

And, of course, many thanks to Ian Henzel and St Sukie de la Croix of Rattling Good Yarns Press. And, a special thanks to Daniel M. Jaffe for referring me to them.

About the Author

Thomas Domenici was the first openly identified gay male accepted for training (1980) in the University of Southern California Counseling Psychology program. After receiving his Ph.D. (1984) he did a post-doctoral fellowship at USC/LA County Psychiatric Hospital working with inpatient and outpatient children who had been sexually abused. Subsequently, he did a two-year fellowship at a private clinic working with incest perpetrators and child molesters. In 1989, he was the first openly identified gay male accepted for training at the NYU Postdoctoral Program in Psychotherapy and Psychoanalysis. He was a co-editor of the anthology *Disorienting Sexuality: Reappraisal of Sexual Identities*: 1995, Routledge, New York.

Printed in the USA
CPSIA information can be obtained
at www.ICGtesting.com
JSHW021740270923
49028JS00005B/159

9 781955 826457